*He saw her walking up the driveway, her son bouncing at her side, and his heart gave a funny little lurch.*

Not for Beth, Logan angrily decided. Ridiculous to feel nervous. It was just annoying, busybody, chatterbox Beth.

He moved away from the window and waited for her to ring the bell before he went to answer the door.

'Hi,' she said, a bit breathlessly. 'We won't stay long. I brought you some dinner.'

She looked like a Christmas light, all bright and beautiful. Her smile warmed him like a fire in the hearth. Whatever dish she held in her hand smelled divine. He didn't want her here, didn't want to care. He needed to be alone with his memories. And she was disrupting his plans.

He took the casserole dish from her. A ragged breath rattled out of him. Warmth, woman, child and food. For a moment, was it so wrong?

Before he could stop himself, the word spilled out of his mouth. 'Stay.'

Dear Reader,

A very warm and cheerful welcome to Special Edition.

It's that time of year again and to celebrate we give you a very festive *Baby Christmas* by Pamela Browning. It's our final THAT'S MY BABY! story for the moment but we hope you've enjoyed these books as much as we have.

Bestselling author Sherryl Woods continues her series THE CALAMITY JANES this month with Gina's story in *To Catch a Thief*. Look out for Emma's story entitled *The Calamity Janes* in Silhouette Superromance next month.

For those of you who relished the MONTANA series, we have the first of six new stories for you— *Christmas in Whitehorn* by Susan Mallery. Look out for the next story in the series in January. Also, as a special treat at this jolly time of year, we have the first story in the WYOMING WILDFLOWERS series from popular author Patricia McLinn. *Almost a Bride* is the first book and the next story will be out in February.

To round off the month we have another wonderful ALASKANS tale from Marie Ferrarella with *The MD Meets His Match* and a lovely story from Sylvie Kurtz called *A Little Christmas Magic* that shows us what Christmas is all about—family!

We hope you enjoy them all.

Merry Christmas!

The Editors

# A Little
# Christmas Magic

# SYLVIE KURTZ

SILHOUETTE®
SPECIAL EDITION™

To Chuck, Axel and Cassie
the best presents in my life

A SPECIAL THANK-YOU
to Margie D'Agostino for sharing her school cafeteria
expertise. Any mistakes in procedures are the author's.

*First published in Great Britain 2002
Silhouette Books, Eton House, 18-24 Paradise Road,
Richmond, Surrey TW9 1SR*

© Sylvie L. Kurtz 2001

*ISBN 0 373 24438 X*

*23-1202*

*Printed and bound in Spain
by Litografia Rosés S.A., Barcelona*

## SYLVIE KURTZ

Flying an eight-hour solo cross-country trip in a Piper Arrow with only the airplane's crackling radio and a large bag of sweets for company, Sylvie Kurtz realised a pilot's life wasn't for her. The stories zooming in and out of her mind proved more entertaining than the flight itself. Not a quitter, she finished her pilot's course and earned her commercial licence and instrument rating.

Since then, she has traded in her wings for a computer, where she lets her imagination soar to create fictional adventures that explore the power of love and the thrill of suspense. When not writing, she enjoys the outdoors with her husband and two children, quilt-making, photography and reading whatever catches her interest.

You can write to Sylvie at PO Box 702, Milford, NH 03055, USA.

Dear Reader,

Christmas at my grandmother's house had always had a magical quality to it. One year, I found myself with two young children and far from my family so I thought they wouldn't have the magical memories of the season I'd had. But I told myself it could be worse—I could be facing a Christmas without my beloved husband and my children. This is how the seed for Logan and Beth's story was born. They both lost so much, yet love found its way back into their hearts. I hope you enjoy their journey of discovery.

May this holiday season find you surrounded by love, and may it feed your spirit with joy!

Sincerely,

*Sylvie*

Sylvie

Readers can reach Sylvie at PO Box 702, Milford, NH 03055, USA or through her web page at www.sylviekurtz.com

# Chapter One

Logan Ward stumbled to the window, yanked up the blinds and flinched at the unexpected morning brightness. A few more blinks brought alien scenery into focus. Snow. A carpet of crystals covered the world—the canted yard, the forgotten brick-red wooden barn, the bowed fence posts meandering toward a stand of pines beyond.

When he'd arrived in Rockville yesterday, he'd expected the cold. He'd known about the snow. He'd even counted on the short, dreary winter days to help make him forget. What he hadn't foreseen was how that same snow would smile in the low-angled light of the sun, and dazzle.

The joyful squeal that had jerked him out of his nightmare skirled through the glass once more.

A kid.

On his property.

He couldn't allow that.

He shoved away from the window and dragged on

clothes. Where had the kid come from, anyway? Didn't he have parents to watch over his welfare? How could they let a child wander without supervision? He plucked his discarded ski jacket from the newel post at the bottom of the stairs, jammed his feet into boots, then yanked open the front door.

The cheer of Christmas carols pulled him to a stop and sawed at his nerves. He hated Christmas, hated the whole damned holiday season.

The narrow country lane separating his property from his neighbor's should have meant peace and solitude. Obviously, he'd been mistaken.

With her fuchsia coat and teal-colored pants, the woman across the street appeared as bright as the decorations she hung.

He hated bright.

And her singing came to him as a free-tripping sound.

He hated bubbly.

As he watched her string lights along the edge of the roof, a sour taste filled his mouth. In his home away from town, he'd hoped to avoid all the festivities, the lights, the wreaths, the whole Santa scene.

As he stood there rooted, disliking the woman he'd never met, a blast of wind cascaded a shower of snow from his roof into the collar of his shirt, reminding him of his mission: the kid trespassing on his property.

"Welcome to New England," he mumbled, wriggling his shoulders to hasten the melting. He turned up the collar of his ski jacket and stepped into the drift of snow covering the stone walkway.

At least the stupid mutt who'd disturbed him last night wasn't still hanging around. Dogs had such needy personalities. And the last thing he wanted was to be needed by anybody—even a dog.

Last year he'd put up with all the Christmas fuss, but pretending had almost killed him. He couldn't bear to face the bustle this year. From now on he'd use the back door and wouldn't wander to the front of the house. And Rockville was definitely out of bounds. Thank God for the Internet and home delivery.

By the time he reached the child, he was more than ready to growl. "Hey, you! Yeah, you. Come over here."

Gripping his bright-red saucer, the boy complied.

"What do you think you're doing?" Logan snarled.

"It's the first snow. Miss Mac always lets me sled when it snows."

"Do I look like Miss MacDonald?"

The boy cocked his head and looked at him with a serious expression for a moment. His daughter, Samantha, had looked at him the same way before answering any question where she risked having one of her privileges curbed. Pain, sharp and swift, tightened his chest until breathing required his full attention.

"You look like the Grinch," the boy finally said.

The Grinch. Green, bitter, empty. That's exactly how Logan felt. "Miss MacDonald doesn't live here anymore, and I don't want you on my property. Is that clear?"

A cantankerous pout creased the child's cold-reddened face. "But I don't got a hill at my house."

"That's not my problem. Where do you live?"

The boy's chin pointed toward the house where the real estate agent had assured him a nice little widow lived. Why hadn't it occurred to him the widow might have children and grandchildren who'd visit? No, his mind, bent on escape, had simply pictured a blue-haired granny, knitting as she rocked herself by the fireplace, quietly, peacefully—alone.

"Mom said I could stay till she called me."

"And I say it's time to go home."

The boy made a dash for the hill, but as he was encumbered by snow pants and the snow saucer, Logan easily caught him on the fly. Feet kicking, the boy fought Logan. "No, no, I wanna stay!"

The boy thwacked his saucer against Logan's knee.

"Ow! Why you little—" Logan snatched the weapon from the boy.

"Let me go!"

In answer, Logan clasped his wriggling prey securely against his hip and marched toward the overbright package perched on a ladder...to the woman who was busily turning the frozen landscape he'd purposely sought into the winter wonderland he wanted to avoid more than anything in the world.

From atop her ladder, Beth Lannigen blew on her bare hands to warm them, then tugged on the string of lights and stretched past her comfort zone to reach the next permanent hook she'd installed along the roof's edge several years ago.

At the sound of crunching footsteps behind her, she smiled. Her six-year-old son was returning from his sledding spree down Eve MacDonald's hill and would want some hot chocolate. She could use a cup herself. "Done already, Jamie? I was going to get the toboggan in a few minutes and join you."

"Is this yours?"

At the booming voice Beth startled and looked down at her unexpected guest. A tall, somber-looking man dangled her squirming son by the scruff of his coat in one hand and held his saucer in the other. "Jamie! What are you doing to my son? Let him go this instant!"

Just as her foot left the top rung to hurry to Jamie's

rescue, a dog scrambled around the corner of the house, tripped over its own feet and slammed into the ladder, knocking it right out from under Beth.

Her heart surged in her throat. Panic bubbled through her like a boiling teakettle. Reflexively she clutched the rain gutter's edge with both hands to regain her balance. For Jamie's sake, she bit down her screech of terror.

Pulse zigzagging madly, she looked down to search for a soft landing area and gulped. Two stories looked much higher hanging from the roof's edge than standing safely on a ladder.

"I'm going to fall." She hadn't meant to say anything, but suddenly disaster seemed inevitable. Visions of broken legs and broken arms danced in her head.

"You're not going to fall," the gruff voice below her said. "Hang on."

Try as she might, Beth couldn't get a good view of what was happening on the ground. Through the haze of fear, only the sounds reached her. Jamie's saucer hit the ground with a thunk, his boots with a plop. Snow crunched. The ladder squealed and rattled as it was righted. And with each second Beth's hold on the narrow gutter was getting more tenuous, her thoughts more frantic. *I can't get hurt. Not in front of Jamie.* That thought alone kept panic, if not completely at bay, at least in check.

"Mom! Come down, come down!"

"I'm okay, Jamie. I'll be right there."

"The ladder's right under you," the gruff voice said.

With her foot Beth reached for the solid feel of aluminum but couldn't find it.

"To your left," the stranger directed.

Muscles shaking from her effort, she closed her eyes and regrouped. As she reached for the ladder once more, her grip slipped. The meat of her palms caught the gutter's sharp side. Pain sliced into her bare hands. Tears burned her eyes. She bit her trembling lips and whimpered.

"Mom! Come down!" The blur of Jamie's bright-green coat caught her side vision as he rushed to the ladder.

"No, Jamie, stay where you are!"

No sooner had she started to speak than Jamie was dragged down from the first rung and set firmly on the ground.

"I'll help her," the stranger said. "You stay here and make sure the ladder stays still."

Her arms shook from her effort to hang on. Her shoulders ached. Her fingers cramped. Tears of pain stung her eyes. She couldn't fall. Not in front of Jamie. He couldn't see his mother in a broken heap. But she wasn't sure how much longer she could hold on. Taking in a shaky breath, she forced herself to speak calmly.

"Jamie, why don't you go inside and get my gloves?"

"But I gotta hold the ladder for you."

Beth swallowed hard and strained to speak in an even tone. "I really need my gloves, sweetheart. My hands are cold."

"O-okay," Jamie said, hesitation making him stammer. "I'll be right back."

When she heard the back door slam, Beth gave a sigh of relief. Then panic surged through her in a sense-stealing wave. As heavy footsteps tromped up the ladder rungs, her hold on the gutter failed. Arms cycling madly backward, breath rushing out of her in a *whoosh,* she fell onto the stranger, taking him and the ladder with her to the snow-covered ground. With his arms wrapped protectively around her, he cushioned her landing with his body, which drew an *oomph* of discomfort from him.

"I'm sorry, I'm sorry, I'm sorry." Thoughts raced like an avalanche through Beth's mind as she rebounded off the hard body below hers and bumped the ladder out of the way. She scrambled around and knelt beside him. He just lay there, eyes closed. His skin was an ashen, unhealthy color. She'd killed him! A fresh wave of alarm flooded her. She grasped the front of his jacket and shook it. "Hey, mister, are you all right?"

"Fine," he grumbled, and reached up to rub his ribs.

The dog, looking like an overcooked, understuffed sausage, crawled over, whimpering an apology. With her hands feeling stiff and cold and stinging with pain, Beth didn't try to pet the animal.

"It's okay," she crooned to the dog. "Are you all right?" The dog rolled over, exposing its pink belly. "Is she yours?"

"No," the stranger barked, as if owning such a scrawny mutt was an insult.

The tone of his voice made her remember what had gotten her into this predicament in the first place. Her concern for his condition flew away and was replaced by her responsibility as a mother.

She stood up, fisted her aching hands and brought them to rest on her hips. The blood in the scratches stung and burned, but her anger blazed hotter.

"Why were you manhandling my son?" A slow throb pulsed in both her hands, bringing out her contrary side. "Answer me!"

"He was trespassing."

The man rose like a disgruntled bear roused from a nap, yet a sense of power and presence radiated from him. As he dusted the snow from his jacket, he scowled at her from beneath dark brows, and she sensed a mighty grip on control under the keen sharpness of his gaze. She couldn't tell what color his eyes were, but whatever the color, *friendly* couldn't be used to describe them.

"Trespassing!" Beth tripped over her tongue as she tried to sort through the barrage of conflicting thoughts assaulting her.

This was her new neighbor? She'd known Eve MacDonald had sold her family home. Eve had been uncharacteristically closemouthed about the new owner, but Beth had assumed nothing would change. Rockville, despite its hard name, was an amicable town. Who was this man with the hurt eyes? Where had he come from? Why was he so surly? The slow burn in her hands turned into a full-blown fire, but her thoughts refused to sort themselves into order. "Jamie's gone sledding there since he was a baby."

The silence between them was iceberg deep. His intense gaze sent a jolt of apprehension skittering down her spine. Who *was* he? Two days' worth of beard darkened his face. Red webbed the whites of his eyes. His pale skin contrasted starkly with his scraggly dark-chestnut hair. He looked like a cross between a ragged bear and a ghost. Normally she'd have found the hurt he tried so hard to hide intriguing, but not right now, not with Jamie's welfare on the line.

"I own the MacDonald property now," he said in a flat voice, "and I'd appreciate it if you kept your son away from my yard."

"What?"

"See that your son doesn't trespass again."

He turned to leave.

"Hey! That's not how we do things around here. Neighbors look out for neighbors."

"M-mom!"

At the tremulous note in Jamie's voice, Beth looked over her shoulder. Jamie had stopped midflight, arms extended, her purple gloves hanging from his hands like scarecrow straw. His gaze was frozen on the snow at her feet. "You're bleeding!"

The instant Jamie uttered the words, the ache in Beth's hands throbbed and the pain doubled. A shower of tiny red drops joined the widening patches at her sides. Slowly she lifted her hands and turned them over, exposing the two red gashes cutting across both her palms.

Whimpering, the dog inched forward, as if sensing Beth's pain.

Her new neighbor rushed toward her, brushed aside the dog with a sweep of his leg, grasped her wrists and frowned as he examined the damage. She tried to snatch her arms back, but as if he were someone people rarely said no to, the strong warmth of his fingers demanded compliance.

"Great! Now look what you've done. Let's get you inside." He spoke to her as if she'd been a disobedient six-year-old he wanted to banish to a time-out corner.

"I can take care of myself."

"Which way to the closest water?" He addressed his question to Jamie rather than to her. His tone suggested he'd rather eat a bowl of broken glass than be here. Not that she blamed him. The sight of blood didn't do much for her, either. But still, that didn't excuse his rudeness.

What he needed was a session of the etiquette class taught by Mildred Wallace at the Historical Society House twice a year. "Politeness," Mildred was fond of saying, "doesn't cost anything, but the dividends will bless you with riches." This man needed a blessing or two. She slanted him a glance. Or three.

"The kitchen." Jamie ran ahead to open the door while her neighbor firmly led her by the elbow.

Until his shadow completely overwhelmed her, Beth hadn't noticed just how tall he was. She barely reached his shoulder. Two of her could fit in his width. He was a stranger. She wasn't sure she wanted him in her house.

"Really, I'm fine," she said, giving him a nervous smile. "I can take care of myself."

"I'm not going to hurt you."

As she struggled to keep up with his ground-eating strides, she blushed. "Well, I didn't think…"

"Obviously not. When did you have your last tetanus shot?"

"Tetanus? I…I don't know—"

"Rusty gutters," he said, as if that explained everything.

Jamie waited anxiously by the door. His normally bright face had turned pale with worry. He tended to become over-protective whenever she got hurt. And the last thing a little boy should have to do was worry about his mother. Beth wanted to put her arms around him and reassure him she'd be just fine, but her neighbor wouldn't let go of her arm and kept her moving forward. She smiled comfortingly at her son and was heartened by his attempt to smile back.

"All I need is a good soaping," she said.

As she stepped into the kitchen, the warmth of the cooking oven and the scent of roasting turkey enveloped her. The dog cautiously poked her nose through the door and sniffed, then followed them in and hedged to the nearest corner. Droplets of blood along with gobs of slush tracked their progress across the kitchen floor.

"Door," the man said.

Jamie doubled back to the door and slammed it shut.

With a swipe of his arm the man pushed away the dirty pots and pans littering her countertop. He definitely needed to be enrolled in Mildred's etiquette class.

"Hey, easy on those. They're the tools of my trade."

Jamie dragged a chair by the sink to supervise the cleansing operation. He shucked off his soggy mittens. His scarf and hat followed in quick succession, leaving his light-brown hair standing up straight from the static. "Mom's a chef."

The man grunted his comment as he helped her out of her jacket.

"Of a sort," Beth added. She dreamed of starting her own gourmet catering business. But that dream was at least seven long months away; more pressing things needed her attention at the moment. Like the somber stranger in her kitchen who was examining her hands with the detachment of a field surgeon.

"If you're going to invite yourself into my home, the least you can do is tell me your name."

She was fast losing control of the situation. How could she have allowed him in when she knew nothing about him? How could she allow him to lead her around as easily as a trained dog on a leash? When he moved her hands over the sink, she winced.

"*Your* home?" The man snapped on the sink's spigots, tested the water's temperature and shoved both her hands beneath the flow. Water splashed onto the worn sleeves of his black ski jacket. "The agent said an old widow lived here."

Beth sucked back a sharp breath and pursed her lips against the sting of water on her wounds. "I lost my husband five years ago, but I'm not exactly ready for the rocker yet."

He gave her such a strange look, something between surprise and dismay, that she didn't know what to make of it. The glance was fleeting, and the raw emotions, whatever they'd been, were quickly hidden beneath the blinds of his dark lashes. He kept her hands under the flowing water and turned to look at Jamie over his shoulder.

"Do you know where your mom keeps her bandages, sport?"

"In the bathroom."

"Do you know what gauze is?"

Jamie shook his head.

"It's the white stuff that comes in a roll."

"It's in the care kit," Beth added between clenched teeth. The water's relentless onslaught stacked burning pain on top of throbbing torture.

"Oh, yeah, I know." Jamie jumped off the chair, bolted out of the kitchen and stomped up the stairs to the second floor. Wet boot tracks marked his path.

"So, do you have one?" Beth asked, to divert herself from the unmerciful agony he was putting her through.

He poked at the swelling flesh around the cut of one hand. "One what?"

"Ouch!" She hissed in a fast breath. "A name. Mine's Beth Lannigen. My son is James Andrew Lannigen, the Third, but I call him Jamie. It suits him better."

"Logan Ward." He jabbed at the skin of the other hand. She bit her lower lip to control the fresh pang of pain. A shaggy lock of his hair fell forward, the spiky ends teasing the edge of his eye. It irked her that, with her wrists imprisoned in his strong grasp, she couldn't reach out and tuck the curl back against his temple.

"Are you quite done, Mr. Ward?" The question came out with more sting than planned. Beth Lannigen *gave* help. Beth Lannigen didn't *take* help. This helpless position disturbed her more than she cared to admit.

"You're going to need stitches."

"Of course not." She tried to yank her hands away from his grasp. With only the slightest pressure of his thumbs, he positioned them back beneath the flow of water. She noticed her pulse then, and how it bumped fast against his fingers. The heat of the water, she assured herself, remnants of adrenaline from her fall, discomfort at having a stranger, a man, in her kitchen.

Jamie returned with the yellow plastic toolbox labeled Care Kit and dumped it on the pine kitchen table. Logan snapped off the water's flow. "Dish towel?"

"I'll get it." Jamie snapped the towel from the oven's handle.

"A clean one, sport."

Dropping the used towel on the floor, Jamie pounced on the drawer where Beth kept her kitchen linens and snagged two fresh towels. "One for each hand."

"Good idea." Logan gave Jamie a crooked half grin. The gesture, so foreign on the grim landscape of his face, caught Beth by surprise. At one point in time this man must have been quite handsome. What had happened to him?

She shook her head. I don't want to know.

Jamie handed Logan a towel and kept the other one for himself. With his tongue sticking out in concentration, Jamie followed Logan's every move as they carefully dried her hands.

Beth's gaze strayed to Logan's hard face. His deep, gray eyes had a haunted quality to them. Yet, despite his unyielding grip and his wild appearance, he had a gentle touch. He handled Jamie with patience yet wasn't patronizing. Did he sense being involved was the best way to deal with Jamie's anxiety? The contradiction of this man's harsh looks and his kind actions revived Beth's curiosity.

"Where did you move from?" she asked, as much to divert herself from his touch and her fanciful thoughts as to alleviate her curiosity.

"Texas."

"Why?"

Looking at Jamie, Logan pointed his chin at the care kit. "Bandage."

Jamie snapped the box's lock open, held up a blue-and-white carton and shot Logan a questioning look. Logan nodded. Jamie scampered back with the prize.

"Can I put it on?"

"I'm going to give you the very important job of hugging your mom while I put this bandage on—just in case it hurts. You know how girls can be. Okay?"

The words seemed dragged out of him by force. As soon as they were uttered, his lips tightened to a straight line, the tendons along his jaw popped into prominence, and his gaze avoided Jamie.

Jamie didn't notice the sudden shift in the stranger. He clamped himself at her waist and hugged her with all his might, making her laugh. "Take it easy, Jamie. I still need to breathe."

Her son readjusted his hold and tenderly snuggled against her, a paradox of softness and energy. Love filled her heart.

Her gaze sought Logan's face, considering once again the contradictions in the gruff man who so gently tended to her hands. For all this man's stern exterior, he did have an extraordinary way with Jamie. Did he have children of his own? A thought flashed across her mind. Had a recent divorce put the dark shadows under his eyes?

"New Hampshire's a long way from Texas. What made you choose Rockville for your new home?"

Logan ripped the carton's top open. "Where's the nearest hospital?"

"There aren't any medical facilities in Rockville."

"You're going to need stitches."

"It doesn't look that bad." Beth looked down at the fresh blood already seeping from the cuts across her palms.

"Trust me, I've seen enough cut-up bodies to know. You need stitches."

She gasped. "What?"

He took the opportunity afforded by her momentary astonishment to walk her backward toward the center of the room. As he followed the strange dance, Jamie giggled. When her knees hit the back of a chair, she sat down reflexively. Jamie's hold switched to her neck, his cheek nestled against hers.

"What exactly is it you do for a living?" she asked, unable to hide her sudden renewal of fear.

"We'll have to use your car." As if he hadn't heard her, Logan placed a layer of gauze across the palm of one hand.

Why, if the prospect of driving her to the clinic held so little appeal, did he insist on doing so? "Really, there's no need. There's too much to do—"

"I don't have snow tires."

"You'd better get some if you're going to survive the winter around here."

"I'm not planning on needing them." Logan concentrated on his bandaging.

"What were you going to do?" She gave a brittle laugh. "Hibernate?"

He didn't answer but put the finishing touches on his bandaging job. "Is this too tight?"

"You *are* planning on hibernating!" Her mouth hung open at her sudden intuition.

The clenching of his teeth brought out the tight ligaments of his jaw, giving her his answer.

"Why?"

Logan reached for her other hand. "That's really none of your business. Where do you keep your car keys?"

Jamie jumped up. "I know. I know." He shot out of the room.

"I really can't go." Beth didn't like the idea of getting in a car with someone she didn't know, especially one who talked of slashed bodies and plans of hibernation. "I've got to baste the turkey and start the rest of dinner soon, and—"

"How long does it have to go?"

"What?"

"The turkey." A hint of impatience tinged his voice.

"A couple of hours. But I've got too much to do—"

"What's more important, taking a chance of developing lockjaw or one stupid holiday meal?"

Once again he left her taken aback. She said the first thing that came to mind. "I've got to finish putting up the lights."

"What difference does it make?" Logan rammed the remnants of the bandage roll into the care kit. The dog pressed deeper into the corner.

Beth had pushed the wrong button, but his crumbling control over his anger and his obvious distaste at being here only made it harder to accept his help. "It's Thanksgiving tradition. Don't you have any?"

For a minute she thought he would forcibly pick her up, throw her over his shoulder and dump her into the car. Instead he placed both his hands on the kitchen table and leaned his weight on them, caging her between his arms. Her heart tripped in sudden panic. His gaze blazed into hers, dark and dangerous. She swallowed hard.

"If you let me take you to get your hands seen to, I'll finish putting up your damned lights. Is that a deal?"

Beth thought better than to refuse. "There's no need to swear."

She couldn't stand the heavy awareness of him so close to her, of the fire in his eyes, of the body heat his anger generated, of the clean scent of soap that wafted pleasantly toward her. Trying to create more space between them, she sank deeper into the chair.

Just as suddenly as he'd trapped her, Logan shoved

away. She silently sighed her relief. She wasn't used to dealing with such blatant male power.

He snatched the baster from the spoon rest on the stove, opened the oven door and doused her turkey with pan drippings. "There. Your bird'll be fine till you get back."

His gruff manner raised her hackles. Even Mildred Wallace with her stiff upper lip and regal propriety would have a hard time edifying this man about the rules of simple good manners. "Am I?"

"What?"

"Coming back."

A dark glower scudded across his face. Beth instantly regretted her outburst. Once again her mouth had spilled out words like an overfilled saucepan before her brain could censor them. Not only had she made a fool of herself, she'd insulted this person who was going out of his way to help her. "I'm—"

"Just *what* do you think I am?"

Beth's cheeks flamed once more. Taking in the worn condition of his jeans and coat, the unkempt appearance of his hair and beard, she shrugged, looked down at the thick, mummylike bandages covering her hands and stared at the thin line of red seeping through. "You don't exactly look, um, presentable."

Logan grabbed the bloody towels from the table, dumped them in the sink and sighed in exasperation. "Listen, lady, I've just moved two thousand miles. I've gotten maybe six hours of sleep over the past few days. I'd much rather leave you alone and go home, but I feel responsible for your fall—"

"The dog—"

"Never mind the dog. I shouldn't have startled you—"

"It's not your fault—"

"I don't want to have to worry about you getting lockjaw, okay? Let me take you to get your hands stitched and get a tetanus shot.'' He placed one of his huge hands over his heart. ''I swear, on my honor, that after you get some stitches, I'll drive you straight home and leave you alone.''

When he put it that way, she had no choice. The least she could do was give him the chance for some peace of mind; he seemed to have precious little of that. Of course, she'd have to pay him back for his kindness. After all, she'd been responsible for her own fall. If she hadn't acted before thinking, she'd have gotten safely down the ladder, and he'd be on his way home. Beth Lannigen owed no debts of any kind. Maybe she'd drop off one of her famous spaghetti casseroles as a housewarming gift. He didn't look like a lemon caper chicken kind of guy.

The throbbing in her hands swept away the rest of her resistance.

''All right, I'll go.'' She nearly choked on her answer.

Jamie came back with her purse in one hand and her key chain, shaped like a chef's apron, in the other. ''Can I sit in the front?''

A fleeting look of pain crossed Logan's face. ''Are there three seat belts?''

Beth nodded, confused by his mixed messages of hurt and helpfulness.

''Air bags?''

She shook her head. Her station wagon was too ancient for those.

With a blank expression he looked down at Jamie. ''I don't see why not.''

With his famous whoop of delight, Jamie charged ahead toward the garage door.

''Hat and mitts!'' Beth yelled after him.

''I'll get some from the dryer,'' Jamie answered, slamming doors as he went.

"What about the dog?" Beth asked, looking at the pitiful creature hunkered in the corner, shivering.

With a sigh Logan crossed over to the animal and gave the dog a quick onceover. "She's fine. Want her outside?"

"No, it's cold. I'll just close the kitchen doors so she can't get into any trouble." Beth rose from her chair.

With a hand on her shoulder, Logan pressed her back down. "I'll do it."

"She needs something to eat."

He slanted her a look that said she was trying his patience.

"There's some leftover meat loaf in the fridge."

Logan poked his head into the fridge and came out with a plate. "This?"

She nodded.

He ripped off the plastic covering and shoved the plate on the floor. The dog looked up at him adoringly, sweeping her ragged tail tentatively against the floor.

"Have at it," he said. The dog greedily gobbled the treat.

Somberly Logan locked the back door and closed the other door leading to the rest of the house, leaving only the entrance into the garage untouched, then came back to loom above her. "Are you ready?"

Beth nodded, keeping her gaze averted from the mesmerizing effect of his haunted eyes. As he helped her back into her jacket, her heart knocked hard once. The dog whimpered. Beth looked at the animal and thought she saw an almost human quality to its soulful gaze. Was the dog afraid to be left alone?

"She'll be all right," Logan said gently.

Once again his gentleness caught her off guard. Reluctantly she got up to follow him. When he took her elbow to guide her to the car, an odd feeling rippled through her.

Tenderness? No, that was wrong. Pity? No, that wasn't it, either.

As he closed the door, she shrugged. Whatever it was, it didn't matter. She had too much to do to worry about her surly neighbor.

But even as she sat in the car and he gently clicked on the safety belt, confusion swirled through her once more. And as he backed down the driveway, Jamie safely sandwiched between them, she wasn't sure at all if she was ready for a neighbor like Logan Ward.

## Chapter Two

Beth Lannigen was the most frustrating woman Logan had ever met—and he'd seen his share of kooks patrolling the east-side streets of Fort Worth. The woman didn't seem to understand the meaning of silence or have heard of its golden qualities. On the drive over to the emergency clinic, she'd talked nonstop about, of all things, Christmas. Even now her mouth worked in a relentless chatter as she directed Jamie out of his coat.

"Mrs. Lannigen?"

Cut off midsentence, Beth swung toward the voice at the entrance to the examining rooms. "Yes?"

"We're ready for you."

"Oh, oh, yes." She started toward the waiting nurse, then swiveled back, setting her jingle-bell earrings jangling. "Jamie, I want you to stay right where you are."

"Okay, Mom."

She put on a stern expression and extended a warning

finger in Jamie's direction. "I mean it. I don't want you to wander anywhere or leave this area."

"Okay, Mom." Jamie took a pack of hockey cards from his coat pocket and sorted through them.

"I mean it, Jamie."

"Mo-om!" He looked up from his cards with a huff of exasperation. "Knock-knock."

A surprise expression crossed Beth's face. "I don't think this is the right time—"

"Knock-knock," Jamie insisted.

A series of emotions flitted across her expressive eyes, stirring equal shots of awareness and annoyance through Logan. She finally relented, putting both him and Jamie out of their miseries. "Who's there?"

"Irma."

"Irma who?"

"Irma big boy now, Mom."

Beth's smile shook at the edges, and tears shone bright in her eyes, making Logan uncomfortable. "I know you are, sweetheart."

She hadn't moved two steps before she spun back again, extending a beckoning hand toward Jamie. "Come with me."

"Are you sure you want Jamie to see his mother being stitched up?" Logan asked. Geez, she was acting as if she were going to have both her hands cut off at the wrists.

She shook her head, took two more steps toward the nurse and turned back. She gave the receptionist a pleading glance. "Will you keep an eye out for my son?"

"I'll do my best." The phone rang, and the nurse gave Beth a perfunctory smile before picking up the receiver.

"I don't want him to leave the reception area."

Understanding suddenly dawned on Logan. Beth was afraid to leave her son with him. What an impression he'd made! He stood up, drew his bulging wallet from his back pocket.

"Here." He stuffed the wallet into her coat pocket. "That's every last dollar I own. I haven't had a chance to find a bank yet. Take it hostage. I'll watch Jamie, and I promise, we'll both be waiting for you when you come back."

Her cheeks flamed, painting her already flushed face bright red. She reached for the wallet, but couldn't get it out with her swaddled hand. "I…I—"

"The nurse is waiting." Logan jabbed his chin in the nurse's direction. "You want to get those hands seen to."

Beth lowered her gaze. "I didn't mean… Okay." She nodded and meekly followed the nurse.

Logan sank back into a chair, crossing one ankle over the other knee. She was a disturbing, disconcerting woman. Something buoyant and festive clung to her. She reminded him of the coziness of sun-warmed rocks on a chilly winter day. Even her hair smelled like the holidays, with its hint of mint. Yet a certain vulnerability edged its way through all the bright packaging as if she, too, held a painful center that hadn't quite healed.

He raked a hand through his hair and massaged the back of his neck. Lack of sleep. How else could he explain the ridiculous thoughts invading his mind? Beth Lannigen wore a pained expression because her hands probably hurt like hell. Nothing more.

He tried to focus on all the things he needed to do to fix the house to his liking, of all the hard work it would take, of the months of mindless effort he'd have to put out, but he couldn't. Thoughts of Beth pierced their way through. And the last thing he needed was someone like Beth Lannigen in his life. He slapped his foot back to the linoleum and shifted his weight.

She wasn't beautiful. Not in the perfect way his wife had been. She was too small, dressed too brightly, talked too much. But there was something about her. Something that roused an unsettling sensation.

Maybe it was the way the powder blue of her eyes made her look so soft and so vulnerable.

Vulnerability meant demands.

He shuddered.

Or maybe it was the way her smile went all the way to the heart of her eyes when she looked at her son, reminding him of his loss.

Had his daughter known how much he loved her?

Or maybe it was the way Beth tried so hard to hide her pain from Jamie, showing Logan a submerged strength that didn't match the delicate package she presented to the world.

Then again, perhaps his brain cells were finally dying from the abuse he'd put himself through for the past two years. He sighed heavily. Whatever the source of his uneasiness, Beth Lannigen was trouble with a capital *T*.

Not only was he stuck in a clinic waiting for her *and* responsible for taking care of her son, he'd promised to hang the rest of her Christmas lights. Christmas lights, for Pete's sake! How could he have let himself be manipulated this way? After he hitched up her stupid lights, he'd make sure he stayed away from her. All this bubbly perkiness and hard-headed stubbornness would drive him stark raving mad.

But he never learned. Knowing she was hurt and living alone with her son, he would feel obligated to keep an eye on her. And the restlessness he felt around her was bad enough without experiencing this damned protective inclination, too.

Once again Logan crossed one ankle over his knee and

his arms over his chest. The stink of antiseptic set his empty stomach roiling. Hospitals all smelled the same. The last time he'd been in one, he'd watched the life breathe out of his little girl.

The institutional stench and the busy sounds behind the receptionist's desk suddenly became too much. He had to move. Spotting a couple of vending machines in an alcove down the hall, he sprang from the chair. "Want something to drink, sport?"

Jamie looked up from his cards. His eyes widened with anticipation. "Can I have a soda?"

"Does your Mom let you have soda?"

Jamie's halfhearted shrug didn't fool Logan one bit. The kid probably hadn't drunk more than a six-pack of the stuff in his entire life.

"Sure, all the time." Jamie headed straight for the big red-and-white machine.

Logan stood beside him, uncomfortably aware of the boy's nearness, of his small, fragile body, of his little boy baby shampoo and wet boot scent, and fished coins from his jeans pocket before thoughts of Samantha invaded his already frazzled brain and soaked it with sadness. With a deft sidestep, he put more distance between himself and the boy. "So what'll it be, sport?"

"Can I have anything I want?"

"Sure."

Jamie cocked his head and concentrated on his selection. "Mom's going to be all right, isn't she?"

"Sure, sport. The doctor's patching her up right now. She'll be good as new."

Logan half hoped the doctor would give her a sedative so he wouldn't have to endure her incessant chatter on the way home. It was bad enough to have her sitting in the car next to him without being overwhelmed by her hummingbird brightness and effervescence every minute of the way. "So, what'll it be?"

Jamie pointed toward an orange drink. Logan stuffed coins into the machine and let the boy press the lit button. The can clanged to the bottom of the machine. Jamie picked it up and popped the top.

Logan opted for a cup of coffee from the next machine over.

They headed back toward the waiting area and sat in opposing chairs. Holding the can with both hands, Jamie sipped from it. As the boy shuffled his feet back and forth along the grime-colored linoleum tiles, the tread of his boots made an irritating noise. But Logan didn't mind. Better the sound of boots than the muted buzzes and clicks of hospital machinery. Resting his elbows on the chair's arms, Logan held the cup close to his nose, edging out the surrounding clinic smells of disinfectant and death with the strong aroma of black coffee.

Jamie's penetrating gaze never left Logan's face. How on earth had the boy managed such a big orange mustache from the can's tiny opening?

"How come you bought Miss Mac's house?" Jamie asked.

"It was for sale." Jamie's eyes were shaped like Beth's—large and open, fringed with long lashes. The hazel of his irises was as soft and gentle as Beth's blue.

"I like my house. Didn't you like your house?"

Logan grunted and took a sip of his bitter coffee. He'd moved because the house held too many memories—the deepest joy, the rawest pain, the greatest betrayal. He'd had to get away.

"How come?"

"Because," Logan answered, knowing Jamie expected

words, wanted comforting. But he couldn't give the boy what he needed. Didn't dare to.

"How come your skin looks green?"

Logan ran a hand along his stubbly cheek. He felt green. Hospitals did that to him. He knew of no way to explain the misery of life to a child, nor did he care to. "You're sure full of questions."

"Mom says you gotta ask questions to learn."

Logan leaned forward and patted Jamie's knee reassuringly. "Your mom's going to be just fine."

When he felt the fragile bones beneath his fingers, he had to force himself not to recoil. Once more he leaned back in the chair, crossed his legs and arms, and nursed the cooling coffee. "So, are you learning a lot?"

"Yep. I'm in first grade. I can read. Want me to show you?"

*No.* "Sure, sport."

Jamie scrambled off his chair and climbed into the one next to Logan. Logan thought Jamie would reach for the Dr. Seuss book on the table littered with magazines and newspapers, but instead he turned over the first hockey card in his stack.

"The Bruins are hot this year. First in their division," Jamie said, leaning his body into Logan's so Logan could see the card. "Brian Dafoe's my fav'rite player."

Logan stiffened against the contact, but didn't move. "How come?"

"He's a goalie and wears a cool mask." Jamie rattled off a bunch of Dafoe's statistics. More by rote than actual reading, Logan suspected.

"Do you play hockey?" Jamie asked, interrupting himself.

"Not anymore. How about you?" The coffee in his cup no longer warmed his fingers.

"Naw, not the real stuff. Mom says I'm too little. But when I'm eight, I'm gonna play in the Mite league. Bobby's brother gets to play. I wish I was bigger already."

*Daddy, please. Everybody's got a bike. Katie and Allison and Jessica. I'm the only one—*

*Katie and Allison and Jessica are all bigger than you.*

*But, Daddy…*

The boy's chatter brought him out of his miserable memory fog. Like mother, like son. Their home probably never knew a moment of peace and quiet. A bullet of envy ricocheted through him. Logan shook his head. No, he didn't want that. He wanted silence and solitude.

"When there's more ice on the pond, I'm gonna go skating," Jamie said. "I'm getting real hockey skates for Christmas. And a new stick. A goalie stick. You got skates?"

"I used to." Probably still did somewhere in those boxes scattered all over his house. He'd bought a pair of skates for himself and another for Sam and taken her skating at the Tandy Center. She'd giggled and laughed every minute of their outings even though she'd spent more time on her bottom than on her blades.

"Maybe we could go together," Jamie said, eyes full of hope.

*Don't look at me that way.* Logan shifted his weight and distracted himself from the growing apprehension in the pit of his stomach with a swallow of cold coffee. "I've got a lot of work to do, sport. Maybe your mom'll take you."

"Yeah, but she won't play hockey." Jamie shuffled his cards, his disappointment clear in the pout of his lower lip and the rounding of his shoulders. "She's a *girl*. She just wants to twirl and jump. That's no fun."

"All the good hockey players practice their skating moves." Logan crushed the empty foam coffee cup and lobbed it toward the garbage can, missing it by a mile. He got up to dispose of it properly, glad to get away from the child who stirred too many emotions with his innocent questions.

Just then Beth reappeared, looking a little green herself.

"Mommy!" Jamie launched himself at her.

Logan joined them. "Take it easy, sport."

"That's okay." Beth crouched to Jamie's level and showed him her bandaged hands. "See, I'm perfectly all right."

The nurse made eye contact with Logan. "She needs to have those sutures removed in about a week. Here's a prescription for something for the pain. The pharmacy down the hall is open twenty-four hours."

Before Logan could say anything, the door closed, and the nurse was gone.

They filled the prescription. Beth waited with Jamie snuggled contentedly by her side and said not a word. Logan paced the tiny space. Her silence seemed worse than her nonstop chatter. Even the bright color of her coat couldn't hide the pallor of her skin. Nor could her smile, directed at Jamie, quite hide the creases of pain around her eyes.

Once in the car and on their way home, Jamie's worry seemed to vanish.

"Knock-knock," Jamie said.

"Who's there?" Beth's parody of perky didn't match the real thing Logan had witnessed this morning. He admired her courage.

"Owl."

"Owl who?"

"Owl aboard. We're going home!"

Jamie laughed at his own joke and peppered his mother with more until she begged for mercy.

Sam had loved jokes, too. Hers ran to the nutty kind.

*Daddy, what do angels do to greet each other?*

*Haven't got a clue.*

*They wave halo.* She'd dissolve into giggles the same way Jamie had. *Get it, Dad? Get it? They wave halo?*

Logan concentrated on his driving. Amazing how well Beth's old beat-up station wagon handled. Snow tires did make a difference.

"Mom?"

"Yes, Jamie."

"What about the tree? You said we'd get one today."

Beth tucked a strand of Jamie's soft-brown hair beneath his red-and-white knit cap. "I think we'll have to leave the chopping to someone else this year."

Jamie's head snapped in Logan's direction without a moment's hesitation. "Can you do it?"

"Umph." Guilt carried only so far. He had to draw the line somewhere. And cutting down a Christmas tree was it. "Why would you want to chop down a perfectly good tree and drag it inside?"

"To decorate it, silly."

Beth's gaze glanced at Logan's knuckles turning white from his hard grip on the steering wheel, then to his face. He forced his grip to relax but refused to look in her direction, even when he felt her question as clearly as if she'd uttered it. His aversion to Christmas was his own business.

"He's right, Jamie. This year we'll get a live tree from the nursery. Then in the spring we'll plant it outside and remember all year what a great Christmas we had."

Logan swallowed a groan. She'd probably plant it where he could see stray tinsel all year. Whatever force directed the universe had a wicked sense of humor. Of all the houses he could have bought, what on earth had made him choose the one next to hers?

"Can I pick out the tree?" Jamie asked.

"You certainly may. But not today, okay? Maybe tomorrow when we go in to town."

Jamie whined his disappointment. "But we always put up the tree on Thanksgiving."

"Your mom's hands hurt. She needs to rest them." Logan silently cursed the edge to his voice. All this fuss over a tree. For what? A holiday that had long ceased having meaning to anyone but merchants.

And kids.

Acid bubbled in his stomach. He tightened his grip on the steering wheel. The anger, always on the edge of erupting, tasted like blood in his mouth. If he didn't vent his fury soon, he couldn't be sure how it would explode. He didn't want anyone to witness one of his descents into hell.

Spotting her house around the curve proved a great relief. Beth didn't know how much longer she could keep up the pretense of cheerfulness. The pain wasn't so much the cause of her discomfort—the drugs were taking care of that—but the tension emanating from Logan had her mind whirling with a thousand questions. None of which were her business, and none of which she should give two hoots about.

But for some inconceivable reason she did. She needed to make sense out of the man who'd bowled his way into her life. After all, he was her new neighbor.

For Jamie's sake, she rationalized.

But that line of thought didn't go far. It was something else altogether that made her mind whirl. Just like the teenage girls who flocked to her at the high school where she worked—"just to talk, Mrs. L., if you've got a minute"—Beth recognized in Logan the signs of a troubled human being. And something in her couldn't help responding.

"We're home! We're home!" Jamie shouted.

Logan pressed the automatic door opener and pulled into the garage. The car had barely come to a stop when Jamie scrambled out of the seat belt, bolted over Beth and out the door before she could stop him. "Jamie—"

"I gotta *go,* Mom!" He continued his mad dash for the bathroom without a backward glance.

Logan switched off the engine and shifted his impenetrable gaze in her direction. "I don't suppose you're the type of woman who takes advice kindly."

Now what would make him say that? Beth considered herself one of the most easygoing people she knew. And he was one to talk. The way he'd forced her to go to the clinic certainly proved *his* stubbornness. "Not any more than you're the kind of man who takes no for an answer."

"I'll give you some, anyway." He removed the key from the ignition and dropped the chef's apron key chain into her open purse. "Rest. You'll heal faster."

"I can't." Didn't he know what day this was? For her, Christmas started Thanksgiving Day. After stuffing the turkey and placing it in the oven to roast came the annual raid of the attic for the multitude of seasonal decorations she kept there. While the turkey cooked, she always trimmed the outside of the house. After consuming an early dinner, they always went out to chop the tree. The day always ended with sipping hot chocolate, stirred with a candy cane, while she and Jamie decorated the tree. As they placed the angel on the treetop, they always sang Christmas carols.

She needed this time alone with Jamie to prepare herself for the official start of the holiday season at the pie extravaganza at the Fellowship Hall. This ritual got her in the Christmas mood. This ritual made her remember her promise. This ritual helped her temper the pain of her loss. "It's Thanksgiving Day."

Logan pressed his hands into the steering wheel. He stared blankly straight ahead and ground his teeth in a tight circle. Beth could almost hear him counting and trying to swallow his anger. What was with him and the holidays?

"What's so important about a damned holiday meal?" His carefully modulated words sounded like shattering icicles.

Unable to round up her scurrying feelings and give Logan a cohesive answer, Beth looked down at her bandaged hands. The nurse had taken off her wedding band to accommodate her swelling fingers, shaving another piece of Jim from her. The ring burned in her pants pocket, and she longed to wear it next to her skin once more to calm the horrifying fear that Jim would leave her heart as he had her life.

"It's a matter of survival," she said finally.

Logan nodded once. In that instant she felt close to him, knew he understood perfectly the effort living sometimes exacted. But even as she wondered how he could, tiredness from the painkiller enveloped her in a weighty blanket.

"I think I will take a nap." She dragged her heavy legs from the car and headed toward the welcoming warmth of her home.

As Logan got out of the car, the vinyl seat shifted. "I'll see to your lights."

"You don't have to." A dullness overcame her, making each movement an effort.

"A deal's a deal. I always keep my word."

A man of honor. Like Jim. She nodded once and watched him leave.

Jamie bounded back into the garage. "Can I help?"

"No!"

At Logan's bark, Beth startled, and Jamie instinctively retreated toward her, lifting his arms around her waist for protection. What on earth had warranted such a forceful reaction?

Jamie's fearful response seemed to make Logan instantly contrite. "I didn't mean to yell at you, sport. Someone has to watch your mom. Since you know her best, I thought you might want to. Will you make sure she lies down and rests?"

Eyes wide, Jamie nodded.

Logan walked away, shoulders hunched as if they carried a massive burden.

"Come on." Beth smiled down at Jamie and squeezed his shoulders tenderly. "Let's go check on that turkey."

"How long till we eat? I'm hungry."

"A while longer." The turkey would be overdone, but Beth didn't care. This whole holiday had a mind of its own this year, and she needed a nap before she tackled dinner.

She led Jamie inside, saw a sprawl of Cheerios on the floor and remembered the bedraggled mutt. The dog was snuggled in the corner, eyeing her with a guilty expression.

"It's okay, girl," Beth reassured. The poor thing's ribs were clearly visible beneath the loose skin of her dull brown coat. "I should have known one slice of meat loaf wasn't going to be enough. Let me get you something else."

The dog wagged her tail tentatively, then looked past Beth expectantly as if she were waiting for someone else to walk through the door. Was she afraid of Logan? Considering his gruff manner, she didn't blame the dog.

"It's okay," she reassured the dog once more. "He won't be back for a while."

Though it surely was a figment of her imagination, Beth thought she saw disappointment in the dog's molasses eyes. You really need a nap, Beth.

Jamie dropped his hat, mitts and coat on the floor and

crouched next to the animal. After a moment's hesitation he gently patted her head. She licked his hand. He giggled and maneuvered closer.

"Can we keep her?" he asked, fast becoming friends with the dog.

"We'll see."

She gave both of them a snack to stave off hunger until the turkey was done. After checking on the bird, she shuffled her way to the living room.

A maze of boxes, spread out on the living room floor, waited for her. She ignored them and plopped onto the couch. A smiling angel with long white hair poked from the nearest box. Beth picked it up and straightened the crooked halo. Jim had bought it for her the first Christmas they'd spent together as husband and wife.

Memories flooded her mind. Like an old movie the colors seemed bleached from the track, leaving everything in black and white. Tears pressed the corners of her eyes. Beth wiped them away before they could fall. As hard as she tried to keep Jim's memory full and vibrant, she recently discovered parts of him were fading.

Not the love. No, that still filled her heart. But the details— his hair's exact shade of brown, the tone of his laughter, which cheek held the deepest dimple. She was forgetting the person who'd been the center of her life since she was eighteen, and the thought petrified her.

But for Jamie's sake she would make Christmas happy. She'd promised.

Next week the Beautification Committee would start putting up the Christmas decorations in town. The parade plans needed finalization, the tree-lighting ceremony needed a few tweaks, the live nativity tryouts needed scheduling, and her sweet-tooth booth for the Holiday Fair needed filling. Not to mention she still had her Christmas shopping to finish, and finding a safe place to hide her goodies from Jamie would take ingenuity.

She would be too busy to cry.

Beth returned the angel to its box, shifted the red-and-blue pillow beneath her head and swung her feet up. Jamie snatched the colorful granny-square afghan from the bentwood rocker and tucked it clumsily around her legs. "Thank you, sweetheart."

"Can I watch a movie?"

"Sure."

Boy and dog sprawled in front of the television. As music from Jamie's video drifted toward her, her eyes drooped. With a sigh she stopped fighting sleep and invited it in. But as images of Jim and Logan mixed one into the other and traipsed across the screen of her lids, she couldn't decide if they were a dream or a nightmare, and in her drugged fog she couldn't stop them.

## Chapter Three

"Where do you want these boxes?"

Logan's deep voice startled Beth. Her attention concentrated on lifting the turkey in its roasting pan, she hadn't heard him come in. She dropped the pan on the opened oven door. Pan juices splattered on her sweater's sleeve, the oven mitts and the only inch of exposed skin between the top of her mitts and her raised sweater cuffs. She yelped.

"For Pete's sake!" Logan tossed the empty light boxes aside, rushed toward her and with a kitchen towel thrust the roasting pan squarely back onto the rack. "If you need help, ask for it."

"I don't need help. I'm perfectly capable—"

"Yeah, with two hands swaddled and a body pumped full of painkillers, you're perfectly capable of hurting yourself."

"I can do it myself...."

Realizing she sounded like a two-year-old, Beth let her voice drift and sagged next to the open oven. Heat swirled around her face, and she was overwhelmed by the scent of burning turkey wings.

The pain pill she'd taken earlier was wearing off. A headache had taken up residence, pounding a jungle beat along her temples. Her hands throbbed. Because she'd overslept, the turkey was overdone and nothing else for her Thanksgiving meal was prepared.

This whole day was turning into a giant disaster. How was she going to make it through Christmas if she couldn't get it started right? And now, to make the whole situation even more unbearable, hot tears gushed down her cheeks.

"Aw, no. Don't cry." Logan crouched next to her, put his hands tentatively on her shoulders and snapped them away just as fast. "I can't stand tears."

"I'm not crying. I never cry." Using the back of one oven mitt, she wiped the salty stream from her face.

He removed the mitts from her hands. "And I suppose this wet stuff staining the poinsettias on your mitts is steam from the turkey."

Beth rested her back against the cabinet behind her and sighed. "It's ruined."

"What?" Logan reached up and closed the oven door.

"The turkey. It's overcooked. It'll be dry. Gourmet chefs aren't supposed to mess up Thanksgiving dinner." What was wrong with her? A little chicken broth and some gravy could rescue the meat. But she couldn't seem to get out from under the dark cloud positioned over her head, and she babbled on like an idiot. "Jamie's hungry. I don't have any dog food. The turkey's ruined and nothing else is ready. We're going to be late for the pie extravaganza."

He closed his eyes, and his head fell forward. Once again, Beth had the impression he was counting in order to keep his temper in check. And once more she got the feeling from the stern set of his face, from the twitch of his jaw muscle and the narrowing of his eyes that he'd rather knock on hell's door than stay in her home.

And worse than that, she wanted him to stay. Him. A stranger. A man. In her kitchen.

With the pain strumming her palms and Thanksgiving falling apart around her like a ruined soufflé, she suddenly realized she didn't want to be alone. And a surly stranger seemed a much better alternative than disturbing Eve's plans with Gus. Eve already did too much for her.

"It's only a meal," Logan said.

"It's *Thanksgiving.*"

After a silence that seemed to last forever and a glare that made her feel like the world's biggest idiot, he said, "What do you need done?"

For a moment she couldn't speak. She could only stare at the enigma of a man crouched before her. She was being selfish. He'd just moved two thousand miles. He was tired. And he probably had a ton of boxes to unpack. "Nothing. You've done enough already."

"And just how are you planning on cooking this grandiose meal of yours?"

"I'll manage." She lifted her hands. "This isn't your fault."

He clenched his jaw.

"Isn't someone waiting for you?" Beth asked, searching for a way to give him an easy out. "Don't you have somewhere to go for Thanksgiving?"

"Don't you?"

She'd refused, as she did every year, at least a half dozen invitations. She couldn't explain to him how important it was for her to be home where the happy memories were. It was as close to Jim as she could get—this time of the year and all the little traditions they'd started together. "It's our special time, mine and Jamie's. We always eat at home together."

For an instant his haunted eyes swirled with emotions, and his sadness touched off chords of recognition deep in her soul. Her hands reached for his and covered them, feeling their chapped cold even through her bandages. He snatched his hands from beneath hers and rose abruptly.

She sprang up and found herself staring at his jacketed chest. Not exactly what she had in mind, but she didn't want to have to crane her neck to look into his eyes.

"What was I thinking?" she said. "Of course you don't have anywhere to go, you just moved here. So you'll stay with us." She whirled around reaching for the drawer in which she kept her table linens. With something concrete to do, some way to repay her new neighbor for his kindness, she brightened. "I'll set an extra place."

"No."

"What?" Looking over her shoulder, she raised both her eyebrows in exaggerated surprise. "You've got someone else you need to bellow at today?"

His body tensed, and Beth quickly tried to cover up her faux pas. Tablecloth in hand, she headed for the table. "Besides, you're right. With my hands bandaged like this, I can't carve, and Jamie's too young to attempt the job."

This excuse was as close as she could come to asking for his help once more. His assessing gaze made her feel like water dropped onto a hot griddle. Carefully, with measured movements, she spread the cloth over the table, giving the task all of her attention. Anything to get away from him and to focus on something less intimidating.

"What do you need done?"

His response held no warmth, but his glacial tone didn't bother Beth. His answer consumed some of the tension his silence had erected. She hadn't realized she held her breath until she found herself having to dole it out in order not to sigh her relief too loudly. To avoid his barbecuing gaze, she swiveled to the counter. "Let me find my list."

Then her body couldn't contain the excess energy percolating in her muscles, and she popped like the bubbles in a boiling pot of water. "I was going to make Duchess potatoes—"

"What? You don't think I can handle Duchess potatoes?"

She stopped midstep and stared at him mouth open. Was he kidding? Or had she managed to hurt his feelings once more? From the serious set of his face, she couldn't be sure. "I'm sure you can handle anything you set your mind to, but for simplicity's sake, mashed will have to do."

As she moved around the kitchen opening cupboards and plucking ingredients from them, her voice tripped almost as fast as the spastic movements of her body, and neither could keep up with her breakneck thoughts. It was crazy. It was nuts. It should feel odd, out of place, to have someone like him in her kitchen. Today of all days. But somehow it didn't.

"The squash casserole needs reheating," she rambled. "Then there's the fall vegetable medley to prepare. I made rolls yesterday. The cranberry mold should be set by now. Let me see—"

Logan grasped her wrist midflight and pulled her toward a chair. "Sit. Your fluttering is driving me crazy."

Beth plopped into the chair. "Well, I—"

"Don't you know how to relax?"

"You're one to talk!" Beth answered with a snort. When he freed her wrist, she placed her hand over the trace of unexpected heat his fingers left behind.

Logan unzipped his bulky ski jacket and pulled it off his

shoulders. When he turned around to drop it onto a chair, Beth gasped and one bandaged hand flew to her mouth. His dark-green flannel shirt hung on his frame like a big brother's hand-me-down. A much bigger brother. "When was the last time you ate?"

He gave her his best glower yet, but so shocked was she by his thin frame, she barely noticed.

"Do you always meddle in other people's business?" Logan headed for the counter where a five-pound bag of Yukon Gold potatoes waited. "How many do you want peeled?"

"Six. Here let me get you—" She interrupted herself halfway to the two aprons hooked behind a door. "Never mind." He definitely didn't look like an apron-wearing kind of guy. Not with that lean male strength so raw and potent and close to the surface, even in his underfed state. An image of him in frills popped into her head, and the absurdity of the picture made her laugh out loud.

"What's so funny?" he asked sharply without looking at her.

"The thought of you in a frilly apron."

He grunted his unamused answer.

Beth had never before known anyone who seemed so lacking in a sense of humor. The thought of him in an apron held some appeal after all. With his hard edges softened by the ruffles and a smile on his lips, he would paint an endearing picture. Her cheeks flamed. To cover up her embarrassment, she zigged to the fridge and pulled the door open.

Somewhere between the clinic and the potatoes, she'd ceased to fear Logan. He might present himself like a bear with a grudge, but below the prickly front, she sensed he hid a troubled soul. When she saw his too-lean frame, she knew she had to help him. With what, she wasn't sure. If nothing else, she could feed him until some meat reappeared on his bones. A few good meals might even sweeten his sour disposition.

She piled containers from the fridge in one arm. A plastic bowl teetered and clattered to the floor.

"That's it." Logan slapped a half-peeled potato and the peeler on the counter, grabbed the contents of her arms and banged them on the table. He grasped her shoulders and marched her back to the chair. "Sit and don't move."

She bounced back up. "I can't. It's not in my nature to watch someone else work and do nothing."

Keeping busy—active, as her mother called it—had been her legacy from two parents devoted to community service. And her saving grace after Jim's death.

"Get used to it. If you keep insisting on using those hands, the stitches will pop open and get infected." He brought his face a mere inch from hers, stared at her like a ghost-story teller around a crackling camp fire. The color of his eyes swirled like smoke over a mystery. She licked her lips against the sudden heat engulfing her. He lowered his voice to a harsh whisper. In spite of herself, she shivered. "Then they'll have to chop your hands off. A chef needs hands to work, doesn't she?"

Without giving her a chance to answer, he whipped back to the potatoes and attacked them with a vengeance.

Well, of all the nerve! She crossed her arms under her chest, squirming with unsettling tension. "Oh, and are you planning on being around every time I need to use my hands?"

He chopped the potatoes with more force than needed and dumped the pieces into a waiting pot, splashing water onto the stove's top.

"Should I call you every time I need a meal prepared, a

box lifted, a…'' She couldn't think of anything to add. ''A shower?''

Uninvited images of his hands soaping her wet body sent a shiver of longing deep inside her. Why? Logan's stiff, mechanical movements offered nothing to swoon over. What was wrong with her? She took the vial of painkiller from her sweater's pocket and examined the label. No mention was made of hallucinations as a side effect.

She fingered the ridges on the bottle's child-safety cap and sighed heavily. She missed Jim, that was all. He'd always made the holidays special—which made his absence today all the more painful and noticeable.

But Logan wasn't Jim. They were as different as a winter blizzard and summer sunshine. She couldn't confuse the presence of one for the feelings she held for the other. No good would come of it.

''Do your hands hurt?'' Logan's voice brought her back to the present. She glanced at the pill bottle.

''No.'' They hurt like heck, but she wanted to enjoy her holiday meal—for Jamie's sake—and not spend it in a drugged fog. She shoved the bottle back into her pocket. ''I'm sorry. I shouldn't take out my frustrations on you. It's just hard…'' She shrugged and concentrated on the dried slush marks on her tile floor.

He grunted and went back to his task.

She watched her somber neighbor move about her kitchen, handling her Calphalon pots and pans with the delicacy a drill sergeant might show boot-camp rejects, wielding her Henckels knives with the finesse of a hunter field-dressing a deer. No wonder he was so thin. He probably ate from tin cans and cardboard boxes. How else could she explain his unfamiliarity with the proper use of kitchen equipment? Yet there was also something in his manner that showed he wasn't completely clueless about cooking.

She tamped back the new set of questions forming in her mind. *I don't want to know.*

The dog kept poking her head in the kitchen, big brown eyes darting from Logan to Beth. As soon as either caught her in the act, she retreated into the living room.

While Beth instructed Logan on the dinner preparations, Jamie switched videos. The words and music of Dr. Seuss's *How the Grinch Stole Christmas* drifted into the kitchen. Her fingers toyed idly with the silverware piled on the table, and her gaze studied Logan's back.

Cuddly as a cactus? That fits. Charming as an eel? Make that an electric one. His heart an empty hole? But why? Garlic on his soul? No, not garlic, but sadness. The kind of deep sadness that could turn off the sunshine in anybody's eyes.

She knew. She'd been there.

Logan turned and caught her staring. Blushing madly, she quickly busied herself setting the table, feeling as guilty as the dog did when she poked her head into the kitchen. What was the mutt's interest in Logan, anyway?

"What else?" He looked at her as if he'd wanted to ask a different question, and she found herself wishing he had.

"That's it. We're all set." She fiddled with a napkin, but his intense gaze didn't lessen. "I'll, um, go get Jamie to wash up."

Despite a rocky start, the meal didn't turn out half as bad as Beth had expected. After consuming a hefty portion of her own, the dog trolled the table like a shark and begged shamelessly for handouts. Neither Beth nor Jamie could resist those liquid eyes. But although the dog spent most of her time next to Logan's chair, he ignored her. And with each mouthful he took, Beth found her curiosity about her new neighbor deepening.

Jamie kept the conversation lively, if one-sided. His

laughter, along with the bright red-green-and-gold napkins and burning candles, gave the kitchen a cheery atmosphere. Logan didn't speak unless spoken to. He ate with concentration, if not gusto, never looking at either her or Jamie directly. Almost as if he were shielding himself from the pleasure a simple meal could afford him.

Jamie interrupted her thoughts. "Knock-knock."

"Who's there?" Beth asked, thankful for the distraction. Logan Ward and his obsession with self-punishment were none of her business.

"Atomic."

"Atomic who?" But the why of his sadness niggled at her like a cake cut crooked begging to be straightened. She angled Logan a glance. Heat flamed her cheeks when he caught her in the act.

"Atomic ache from eating too much!"

Beth laughed with Jamie. "Do you have room for pie?"

Jamie pretended to ponder the question and flashed her a mischievous grin. "Maybe just one piece. Or two. I hope Mrs. Parker made her chocolate pie again. I'll get my coat."

He scampered away.

"How about you, Logan?" His name tasted strange on her tongue. Not altogether unpleasant, she decided. "Room for dessert? The pie extravaganza at the fellowship hall lives up to its name. More pie than any one town can consume."

For a moment so small Beth thought she'd imagined it, something warm and volcanic flared deep in Logan's eyes. And if she hadn't witnessed his surliness all afternoon, she might easily have mistaken the look as the kind a man gives a woman who interests him. But on second glance she saw nothing in his dark-gray eyes but a thick slab of ice even the sharpest pick couldn't get through. The figment of warmth had been nothing but her overactive imagination and her loneliness in action. So why the strange sense of disappointment?

Shaking her head, she gathered her plate and rose. *You're really losing it, Beth.*

Logan cleared his throat and took the plate from her hands. "I'd better start on those dishes for you."

"I'll wait for you here," Logan said as he turned off the car's engine.

"You'll do no such thing. It's freezing out here, and you're not used to the cold. Besides, Jamie can't reach the handle on the front door, and you're the one who keeps insisting I shouldn't use my hands."

His jaw ached from all the teeth grinding he'd done during the day, but rather than argue and prolong his ordeal, he pocketed the keys and followed her to the town hall. The sooner he got her to eat her blasted pie, the sooner he could get her home again.

The fellowship hall was on the second floor of the town hall building. Beth informed him the narrow, creaky stairs they scaled were more than a hundred years old and gave him more history on the building than he cared to know. The noise of festivities grew with each stair they climbed, souring his already irritable disposition.

People, a mass of them, were stuffed into the hall. Coats were piled onto the stage at the back of the room. Children raced and yelled and laughed, grating on his already raw nerves. Adults stood or sat in clusters talking, shifting now and then like the image in a kaleidoscope to visit with a new set of people.

The scent of age and wood wax was overtaken by the cloying aroma of sugar. His stomach protested. Table after table rimmed the perimeter of the room. Pie plates were set close to the wall. Precut pieces from the pies waited on paper plates to be sampled. Beth was right. There was enough pie to feed a third-world country.

And Logan wanted to be anywhere but here.

At least there were no wreaths or poinsettias or bright lights trimming the place, only decorative gourds and fake autumn leaves artfully spread from straw horns at each of the tables.

Jamie discarded his coat at his mother's feet, then raced away to join a pack of boys his age creating chaos in one corner.

"What kind of pie do you want?" Beth asked as he helped her out of her coat and held on to it. The last thing he wanted was to have it disappear in the mound on the stage. His game plan was to leave as soon as possible, not waste an hour looking for a coat.

"What kind did you make?"

She blushed, bringing too much warm life to her China-doll skin. "Apple cranberry with a crumb topping."

"That's fine."

As she made her way to one of the pie tables, it didn't take long for Beth's bandaged hands to be noticed. She was swept away in a wave of humans like a duck riding a wave in a storm. She was fussed over and questioned, and curious glances kept darting in his direction. A few brave souls tried to engage him in conversation. He kept it short and snappy, and soon interest dwindled. Bits and pieces of conversation floated to him and didn't do anything to set his mind at peace.

"…Beth's latest stray."

"He's staying at her place?"

"No, no, he bought the MacDonald property across…"

"…no snow tires—"

"—all-season radials work just as well, if you ask me."

"No one asked you."

"...a dog, no kids..."

"...from Texas."

"What does he do?"

"Don't know. She didn't say. But if things are on par, he's just another fixer-upper...."

And Logan stood there in his corner frowning, hating every minute of the evening. Just what he needed, the whole town meddling in his business.

After what seemed like an eternity, a teenager whose blond hair was bedecked in dreadlocks sat at the piano on the stage and banged out a few chords to draw attention to himself. A sturdy matron who looked to be about sixty clambered onto the stage and went to stand next to the piano. She patted the long brown curl of her outdated flip hairdo and smoothed the lapel of her bright-red jacket.

"Hello!" The microphone shrieked with feedback. Someone adjusted it for her. "Is that better? Great. I trust everyone has helped themselves to pie."

She nodded and smiled regally, like a queen to her benevolent subjects.

"Louder, Mildred. We can't hear you back here."

"Turn up your hearing aid, Carl."

A chuckle ran through the room.

"I'd like to call your attention to the table by the main doors," Mildred continued, pointing her manicured fingers vaguely toward the back of the room. "The Beautification Committee has placed sign-up sheets for volunteers. We would really appreciate a good turnout in order to make this the best holiday season ever."

A grumble traveled through the crowd.

"Now, now. With the SuperMart going up next door, we've got to do all we can to keep our town together."

A fist went up and pumped the air. "Darn right we do.

Remember to 'Wrap It Up Locally.' It's gonna benefit us all.''

A murmur of agreement swarmed through the room.

Mildred patted her hair again. "All right, with business out of the way and pie in our bellies, all that's missing is the right note to get us all in the holiday mood."

Mildred turned to the kid at the piano. "Ready?"

The kid nodded and struck a few chords.

Then they did the worst thing of all.

They sang.

Christmas carols with sleigh bells and Santa Claus and enough merriment to choke a dozen reindeer.

And just when Logan thought he couldn't take another second more of this holiday cheer, Beth came toward him with a protesting Jamie by her side, and a part of him breathed easier.

"I wanna stay!" Jamie whined, dragging his feet.

"I'm sorry, Logan." Beth's regret showed in the softening of her powder-blue eyes. "I shouldn't have brought you here."

"I didn't even get any pie," Jamie continued.

"We'll get some at home."

"Bobby—"

"That's enough, Jamie." She handed the boy his coat and took hers from Logan's arms. "Let's go home."

And though he knew she belonged here in all that community and glee, he could have kissed her for walking away from it all in order to free him from his torment.

Logan stuffed his hands deep in his jacket pockets and buried his chin in his jacket collar to keep out the cold air. The crunching of his boots on the snow was the only sound disturbing the quiet of the night.

He'd forgotten how much he liked that sound. He'd been

seventeen the last time he'd felt snow beneath his boots. His grandfather had died that spring, and his mother had sold the cabin in New Hampshire without listening to her son's objections. With it had gone some of his fondest childhood memories—hockey on the pond, fishing in the summer and his grandfather's love. Logan had never known his father, and his mother never tired of letting him know she worked two jobs just to keep food on the table and a roof over his head. She didn't have time to love him, only to resent him.

Logan stepped high over the downed rail in the fence bordering his property. He took a few strides forward, then turned back to secure the rail into its hole in the post. Not that it would stop Jamie from trespassing. A quick glance at Beth's house brought regret. The lights he'd cursed while installing shone a bright beacon in the dark night. With determination, he turned his back on the festive spectacle, resuming the dour track of his winter memories.

When Julia had come into his life, he'd thought he would finally have his dream of a real family, but she'd come from a loveless background, too, and hadn't known how to give what she'd never received. He'd been twenty-two and still full of hope then—he was going to change her mind, change the world, make a difference. What a crock!

The dream had proved a mirage. Julia had cried when she found out she was pregnant and hadn't stopped crying even after their child was born. Logan had known then his dream would forever remain an illusion. But he'd been determined his daughter wouldn't suffer the way he and Julia had. He'd spent his days showering Samantha with love and time, hoping she would never notice the shaky foundation on which their family stood.

Family.

Watching Beth and Jamie together, he'd felt that longing

surge forward once more. Must have been the combination of hot food and her warm kitchen. He hadn't eaten a meal like that since…since he couldn't remember. He hadn't felt so much warmth in forever either. And instead of gratitude for Beth's compassion at the pie extravaganza, he seethed with renewed anger.

Damn the woman, anyway. Hadn't he predicted she'd be trouble from the moment he'd seen her perched on that ladder with all those bright decorations around her?

Logan hunched his shoulders and kicked at the snow. What had possessed him to share a meal with his neighbors? To drive them to their blasted pie gorging event and subject himself to all those curious stares and whispered questions?

Hunger, came the answer.

He didn't like the thoughts forming in his mind and tried to blast them into nothingness. But the more he tried not to think of Beth, the more his addled brain filled with images of her.

*Logan.* The echo of Beth's voice still reverberated in his mind. He wasn't used to hearing his name said without rancor or regret. And when she'd said his name at the table, he'd felt the sharp pangs of a man's hunger for a woman's touch.

But thinking along those lines was dangerous. Deadly. Someone like her couldn't offer him what he needed, and he couldn't give her anything at all.

He turned the corner of his house, glad to be back at his cold home where he could nurse his misery in peace. The sadness of the house had appealed to him—the gray exterior, the equally dismal interior, the creaky stairs and all that age-dulled woodwork to be refinished. The sheer amount of physical work needed to whip the place into shape would keep him too busy to feel.

On the first step to his front door he stopped in his tracks. There, waiting for him, was that damned mutt again.

As if Logan were her long-lost master, the dog shot up and wagged her rear. She had a spaniel's tail, a terrier's short-haired, dark-brown coat, ears that couldn't decide if they wanted to stand up straight or flop over and the most insipid grin imaginable on an animal.

"Oh, no!" He reached the dog in two steps. He tried tugging on the hair around her neck to get her to move. "Go on. Shoo!"

The thing couldn't weigh more than twenty pounds, yet she refused to budge. In a change of tactics, he moved to the rear end and pushed. The dog hunkered down, making it impossible to shift the beast. "I've reached my limit of goodwill today. Go home where you belong. Go to Beth's. She'll take you in."

Logan grabbed the scraggly mutt by the middle, but when he tried to lift the animal, she snarled at him and threatened to bite. "Fine. See if I care. You're not coming in. That's final. And it's going to get mighty cold out here."

The dog cocked her head, making her eyes melt the way only dogs could. "Forget it. I haven't got an ounce of charity left."

Logan opened the door, walked into the house and slammed the door behind him. From the empty front parlor, he peeked outside. The dog lay curled near the door, nose buried in the intersection of her back and front feet, tail covering the whole like a pitiful blanket.

Why should he care if the stupid dog had confused him for someone he wasn't? The dog wasn't his. She wasn't his responsibility.

He trudged to the kitchen on the other side of the hallway. Boxes still lay haphazardly on the floor, but Logan didn't pay them any attention. He picked out a screwdriver from his toolbox and attacked dismantling the cabinets. The front panels would have to be sanded before he could cover the walnut stain with clean white paint. The faux-wood counters would have to be replaced. The gaudy harvest-gold and avocado-green wallpaper would have to go. And the hardwood floor, the kitchen's best feature, would have to be refinished.

While his mind ran along the long list of tasks he'd have to do to modernize the house, he swiveled to reach for the first cupboard door and caught a glimpse out the front bay window.

Across the moonlit snowy landscape shone Beth's sea-foam-green house. This wouldn't do at all. Tomorrow he'd install blinds.

But like a masochist he couldn't tear his gaze away from the warm lights shining from the upstairs windows. Was she tucking Jamie in for the night? Did Jamie fuss over baths the way Samantha had? How many stories could he con Beth into reading him before falling asleep?

Logan twisted away from the window and concentrated on the stubborn screws holding the brass hinge in place. Ramming the screwdriver into the screw's head, he wrenched with all his might. A night spent toiling at wood-work would cure the tightening spiral of his crazed mind.

He didn't want Beth in his life. He certainly couldn't handle having Jamie around to remind him of what he'd lost. No, he *needed* to be completely alone.

But even the relentless physical exertion couldn't drown out the fierce buzzing of his thoughts, and after an hour of trying, even his nightmare-filled sleep seemed a pleasant option.

He shuffled to the front door and checked the lock. A peek outside the window showed him the dog still there, shivering madly, a soft, pitiful whine becoming a yip in frozen intervals.

Swearing, Logan unlocked the door and yanked it open. "Okay, you win. In you go." He marched her to the laundry room, took a towel from the pile on the washer and placed it on the floor.

"Don't think this is permanent. Tomorrow you go."

As Logan closed the door, he could have sworn the mutt wore a smile of triumph.

He dragged himself up the stairs, cursing his wretched fate. First the kid, then the woman, now the dog. "You're turning into a regular doormat, Ward."

He snapped on the bathroom light and reached for the toothbrush in his toiletry kit.

Things could only get better. He had no reason to see Beth or her son again. Tomorrow he'd take the mutt to the pound and be done with her. Then he'd have the blessed isolation he wanted.

Yeah, things could only get better.

## Chapter Four

"I'm ready, Mom." Jamie, clad in his favorite blue polar fleece pajamas, bounced on his bed. "Read me the Christmas bear story."

With a determined movement Beth reached to the bookshelf and pulled out Jamie's request. Her hands were hurting, and she wanted nothing more than to swallow another painkiller and curl up in bed. But Jamie expected this ritual, and she didn't want to disappoint him. "Okay, but only one story tonight. It's late."

"Awww." But his protest was halfhearted. As he snuggled against her, his eyelids already drooped.

Beth read the story and slipped out of his bed to settle him in the for the night.

"Why is he such a Grinch?" Jamie asked, stifling a yawn.

"Who?"

"Logan."

"It's Mr. Ward to you. I don't know."

Jamie stretched his arm to reach his stuffed panda bear on the night table beside his bed. "Is his heart two sizes too small like the Grinch?"

"I think maybe he just forgot how to use it." Beth tucked the blanket and comforter around both Jamie and the bear.

"Do you think he'll be my friend?"

That didn't seem too likely. "I don't know."

"Knock-knock." Jamie's laugh, so spontaneous and free, never failed to warm her heart. To hear his laughter ring through the house, she'd do anything—even sit through the obnoxious knock-knock jokes that had become part of their bedtime ritual.

"Who's there?" she asked.

"Butch."

"Butch who?"

"Knock-knock." Another fit of giggles escaped Jamie.

"Who's there?"

"Jimmy."

"Jimmy who?"

"Butch your arms around me and Jimmy a kiss!"

Laughing, Beth complied to her son's request and re-tucked the covers around him.

"Knock-knock," she said.

"Who's there?"

"Donnalette." Beth snapped off the bedside lamp.

"Donnalette who?"

"Donnalette the bed bugs bite!" Using her fingers as mock biting bugs, she tickled Jamie. She couldn't help smiling at his laughter.

She bent down and gave him a kiss. "Good night, sweetheart."

Jamie yawned again and closed his eyes. "Good night, Mom. Can we get a tree tomorrow?"

"We'll see."

Beth paused for a moment at the bedroom's doorway and looked at her son's sleeping form.

Jamie loved life—everything about it. Except maybe her culinary experiments, but she suspected even those protests were more show than real. His adventurous spirit gave him a knack for finding trouble, but Beth had learned long ago that worrying didn't keep things from happening, it only hampered enjoyment of the precious people who could be taken away at any time.

The way her parents had. The way Jim had.

Jamie's need for her would diminish soon enough. She had to enjoy him while she could. Even without his father, Jamie would have a childhood filled with bright memories. She'd make sure of it.

Quietly she closed the door and headed for her room. Picking up the blood-stained pants she'd worn that morning and plodding downstairs to throw them in the washer and lock up required an effort of will. On the floor in the hallway, she spotted the coat she hadn't had the energy to hang up earlier. Seeing the darkened bloodstains, she decided to throw it in the washer with the pants. With a tired sigh she dumped her small load on the floor and selected the settings on the washer. While the water gushed into the basin, she picked up the pants to spray them with stain remover. Next she reached for the coat. The pocket bumped against the appliance with a thud.

"What?" Beth reached inside the pocket. Her bandaged hands made the operation clumsy. The object inside popped out and plopped to the floor. Logan's wallet. She'd forgotten to give it back to him.

Beth crouched to pick it up. The thing was already

opened. It wasn't as if she were being nosy. She looked at the Texas driver's license showing through the plastic window. Not bad for a DMV picture. The photo had obviously been taken several years before. His face showed a healthy tan, and a semblance of a smile graced his lips. His hair was trimmed in a neat military style. What had happened since then to change him so much? So, okay, she was curious. Curiosity was normal, healthy behavior.

The washer's noise changed from a gush to a chug. Beth dumped her coat in and closed the cover. Wallet still in hand, she headed for the living room. Going through the compartments wouldn't really be an invasion of privacy, not if her perusal was undertaken with the right attitude. She wanted to understand the man, not use the information against him. After all, he was her neighbor. And Jamie would be going to his house to take leftovers.

Her conscience debated ethics, but curiosity won out. Sitting on the sofa, she awkwardly pulled out the photo gallery from the back compartment. She found five cropped pictures.

The first was a beautiful, smiling girl about Jamie's age. The wide smile with its missing front tooth reached all the way to her deep-hazel eyes. A bright-red bow sat slightly crooked on her long, dark-brown hair. Her coloring was darker than Logan's, but she recognized him in the little girl's face. His daughter?

An old man with silver hair holding a line of trout smiled at her from the second picture. A woman with intense brown eyes stared at her from the third. Beth looked at the little girl's picture again and recognized the woman's coloring. His wife?

What had happened to his family? Divorce? Had it been bitter and etched the pain on his face?

As she turned to the fourth picture, Beth gasped. Logan

stood in a policeman's uniform, surrounded by a group of smiling kids holding a sign that read, "Thank you, Officer Ward." She dropped the plastic sleeve.

A cop...like Jim.

Questions zoomed so fast in her head she couldn't make any sense of them. Had something happened to him on duty? A heaviness settled over her heart. She almost wished she hadn't given in to her curiosity. Seeing Logan in uniform brought back too many memories of the past.

She picked up the dropped plastic sleeve. The last photograph brought a smile to her lips. An ice-skating rink decked out in full Christmas cheer filled the background. In the foreground, Logan and the girl hammed it up for the camera. The man was gorgeous when he smiled! At one time he must have enjoyed the holidays.

Suddenly Beth came up with a wonderful idea.

A perfectly brilliant plan.

After all 'twas the season to be jolly. If Logan couldn't find his heart at this time of the year, when would he?

"Beth..." She could almost hear Jim's voice caution her. "Leave it alone. Not everybody wants your interference however well-meaning it is."

She looked up at Jim's framed picture on the mantel.

"But, Jim, he needs help."

She could imagine Jim's gaze rolling toward the ceiling the way it had whenever she'd come up with one of her grandiose schemes. Then he'd hug her close. "What am I going to do with you?"

"Love me, Jim. Just love me." And he had.

How she missed him! Tears prickled the corners of her eyes, and she hugged herself to ward off the chill suddenly permeating the room. She missed him as if he'd left her yesterday instead of five long years ago.

Generous to the end, Jim's last thoughts had been for her and Jamie.

Beth swiped at the tears before they could fall. He'd made her promise never to cry for him. He'd made her promise Christmas would always be a time of joy.

That promise seemed harder each year to fulfill.

She looked down at the picture of the man and the girl in her hands and knew she had no choice. Logan Ward became one more project on her Christmas to-do list.

For Christmas, she'd teach him to smile again.

She had a feeling she'd have to wrestle all of her holiday imagination to accomplish the task. But if she managed this minor miracle, maybe she'd find her spirit again and keep her promise to Jim for one more year.

Other than the squashed breakfast bar Logan found on the passenger's side of his car, there was not a crumb of food in the house. He fed the raspberry mush to the dog and would have given half of his possessions for a hot cup of coffee. His glance strayed to the kitchen window, to Beth's house. He rejected the notion with a grunt. No way. He didn't need coffee *that* badly. His neighbor's effervescence on top of the dog's misplaced infatuation would be too much to endure.

Without a phone, though, a trip to town was unavoidable. He needed to drop off the U-haul trailer at Gus's Country Store, leave the dog at the local pound and brave the grocery store for basic staples.

"Might as well get it all over with in one trip."

Logan fashioned a makeshift collar and leash from a piece of rope he found in his toolbox. As he approached the dog, noose in hand, she cowered in a corner of the kitchen and growled.

"I'm not going to hurt you," he said, disgusted. Crouching beside her, he held the rope loosely, letting her sniff it. "I don't hit women, children or animals—only thugs, and even then, only when there's no other choice."

She licked her lips in a nervous manner and lowered her head submissively, looking at him as if she didn't quite believe what he was saying.

"I'm taking you to a place where they'll take good care of you. You'll have your own dry and warm space, a balanced meal and fresh water. And if you look cute enough when people come to visit, you might even get a family to take you home."

She licked his fingers and batted her tail against the floor in a timid half measure.

"Here there's gonna be nothing but dust and mess for months and months. And that's not very healthy. Not even for a mangy mutt like you. Hear what I'm sayin'?"

She scooched a little bit closer and cocked her head as if she understood every word coming out of his mouth.

"Chow's gonna be lousy. Hours are gonna be hell. Living conditions, the pits."

She cocked her head the other way.

"Now, Beth...she'd take you in in a minute. But I've got a sneaking suspicion you'd just end up here like you did last night. So it's really best this way."

She tentatively placed her muzzle on his knee and rolled those liquid eyes up at him.

Those eyes, that expression, made him think of Sam, and he swallowed hard. His daughter had known just how to manipulate him with a look and a smile. He'd never minded. She was his life, and her happiness had been his goal.

"It's not gonna work." He slipped the noose over the dog's head, feeling the cold, empty darkness inside him. "I just don't have anything left inside."

\* \* \*

"What do you mean you don't have a pound?"

Beth froze as her heart gave a lurch of recognition at Logan's outraged bellow. She'd been humming along with the Christmas carols playing over the speaker at Gus's Country Store—which had started out as a hardware store, but now contained a bit of everything. At the sound of Logan's voice she stopped her inspection of the two potted evergreens she'd been comparing and headed toward the counter island in the middle of the store.

"I'm telling you, you're gonna have to go down to Nashua or up to Bedford to find an animal shelter. Best I can do for you is post a notice on the bulletin board."

Gus Leonard was working hard to keep his temper under control, but his skin was reddening, and one end of his gray mustache twitched at every other word. He was strong and fit, for a man of sixty-odd years, and usually didn't take any guff from anyone, but Gus also prided himself on his customer service, and Logan, for better or for worse, was presently a customer.

Logan stood with the dog held firmly like a football under his left arm. His stance was confrontational yet defensive. Even if she hadn't seen the picture of him in uniform last night, she might have guessed cop as his occupation by the way he seemed poised and ready for action.

"Is there a problem?" Beth asked, joining the two men at the counter. She should walk away, leave him alone to handle his own problems, but she couldn't. He was on her to-do list now, and although she hadn't quite come up with a plan for his reformation yet, she felt he was her responsibility. Besides, it felt strangely good to see him again.

"How'd you get here?" Logan barked at her and speared her with his stormy gaze.

Beth recoiled half a step at his unexpected outburst, then tilted her chin up. "I drove."

"Your hands. You should have called me."

"My hands are fine." She twisted them around and wiggled her fingers to prove her point. For a man who professed to want to be left alone, he was certainly showing an awful lot of interest in her welfare. That was good. It meant there was hope for him still. "You don't have a phone."

He grunted, then turned back to Gus. "So what am I supposed to do with the dog?"

"I suggest you get a collar and leash. Aisle four in the back. Alex Green isn't too keen on strays, and he's the officer on duty this morning."

"What does he do with them? Take them to the pound?"

Gus reached around Logan's body to ring up the gallon of paint and paintbrush Donna Toledo hesitatingly handed to him. "Fines the owner."

"She's not mine."

Gus's bushy eyebrows rose and he huffed. "Seems to me you're the one holding her."

The dog's tail swept Logan's black ski jacket with a swish-swish, and she licked his jaw. Logan swiped a hand at the unwanted canine's public display of affection.

"And what's with this Christmas music? Thanksgiving's barely over, for Pete's sake." Logan's gaze radiated anger and resentment that far exceeded what was warranted by the situation, making Beth uncomfortable. She had to get him out of here.

Gus handed the paper bag filled with Donna's purchases to her. "It's tradition. Customers expect it, to get 'em in the right holiday mood."

Before Logan could reply, Beth took hold of his jacket sleeve and pulled on it. "Don't mind him, Gus. Logan is a little bit holiday-challenged. We'll be in the pet section."

Putting Logan on her to-do list was one thing; handling

him, quite another. She'd have her task cut out for her, excavating all those layers of protective anger to get to his true heart. In her mind she saw the picture of him with the little girl, both of them smiling. It would be worth the effort to see that smile in living color. Getting him to keep that dog, she sensed, would be an important first step to his reformation. Speed, she decided, was the answer.

"Where's Jamie?" Logan asked as she led him toward the pet section. The scent of mothballs and paint and fertilizer came and went as they walked.

"Looking at hockey equipment."

"You let him go by himself?"

Beth sighed her exasperation. "It's a small town. Everybody knows everybody. Jamie's safe."

"A small town doesn't guarantee safety." His voice sounded like a velvet growl, making her wonder once more about what had happened to him in Texas.

"It does if you're Jim Lannigen's son."

After Jim's death every cop in town had made it his business to see to Jamie's safety. When Jamie was in town, he couldn't spit the wrong way without the fact finding its way back to her. On father-son outings, one of them always volunteered to act as a stand-in. And every Wednesday night, Glenn Harris, a part-timer with the Rockville P.D., showed up to take Jamie to the Cub Scout meeting, even though he didn't have a son among his brood of cherubic offspring. A tug of regret pulled at Beth's heart. She missed Jim so much.

Logan slanted her a curious look but didn't ask any questions. Beth was grateful. Talking about Jim selfishly made her want to cry for all she'd lost, and she'd promised him she wouldn't cry. She stopped at the pet supply section of the store, blinked several times to sweep away tears before they could form. Logan's restlessness was contagious, and she found her attention wandering and her body filling with tension as she tried to study the available merchandise. Speed, she reminded herself. Don't give him a chance to think about how else he can dispose of that dog.

"You're not going to have much of a choice," she said, picking up a red collar from the hook. She slipped it around the dog's neck. Her cheeks flamed when she accidentally bumped her hand against Logan's side. "It's red or blue. Do you have a preference?"

"No."

Beth patted the collar into place. "There, that fits. Do you have any bowls?"

"Bowls?"

"Yeah, you know, for dog food and water."

"No."

She turned back to the display and started stacking her selections in her arm. "You'll need a leash, bowls and a bed—"

"She doesn't need a bed. She's not going to be around that long."

Beth stubbornly held on to the green-and-white-plaid pillow. "She's got to have someplace to sleep in the meantime."

Logan grumbled something she couldn't quite hear, and she secretly smiled. If the dog could stay with him for just a few days, he'd start thawing. Who could resist that sweet brown face, those liquid eyes? "You'll need dog food, too, but I'd get it at the Market Basket. More choice."

Beth added a brush to her selections, then picked up a rope puppet and squeaked it at the dog who responded with canine glee. Logan grabbed the puppet from Beth's hands and returned it to the shelf. "That's going to drive me nuts."

"Um," she said, scratching the dog's jaw, "let's find

something that doesn't squeak then.'' She picked out a raw-hide bone, a tug toy and a small ball. As they left the pet aisle, she grabbed a bottle of shampoo.

Just then Jamie came bounding down the center aisle. ''Mom, Mom, they got skates my size and they fit. Darlene helped me try them on and everything.'' He skidded to a halt. ''Logan! You're here.''

''Mr. Ward,'' Beth corrected.

''Mr. Ward.'' Jamie reached for the dog, who squirmed madly in Logan's arm. ''You brought your dog. Did you give her a name yet?''

Logan crouched, holding the dog by the collar but letting boy and dog greet each other. ''She's not going to be around long enough to have a name.''

''Max.'' Eyes scrunched and giggling, Jamie dodged Max's busy tongue. ''That's what I'm going to call her.''

''Max is a boy's name,'' Beth pointed out. She shifted the dog pillow in her arms. ''This is a girl.''

''She looks just like Max.''

Beth frowned. ''I don't know anyone named Max.''

''The Grinch's dog. In the movie.''

Beth blushed. ''Jamie—''

Logan pulled off the price tag from the leash and collar and handed the leash to Jamie. ''Why don't you hold her while I go pay for all this stuff.''

''Can I really? Can I take her outside? Bobby's at the Toy Barn.'' Without waiting for an answer, Jamie took the dog's leash and stood up. ''Come on, Max. Come on. I'll be back to help you pick out a tree, Mom.''

''He'll be all right,'' Beth assured Logan. ''The Toy Barn is right next door, and he knows to stay on the side-walk.''

Logan grunted an answer and headed toward the cash register. He patted his pocket and came up empty. It was then Beth remembered his wallet still lay on her living room coffee table. "Let me get this. I'll return your wallet as soon as we get home. Gus, add a potted blue spruce to the bill."

Gus glanced from Beth to Logan and back again. "Sure thing."

She wrote out a check while Logan helped Gus bag Max's things.

"I'll put a notice on the bulletin board," Gus said as he slipped his glasses from his forehead to his eyes to peer at Beth's check.

"I appreciate that. I should have a phone by Monday."

A phone. Another good sign. He wasn't cutting all ties to the living.

"If I hear anything before then," Gus said, "I'll let Beth know."

Logan nodded and turned to her. "I'll get your tree."

"Thanks, that's awfully nice of you."

He ground his teeth. She flashed him a smile.

He returned a few minutes later with a blue spruce. "How's this one?"

"Perfect."

She grabbed the dog pillow and followed Logan out of the store. Suddenly she knew just what she was going to do.

Little by little she would expose him to the community, and just as with an allergy serum, he would get used to human contact. Before he could realize what had happened, he would be one of them.

She smiled again, hugging the pillow closer, feeling quite pleased with herself.

## Chapter Five

The doorbell rang, but Logan ignored it. He wasn't expecting anyone, and after the living hell Beth had put him through this morning, he deserved some peace and quiet. He reached up and stripped another layer of the gaudy harvest-gold and avocado-green flowered wallpaper off the kitchen wall.

Beth had followed him to the Market Basket and introduced him to every blessed human being in the store. She'd fussed over his selections, chided him about proper nutrition and pretty much made him wonder what had possessed him to move here in the first place.

The doorbell's *ding-dong* reverberated once again through the empty house. He glanced at the dog sleeping contentedly on her pillow.

"Some guard dog you are."

She cracked open an eyelid and batted her tail against the floor.

Logan dumped the gluey mess of wet paper into a bucket.

"So there you are." Beth's voice made him swing around in surprise, scraper forward at the ready. "No wonder you didn't answer the doorbell. Need any help?"

"No." Logan turned back to the wallpaper. He'd have to remember to lock the front door from now on. Where had he gotten the idea that New Englanders were reticent?

Beth cleared a space on the counter littered with grocery bags, screws, hinges and dog paraphernalia and placed a casserole dish on the faux wood. "Three hundred fifty degrees for about forty minutes, and you'll have a piping-hot meal. I don't suppose I can convince you to make a salad to go with that?"

"I don't take charity."

He'd gotten more casserole dishes from the local church ladies than he ever wanted see again after Sam's death. Just the shape of the pan with its foil cover was enough to rack a shiver of nausea through him. Give him a steak and potato any day. At least they had recognizable shapes, substance and weren't indecipherable blobs held together by some tasteless saucy goo.

"It's not charity," she protested, but her blush belied her intent. Did he have *sucker* written all over his face?

"I'm testing a new recipe," she went on, fluttering about his kitchen like a damned hummingbird, "and Jamie doesn't like spinach. I thought maybe since you were still in the middle of unpacking and probably wouldn't take the time to cook yourself a decent meal that I'd see if you wanted to test it for me. I'll need a detailed report on taste, texture, consistency—"

There would be no report if he could help it.

"Where's Jamie?" Was she in the habit of leaving her

son alone? Didn't she realize he could be snatched away from her in the space of just a second?

"He's at his friend Bobby's house." He caught her muted reflection on the refrigerator door. Confusion rucked her forehead, but he wasn't about to enlighten her. It wasn't his business.

"How's Max doing?" she asked as she inspected the insides of his bare cupboards.

"Max?"

"Your dog."

"She's not mine," he grumbled, plopping another ball of soggy wallpaper into the bucket.

Max, the traitor, popped her head up and grinned inanely up at him.

"If you say so." Smiling, Beth dug awkwardly into her purse and brought out his wallet. "You do have plates, don't you?"

"Somewhere."

He wished he'd never handed her his wallet, giving her a ready excuse to bother him. Ten to one she'd taken a gander at every piece of paper in there. And someone like her was bound to be filled with questions. Her curiosity was there in those big, powder-blue eyes. How long before she pecked at him like all those frenzied reporters after the trial?

"Mr. Ward! Mr. Ward!" They'd chased after him mike in hand, cameras whirring. "Tell us about the day your daughter was killed."

And they'd wanted all the excruciating, titillating details to feed the excitement-starved masses on the five o'clock news. And maybe, just maybe, they'd also wanted to scoop the ugly truth that some of the blame should be cast his way.

"Yes, I was there."

"Yes, I'd just let her go."

"First time on her brand-new bike."

"Yes, I saw the truck hop the curb and smash into her."

And I would have taken her place in a heartbeat, if I could have. But they'd never asked *that* question.

"Mr. Ward, how does it feel to know the person who killed your daughter is now a free man?"

"How do you think it feels?"

It feels like hell. Every day. Every hour. Every minute.

The raw, jagged wound reopened inside him, bleeding shame and guilt and anger all over again.

"Where do you want me to put your wallet?" Beth asked.

"Anywhere. It doesn't matter." He jabbed the scraper, taking part of the sheetrock along with the wallpaper.

The dog whined and scrambled to her feet.

"Logan? Are you all right?"

He turned toward Beth and forced the semblance of a smile. "I'm just fine. I'd really appreciate it if you left."

She fiddled with the zipper on her coat, sliding it up and down as if she couldn't make up her mind whether to stay or go. The *zzz-zzz-zzz* sawed at his already skinned nerves.

"Three-fifty for forty minutes," she said.

He nodded and turned away, scraping without really seeing what he was doing. His hand shook slightly, zagging the shriveling paper into a squiggly eel. The dog sat at his feet and pawed at his work boot.

"I'll check on you tomorrow."

"I don't need to be checked on." She was a trial. True purgatory. Flaying him with reminders of his failings. "I told you I'm perfectly fine."

"Okay." Beth hesitated. "If there's anything I can do…"

"There isn't." The last thing he needed was a meddling female in his sanctuary.

"I'm right next door, if you need anything."

"I won't."

She started toward the hallway, then stopped. "Logan?"

"What now?" His throat was raw. His hand was white as it clutched the scraper. His body rippled with his intensifying pain. He needed a stiff drink, a whole bottle of straight-cut bourbon, except that he'd promised himself he wouldn't travel down that road. Whatever came, he was going to face it straight on and sober. The same way Sam had been forced to face that truck.

"I understand."

He snorted and attacked the wall once again. "How can you when your little world is all sunshine and song?"

"Because someone who's been to hell and back recognizes a fellow traveler."

The growl of anger snarled inside him, slashing at his gut, burning hot and red. "How dare you presume...?" Then he remembered she was a widow. "It's not the same thing. It wasn't your fault."

"Maybe. Maybe not."

Her voice was soft, holding not a hint of accusation, but a familiar chord of torment. He couldn't help himself, he looked at her over his shoulder, saw the fragility behind the smile, the vulnerability behind the ebullience.

"He was the center of my world," she said, gulping in a breath of air. The blue of her eyes became brilliant stars with the shine of unshed tears. "I loved him more than life itself. But I didn't see the cancer eating at him. What if I'd seen the signs earlier? Could I have saved him then? Would he still be here if I'd insisted he go to the doctor sooner?"

He couldn't bear to watch her pain, yet he couldn't look away from the mirror of his own misery.

She shrugged. Her gaze dropped to her bandaged hands where her fingers twined as if seeking support one from the other. "I've asked myself those questions a thousand times. I'll ask myself a thousand more. Maybe I'll never stop asking. But it won't change the outcome. The one thing I do know is that killing myself isn't going to bring Jim back. And if I had to bear the load alone, I'd have crumpled from the weight long ago."

Her gaze crept up, sought his. Her eyes were ablaze with fervency. "You don't need to lock yourself away. You need to let people in."

He said nothing, couldn't say anything. No argument would convince her of his compelling need to work and sweat and be completely and utterly alone with his loss.

She hitched her purse up on her shoulder. "Anytime, Logan. I'm there. I mean it."

This time she left. He opened his mouth but couldn't think of what it was he needed to say. And when the front door clicked closed, he turned back to the hideous wall-paper, scraping until his hand hurt, dulling the pain and anger, and toning down the insistent voice that nagged at him. The little dog's body shivered against his leg, but he didn't have the strength to bend down and pet her.

Finally giving in to the hounding urge, knowing all the while there was no way she could hear him, Logan rested his forehead against the bared wall and exhaled a low, long puff of breath. "Beth…"


Beth knew she was driving herself into a frenzy for nothing. What was said was said, and there was no taking it back. Still… She peered once more out the living room window at the gray farmhouse across the street. The light in the kitchen burned bright in the darkness, but she could see no movement from this distance.

Acting on intuition, she'd said too much. But when she'd seen him standing there, trying so hard to hide his pain, she couldn't help herself. She'd recognized the signs of someone in deep mourning. For his wife? His daughter? Both? Her heart went out to him.

Eve had been there for her after Jim's death. How many times had she told and retold all of her stories to the patient Eve? Beth had simply tried to pass on the favor by being there for Logan. Instead she'd managed to drive him deeper into himself.

When she'd gone back the next day with another meal, he'd ignored the doorbell, and this time the doors—front and back—had been locked. She'd left the food on the doorstep and had found the empty dish this afternoon when she'd returned with yet another peace offering. Again he'd refused to answer. Again the doors had been locked.

Sitting on the sofa, she looked up at Jim's picture on the mantel and could almost hear him tutting at her. "I told you this would lead to no good."

"But, Jim, I can't just leave him to drown like that."

This time Jim's photograph only smiled back at her. She sighed and looked away. "I'll give him one more day. He said he'd have a phone tomorrow."

In the meantime she had a ton of things to do—bills to pay, phone calls to make, menus to go over. After peering in on Jamie, she sidestepped her office and elected to go to the kitchen instead. Pulling out a recipe file, she decided to experiment with a batch or two of muffins to keep her mind off her sorrowful neighbor. Something tasty, yet nutritious she could slip by Jamie's "yuck-radar." Maybe she'd even drop a few off on Logan's doorstep in the morning. The man needed more flesh on his bones.

When she headed to bed a few hours later, she noticed that Logan's kitchen light was still burning bright. And even though she had to get up early to go to work, she couldn't seem to fall asleep. Her mind ran round and round with thoughts of Jim and the picture of him fading in her memory, of her desperation to color in all the details, of their love, of his death, of her loneliness.

She punched the pillow and flopped onto her side. "I'm not lonely. I've got Jamie. I've got my work. I've got lots of friends...."

Then inevitably her thoughts turned to Logan and the raw wound of sorrow she'd spied deep in his eyes, his punishing self-isolation, his control strung too tight. When that control broke, someone needed to be there. And somewhere in the fuzzy haze between sleep and waking, she understood that helping Logan find his foothold on life once again was as important to her well-being as to his.

Logan was using the window seat at the kitchen's bay window to rest while applying a fresh piece of sandpaper to the sander. Max had hopped up next to him and surveyed the operation. She looked a bit dazed. Logan could relate. He wasn't feeling particularly sharp, either. And that's just how he wanted things to be. Sleep would only bring nightmares, and he couldn't handle them right now.

"I told you the hours were gonna be hell."

Max sneezed.

"I warned you about the dust, too."

The stupid mutt just wagged her tail as if he'd said something profound. "You're not too bright, are you?"

Max huffed her indignation and lay down on the seat, tail curled over her muzzle.

Logan concentrated on his task, on every ache of his overworked muscles. He kept his gaze locked on the sander, on the sandpaper, on his hands. When his gaze tried to creep up, he forced it back down. Then he told himself it was to see if the dog was still there. Even when he looked past the mutt's head to the outside, he told himself it was to check on the weather. The clouds *had* looked ominous during the afternoon.

The inky blackness against the windows reflected his own gaunt image. He hadn't shaved in a couple of days, could probably use a shower and a change of clothes. But even his own base evaluation of his scruffy condition didn't prevent him from penetrating the darkness of this winter's night and finding the shadow of Beth's house. She'd turned off all the colorful lights when she'd gone to bed at eleven the night before. Yankee thriftiness, he was sure, not due to any consideration of his dislike of their brightness.

"I wonder if she'll feed us again today."

Max sat up and looked out the window with him.

When a bedroom light went on, quickly followed by a second one, Logan froze. His heart pounded in his chest. Seeking a clock, he zeroed in on the stove. Five-thirty. Something was wrong. Had to be. Why else would they be up so early? Was Jamie sick?

"It's none of my business." He fiddled with the sandpaper. It refused to cooperate. With a growl he rammed the sander onto the seat. Swearing, he got up and donned his coat.

"What if she does need help?" he asked the dog. "With her hands all cut up and bandaged…"

Max barked her approval, hopped off the seat and followed him to the front door.

"Stay." He dragged on his coat. "The last thing I need is you to add to the confusion."

Max whined, but Logan shut the door in her face, anyway. He hiked his collar up and trudged across the street to Beth's house, cursing himself with every step. Pounding on the door, he called himself every name in the book.

"What's wrong?" he asked when an out-of-breath Beth answered the door.

"Wrong?" She frowned as she pulled a purple, teal and royal-blue ski sweater over a white turtleneck. "Nothing's wrong. What made you think something was wrong?"

The sweater's bright colors brought out the blue of her eyes. Logan couldn't look away from the mesmerizing brightness. "Why else would you be up so early?"

She blinked twice. "It's Monday. I've got to go to work."

"But it's five-thirty."

Beth gave his coat sleeve a firm tug, drawing him inside, then shut the door. Warmth surrounded him and the aroma of fresh coffee teased him.

"I've got to be at school by six-thirty."

Saying the words seemed to act as a reminder. She glanced at her watch and sprang into action. Her magnetic energy towed him behind her, and he followed her to the kitchen.

"I thought you were a chef."

"I'm the food service manager at the middle school. We've got a breakfast program."

She took two mugs from a cupboard, filled them with coffee and handed him one. After a quick sip from hers, she was fluttering again—from fridge to pantry to drawers—as she put together a lunch. One by one a peanut-butter-and-jelly sandwich, carrot sticks, apple and an oatmeal cookie with an M&M smiley face found their way into a brown paper bag.

Did Jamie trade or did he hang on to that cookie? Sam would have ended up with twice the cookie's worth of chips and cheese curls. She kept telling him she was sweet enough as it was and needed a good crunch. She'd laughed at the idea of carrot sticks instead of chips. "Oh, Daddy." She'd shaken her head as if he didn't have a clue.

"What about Jamie?" Logan said, jarring himself from the memory.

"What about him?" Beth ripped a piece of paper from the pad on the fridge, scribbled a note, ending with a doodled heart, and tucked it on top of the lunch.

It was the heat, he decided. Or maybe the fact her coffee tasted much better than his. Something had him suddenly on edge and grinding his teeth. "Do you leave him here by himself?"

"Of course not." She was gathering coats, mitts and hats. "I drop him off at Eve's, and she walks him to school."

"This is too early for a kid."

Beth stopped her active buzzing and slanted him a narrowed look. "He goes to bed at seven-thirty on weekdays, so he gets plenty of sleep. Anything else on your mind this morning? I've really got to go check on Jamie's progress."

He should quit while he was ahead, but he couldn't seem to stop the mad impulse to push and question and...know. Know what? He was going crazy. Stark raving mad. These people were strangers. Noisy busybodies. Why should he care? "Why don't you get someone to come to your house?"

"I tried. But it's too far out."

Fuss, fuss. Check and recheck. Beth's hands never stopped. Now it looked as if he'd made her uncomfortable in her own home. He definitely should head back. She didn't need him. Everything was under control.

Except him.

"Why don't you move closer to work so you don't have to leave so early?"

This time Beth didn't hold back her exasperation. She

sighed the mother of all sighs and shook her head. "It's my house. All my memories are here. And just what business is this of yours?"

His jaw tightened. His fists stiffened. "None."

"Knock-knock." Jamie's voice bounded ahead of him as he pounded down the stairs. In stocking feet, wearing jeans and a T-shirt dotted with silk-screened bugs, he came sliding to a halt between Beth and Logan, clasping a pant leg from each adult in his hands. His light-brown hair was still mussed from sleep.

"Who's there?" Beth asked, giving her son a smile much too bright for the early hour.

Logan had to look away and found the cream-colored stoneware mug with its blue-and-green snowflake design still gripped in his hand. He downed half the coffee, burning his palate in the process. Concentrating on the aroma, on the taste, he tried to distract himself from the sturdy, yet fragile feel of Jamie's fingers scrunched around his jeans, of Beth's soft strength, of their nearness, of the buzz of anxiety rising to his chest like a swarm of Africanized bees.

"X."

"X who?"

"X for breakfast?"

Beth ran a hand through Jamie's hair. "I made some muffins last night to bring to Eve's."

"Mo-om." Jamie twisted his head away from her busy fingers. "What kind?"

"Peanut butter and raisin."

"Old recipe?"

"New recipe."

Jamie scrunched his face. "Oh, yuck!"

"More peanut butter."

Jamie brightened and let go of Logan's pant leg to lift up a couple of fingers. "I'm gonna have two."

"Not if you don't hurry up and get ready. Where's your backpack?"

"In my room."

"Your shoes?"

"In my room."

"Up you go, then." She gave Jamie a playful swat on the bottom and sent him pounding up the stairs like a two-ton elephant.

"And put on a sweatshirt," she called after him. "It's too cold for just a T-shirt."

"Mo-om."

"Five minutes," she warned, and flitted once more toward the kitchen counter, making Logan feel like a voyeur in this domestic tableau.

Time for him to leave.

"Wait, don't go yet."

Already halfway down the hall, he waited. Paper bag in hand, Beth rushed after him. "Here. I thought you might like some breakfast. One meal a day really isn't enough when you're working so hard."

All bright-eyed and pink-skinned, she looked at him expectantly, the bag of muffins dangling between them like laundry on a line. The scent of brown sugar and peanut butter and something else altogether drifted toward him, teasing, taunting, stirring.

"It's not charity," she said, thrusting the bag into his chest. He had to lift an arm in order to catch the muffins before she released the bag. "I told you, I experimented. There's no way we can eat three dozen muffins on our own. And you need it more than the squirrels."

As if to prove her right, a hunger pang twisted his gut, and his stomach growled. Embarrassed, he nodded once and turned to leave. As he wrenched the doorknob, Beth's presence buffeted him with its warmth. The unexpected need to draw her nearer rattled through him.

"Thanks," she said.

"For what?"

"For coming over when you thought we needed help." She blushed. "I'm not used to—" her voice caught "—having someone worry about us."

He shrugged and shifted his weight against the warmth creeping into his solar plexus. He itched to go, but couldn't seem to make his feet move. "Thanks for the muffins."

"You're welcome."

She smiled, and the bright punch of it hit him square in the stomach. His breath vanished. His thoughts scrambled. Somehow he managed to step through the door without stumbling. "I'll let you get to work."

"We should be back by three-thirty."

He nodded, turned away from the cozy house, from the warmth, from the confusion, and hunched his shoulders against the crisp bite of morning air. The bag of muffins thumped against his thigh as he walked, adding a lively swish to the crunch of snow beneath his boots.

Dawn was starting to pinken the horizon. It would be a sunny day. And already he was looking forward to the afternoon.

## Chapter Six

"How do you like your new neighbor?" Eve McDonald chirped before Beth could even say hello.

Ignoring her best friend, Beth made her way up the walkway to the cottage located just off the town center. With its pale-pink paint and off-white trim, Eve's tiny home reminded her of a dollhouse. Jamie ran ahead and launched himself into Eve's waiting arms.

Chic as usual, Eve was already dressed in black pants, a raspberry wool jacket and a matching raspberry turtleneck. Her gray hair—Eve didn't believe in coloring—was closely cropped. Her only requirement in a hairdo was that it be easy to coif. But on her the boyish style looked good. From afar, she looked younger than her fifty-five years, but upon closer inspection, her lined face revealed the hard road her life had traveled. Abandoned by a fiancé, she had supported her mother after her father's early death and nursed her mother through the last years of her life.

There hadn't been much joy in Eve's life until she'd discovered her skill at selling real estate. She'd done well for herself in the past few years, bought the little cottage of her dreams, and had chosen to slow down and work when it suited her.

And it never suited her if she had an inkling either Beth or Jamie might need her. Because Jamie's grandparents refused to visit and because Eve relished her role of surrogate grandmother, Beth had allowed the relationship to flourish.

The one tiny thorn between them was Eve's propensity toward matchmaking—a sorely deficient propensity, judging by her past efforts.

Eve greeted Jamie with a bear hug and a kiss. "Hi, sweetie. I've got hot cocoa waiting for you in the kitchen."

"With marshmallows?"

"Of course."

"Yippee!" Jamie discarded his coat and zipped toward the kitchen.

"You're spoiling him." Beth dropped Jamie's backpack by the door.

Eve beamed at her as she closed the front door. "What do you expect from a free baby-sitter? So what do you think of your new neighbor?"

"Logan? He's the grouchiest bear I've ever seen." Beth hung Jamie's coat on the rack beside the door and fervently hoped Eve wouldn't notice the sudden heat burning her cheeks.

"Logan, hmm." Eve crowed with delight. "I knew you'd like him."

"Like him! Are you nuts?" Beth stuffed Jamie's mittens into his coat pockets and found it hard to concentrate on her usual routine to make sure Jamie wouldn't forget anything when Logan's grim face kept popping into her mind.

"As soon as I saw him, I knew he'd be perfect for you."

Had Eve orchestrated Logan's purchase of the house? Of course not, even Eve wasn't that calculating. But she wasn't past using her real estate contacts to try to set Beth up. Beth would never understand why, since Eve herself seemed to have an aversion to marriage. Hadn't she turned down Gus's offer twice now? And the last thing Logan Ward was perfect for was marriage.

Beth snorted. "Perfect? Just what have you been putting in your coffee?"

"So you don't like him?"

Frowning, Beth searched through her purse for change and came up with enough for Jamie's milk purchase at lunch. Like Logan? "Of course not. He's rude and socially inept."

Nodding once, Eve smiled. "That's what I thought."

"You're wrong." Beth waved a finger at her. "Just like you were wrong about Alex Green, and that horse doctor you sold the Borealis Farm to and that businessman who bought the town house from you."

Eve shrugged. "If you say so. But I've got a feeling…"

"I don't have time for one of your 'feelings' this morning, I'm already running late." She handed Eve Jamie's milk money.

Eve pocketed the change. "He's a hero, you know."

"What?"

"Logan Ward. He's a hero."

Curiosity tugged at her, but time was short and she had to get to work. Still… "How do you know that?"

"You'd be surprised at the information you can find when you're surfing the net."

"Surfing the net? Eve, you amaze me."

Eve feathered the short hair over one ear with her fingers. "Well, I couldn't sell my home to just *anybody*. It's been in my family since 1865."

"So you checked him out?" Now Beth's curiosity tripped at hyperspeed. What else had Eve discovered? Maybe she'd have an answer to Beth's most burning question—what had caused Logan so much grief? Would there be time to visit the middle school's computer lab after work and run a search of her own?

"Mom, Mom, where are the muffins?" A running Jamie collided with the decorative table in the hallway. The phone crashed to the floor with a series of choked rings, the glass bowl with a mighty shatter. Leaves and pinecones and bits of cinnamon bark scattered all over the hardwood floor and the blue-and-burgundy runner.

"Jamie!"

Her son, skidding to a belated halt, had the decency to look crestfallen. "I'm sorry, Miss Mac."

He bent down to pick up the broken pieces, but Eve and Beth both pushed him away.

"That's all right, sweetie," Eve said. "Why don't you go get me the broom and dustpan."

"Let me." Beth tried to pick up the bigger glass shards, but the bandages on her hands made the task awkward.

"Why don't you take care of the phone?" Eve said as she gave Beth's hands a gentle nudge away from the glass mess. "You'll have to tell me all about your little adventure."

"Adventure?"

"Your hands. You ran out before I could catch you last Thursday. The rumors running around town range from third degree burns from one of your experiments gone bad, to having been attacked by a drifter, to a mauling by a wild dog."

"Wow." Beth straightened the lace doily and reset the telephone on the table. "Not even close to the truth."

"That's what I figured."

Jamie sheepishly handed Eve the broom and dustpan.

"Here," Beth said as she gave her son the bag of muffins. "Walk, please."

"Yes, Mom."

Beth strode to Eve's desk by the window and picked up the wastebasket beside it.

"I heard you had to pay for Logan's dog supplies. Something about his wallet being at your house…"

Beth shook her head. "You're too much. How was your weekend trip to Boston?"

"Obviously not as exciting as yours."

"Eve…"

"Did you hear about Big Bill?" Eve swept the glass and potpourri with bold strokes into the dustpan.

"No, what happened?"

"A pipe burst in the town hall basement last week and it flooded."

"I heard about that." Beth crouched and held the wastebasket for Eve, wondering where her friend was going with this unexpected sidetrack. It wasn't like her to just let go of such juicy gossip.

"Big Bill slogged through all that cold water, and now he's in the hospital with pneumonia."

"How awful! I'll have to make him some chicken noodle soup."

"All the decorations for the downtown beautification were ruined. Might have to do without this year."

"I'm sure the town'll figure something out."

"That new superstore is already affecting sales along the common."

"There's the Holiday Fair in a couple of weeks. That's always a big draw."

"Um, maybe." Eve looked up from her task and speared

Beth with an amused look. "You're not going to ask, are you?"

"And reward you for baiting me? I don't think so." But she was dying of curiosity. What had Logan done to become a hero? Was it related to his loss, to his move? She'd get Eve to spill her guts later. Under the spell of a brownie high, Eve might not even think to crow about her victory over Beth's interest in her surly neighbor.

Purely practical interest, of course. He was, after all, the biggest project on her Christmas to-do list. The more she knew about him, the easier it would be to help him find his heart again.

Eve scooped the last of the glass shards into the garbage can.

"I'm sorry about your bowl," Beth said. "I'll replace it."

"Don't give it another thought. I never liked the thing. Mildred gave it to me for my birthday, and I felt I *had* to put it out in case she came over."

"What'll you say when she asks about it?"

Eve gave a raucous laugh. "The truth, of course. That it was Jamie's fault."

Beth contained her smile and quirked an eyebrow. "She'll just replace it, you know."

"I'll casually mention my allergy to potpourri."

"You are something else." Beth reached across the garbage can and hugged her friend. "Thanks for looking after Jamie. It means the world to me to know he's safe."

"It's my pleasure. He keeps me young." As she straightened up, Eve's eyes twinkled with mischief. No wonder she got along so well with Jamie. They were two of a kind. "Drop by after school?"

"I'd love to, but I've got too much to do."

"I see." Her smile took up most of her face. "Have to rush home, do you?"

Beth laughed. "You are an evil woman."

Eve shrugged as she hung the dustpan on the broom handle. "With the best of intentions."

"And that's your redeeming quality. But don't push it this time," Beth warned.

"I just want to see you settled and happy."

"I am settled and happy. Logan's just a project, not a prospect."

"If you say so."

"I just met him."

"He's already a project."

Beth shook her head. There would be no winning with Eve. "Don't linger too long at the park. I don't want Jamie to be late again."

"Who, me, linger?"

"Yes, you." Beth swung her purse onto her shoulder and exited the front door.

"So what are you cooking Logan for dinner?"

"Sole almondine with asparagus and dilled potatoes."

Eve frowned. "Oh, dear, that doesn't sound right."

Beth laughed as she waved Eve goodbye and ran down the walkway to her car. "Got you! Have a good day."

"Try your parmesan chicken instead," Eve called after her. "I want a full report tomorrow."

Logan's status as a hero occupied Beth's mind as she drove to the middle school. She would have pondered longer on the tantalizing tidbit Eve had offered her, but circumstances prevented anything more than a fleeting thought here and there.

The middle school's walk-in freezer had gone on the fritz again over the long weekend. Thankfully, the unit's stone floor had retained the cold, but she now had three hundred pounds of ground beef to rescue before it thawed all the way. To make matters worse, two of her workers had called in sick.

Lasagna, chili, chop suey, burritos, tacos. It was going to be a long day. And dissecting Logan's past would have to wait until later.

She was late.

Logan spackled another nail hole on the kitchen wall and resisted the urge to check the stove clock once more. Eve MacDonald's vast collection of bird prints—he'd seen them on the pictures she'd sent—had left a series of evenly spaced holes along one wall. They needed to be taken care of before he could finish sanding the walls in preparation for a base coat of paint. As he scooped another glob of Spackle, his gaze locked with the clock. Almost five.

It didn't matter. Beth was old enough, wise enough, able enough to take care of herself, he rationalized. But she *had* said they'd be back by three-thirty. Had something happened? Had working popped some stitches? Beth didn't strike him as the sort of person who did anything halfway— bad hands be damned. She'd probably overdone it.

"Just like her." He spackled another hole in the wall. "Not that it's any of your business, Ward."

Like a heat-seeking missile, his gaze fixed on the clock once more. At the rumble of a car driving up the street, he peered out the window. Beth's station wagon. He plopped the scraper into the can of spackle, then wiped his hands on a rag.

"Max," he called to the dog, snoozing on the pillow. "Don't you need to go out for a business trip?"

She grumbled and recurled her tail around her body.

He tried bribing her with the ball, the bone and the tug toy and got not even the bat of an eyelash for his troubles.

Which just went to prove you couldn't depend on anybody for anything.

He tied the leash around the collar and gave it a tug. "Up you go."

With a yawn and a back-rounding stretch, Max finally relented.

By the time he had the dog out the front door, the garage door at Beth's house was closing. Disappointment sighed through him, but he dismissed it with a careless shrug. He didn't care. Why should he?

Logan unleashed the beast and stood at the door, heat warming his back, cold frosting his front, watching the lights go on one by one at Beth's house. Max sniffed around, did her business, then trotted back inside and sat down next to him, looking up expectantly.

"What?"

"Woof!"

"You can go back to your nap."

She wagged her tail and danced around his feet.

"I don't know what you want."

"Woof!"

"Woof to you, too."

With a last glance at Beth's house, he reluctantly closed the door. Max followed him as he returned to the kitchen. She happily accepted the bone he offered her and chewed it with relish.

"Guess we're on our own for dinner tonight." He rummaged through the dry goods still packed in their Market Basket bags. "Soup or macaroni and cheese?"

Tipping her head to one side, Max actually seemed to be pondering his question.

Logan dropped both back inside the bag. Neither sounded appealing. He went to the fridge, cracked open a can of Dr. Pepper. A short, sharp grunt escaped him as he recalled Beth's lecture on the drink's nutritive value. He tipped the can in mock salute in the direction of the bay window. "Sugar and caffeine. Pure fuel for a working body."

But for some reason the soda didn't taste as good as usual, and it irked him.

An hour later he was done with the spackling, had cleaned all of his tools and was once again considering the merits of boxed macaroni and cheese versus canned clam chowder.

He saw her then, walking up his driveway, Jamie bouncing at her side. His heart gave a funny little lurch, and his pulse quickened. Not for Beth, he angrily decided as he tossed the can and box back into the bag, for her cooking. The woman did know how to put a meal together—even if her repertoire was limited to casseroles.

He moved away from the window and waited for her to ring the bell before he went to answer the door.

His palms were sweaty, and he wiped them on the side of his jeans. Ridiculous to be so nervous. It was just Beth. Annoying, busybody, chatterbox Beth. But he *had* scared her with his early visit this morning. And it was only right to apologize. And he couldn't do that unless he opened the door. Besides, he was hungry, and here she was with a hot dish in her hands. Hands that were hurt because of him. So it was only right he should ask about them, especially after her first day of work. And, damn it, she had gotten home late, making him worry about her for nothing.

He'd worked himself up to a barking mood. For Pete's sake, Ward, just open the damn door.

"Hi," she said a bit breathlessly.

She looked like a Christmas light, all bright and beautiful with her cold-reddened skin, candy cane earrings and reindeer-adorned sweater under that fuchsia coat. Her smile warmed him like a fire in the hearth. And whatever dish she held in her hands smelled divine.

"Can I play with your dog?" Jamie asked before Logan could say anything.

"She's not my dog."

When Max came trotting into the hallway, tail wagging, Jamie dropped to his knees and held out his arms. "Can I still play with her?"

This time the quickening of Logan's pulse, the sudden clamminess of his palms were due to fear. A kid. In his house. Get a grip, Ward, he told himself. What can he get hurt on? A cardboard box? "Sure, sport."

Max had already taken charge. Jamie giggled while she gave his cheeks a good tongue-lashing. She then leaped out of Jamie's arms and trotted to the kitchen, looking back every few steps to make sure her entourage was following.

"We won't stay long." Beth raised the casserole dish in her hands. "I brought you some dinner."

Logan waved her in and closed the door behind her. "More testing?"

Beth looked down at the casserole in her hands. Was that a blush under the red kiss of winter air?

"Um, no. I've decided you're too thin. Besides recipes are usually for four, and there are only two of us. And I don't like eating the same thing two days in a row."

If that was a portion for two, she went by a different set of measures than most people. The three of them could pig out on what she'd brought and still have leftovers. Once they arrived in the kitchen, Max poked her nose around Logan's legs and sniffed up at the casserole.

"Are you feeding that dog? The bag of kibble still seems awfully full."

"She's fussy. Won't eat that stuff." Straight-faced, Logan couldn't resist teasing Beth. She took her food much too seriously. "Max here loves your casseroles, though."

As if to prove him right, Max licked her chops with delight.

"Well, at least someone appreciates my effort." Beth's small burst of laughter and her gentle smile unexpectedly ricocheted inside him.

She handed him the dish. "Half an hour on three seventy-five."

Frowning, he shoved the casserole in the oven and set the temperature and timer. Confusion jumbled his thoughts once again. She'd taken the ribbing good-naturedly. She hadn't gotten mad or burst into tears like Julia, his ex-wife, would have. Is that what he'd been after, female shrapnel to put his wayward thoughts on the right track again? He didn't want Beth here, didn't want to care what happened to her, couldn't get involved, not with her, not with a child as part of the equation. He needed to be alone with his pain and his memories. And she was disrupting his plans.

But there was something about her that aroused all of his protective instincts, instincts that had proven defective, instincts he needed to curb if he were to survive. Was it her small size? The fact she was all alone so far from town? Or was it because of her son?

Logan glanced at the boy and dog playing with the tug toy in the cleared area by the bay window. Jamie's vitality reminded him of Sam's no-holds-barred approach to life. He had an angel's face, but his hazel eyes twinkled like the devil's. He was Dennis the Menace with brown hair. He could have been Sam.

Sam would have loved Max, too. She'd be giggling like Jamie, enjoying every second of the game. After two minutes she'd have been begging, "Daddy can we keep her? Can we?" And he'd have told her yes because refus-

ing her anything was difficult. Something inside his chest
wrenched hard, and he reached a fist to his heart to relieve
the agony.

"A little green stuff wouldn't kill you," Beth said, removing her mittens and stuffing them in her coat pocket.

Still caught in the web of his memories, Logan grumbled
something. Green stuff? What was she talking about?

"Lettuce. You know what that is, right?"

Food again. The woman was obsessed. "It's healthy.
Who needs that?"

"Right. Not good for self-flagellation."

Without meaning to, he cracked a gruff chuckle. She
wouldn't understand. How could she? Her son was hale and
hearty and by her side. But he didn't want to get into a
discussion with her, so he let the comment pass. "You're
right there. I never expected the chow to be so good in
purgatory."

"I'll take that as a compliment." And she did look in-
ordinately pleased. "You know, if you told me a bit more
about yourself, I could be sure and whip up a dish you'd
really hate. That way you could have the jail-like feel you
seem to be going for."

Food, that was the way to deal with Beth. Keep the conversation on food. "I never cared much for brussels sprouts
or sweet potatoes."

A gleam of pure challenge sparkled in her eyes. "You're
on, cowboy. Brussels sprouts and sweet potatoes."

"You wouldn't."

"I would. It's going to have to wait till the weekend,
though, because I've got technical problems at work this
week."

"Is that why you were late?" He tossed the question as
if he couldn't care less about the answer, yet he could feel
the quickened hammer of his heart against his ribs. Dis-

tracting himself by rummaging through the fridge, he grasped a can of soda to offer her, then rejected it for a bottle of sparkling water.

"If I never see ground beef again, I'll be happy," Beth said with a shake of her head. "On top of my regular food service, I had to deal with three hundred pounds of hamburger today because the walk-in freezer decided to take another vacation, and there's no money in the school budget for a new one."

With a muffled thanks, she took the bottle he offered her and sagged against the counter. There were tired lines beneath her eyes. Her bulky coat exaggerated the raised and stiff stance of her shoulders, as if a deep ache resided between her shoulder blades. When she reached to twist the cap off the water bottle, the bright red streak on the bandage caught his attention.

Blood.

He knew it. She'd overdone it and popped her stitches. Why couldn't she have taken a couple of days off instead of pushing herself to go to work?

"You're bleeding," he said gruffly. He reached her in two steps, snatched her hand and peered at the bandage.

"Tomato sauce," she said, laughing. "Lasagna, tacos, burritos. That's an awful lot of tomato sauce."

Relief crested through him. "I've got some gauze around."

Cheeks flushed, she snatched her hand away. "It's not necessary."

"And how are you going to manage the task on your own?"

Why was he pushing her? If she wanted to sleep with dirty bandages, what was it to him? Still, he didn't give her a chance to protest, or himself a chance to analyze his motives, but dug through the packing carton in which he thought he'd seen his first-aid supplies. "Take off your coat and make yourself comfortable."

Out of the corner of his eye, he could see her hesitate, then relent. "Well, gee, Mr. Ward, choices, choices. Which chair to use?"

"I'm afraid it's the counter or the toilet." He slanted her a glance and couldn't understand what possessed him to add, "Or my bed."

He was enormously pleased at the fiery coloring of her cheeks. No mistaking it for cold this time. She was so sure of herself, so competent, so balanced, it was good to see her flustered. Except that it gave her face an endearing quality and sparked a troublesome need to touch that beautiful pink skin. Before he could talk himself out of the foolish idea, he grasped Beth by the waist and lifted her to the counter. A sound of surprise escaped her, and she held on to his shoulders to keep her balance.

She was small and light and warm, so warm. At this angle, her mouth became the center of his focus, unleashing a rabid hunger from a forgotten depth inside him. She was a woman with a child, he reminded himself. A young child. He couldn't afford to be involved in that kind of situation.

But he was a man. Damned or not, there was a fact he couldn't argue. And in spite of all the abuse he'd put himself through in the past couple of years, it looked as if he was still a healthy man.

"Mom, look. Look at Max."

Jamie's voice knocked sense back into Logan. He scurried away like a rat that had almost been trapped, and located the box of bandages in the packing carton.

Jamie held the tug toy in the air, and Max jumped to retrieve it. She hung in midair when Jamie didn't let go. Logan cringed even though the dog looked sturdy enough to survive the three-inch fall, even though he'd done the very same thing and worse with his grandfather's terrier a thousand times while growing up.

"On the floor, Jamie," Beth chided. "You wouldn't want Max to get hurt."

"But she likes it."

"Jamie."

"Okay, okay." He lowered the dog, and they resumed their tugging game at a lower level.

As Logan unwound the soiled bandage from her hand, Beth shifted her weight from hip to hip, then settled on knocking the heel of her boot against the cabinet frame below her and talking at a rapid pace. "Not only was the freezer not working, but two of my workers didn't show up. The flu. They say it's going to be bad this year. And it's starting early, too. A good quarter of the kids are out with it. Have you had your flu shot?"

He grunted. Getting a flu shot was the farthest thing from his mind. She wasn't going to start meddling with his health, too, was she?

"Then there was Sasha—"

"Sasha?"

"A student. An eighth-grader. She's having a real tough year. Divorce. Her mother and father are using her as a go-between. She doesn't want to take sides, and hearing both of them badmouth each other is really wearing her down. I could tell she needed to talk, but I had all this ground beef to deal with."

"Mmm." He'd bet his dinner Sasha had managed not only to win some of Beth's precious time, but gone back to class feeling better. "Lasagna, tacos and burritos."

"American chop suey, too. Then the office wanted an update on the staff Christmas party. As if I had any time to even think with all that ground beef to deal with, let alone plan a party for a hundred. And if that wasn't bad enough, Laura came in, nagging about the concert next week.''

"Laura?''

"Laura Darlington, president of the PTA. Not only for the middle school, but also for the elementary school. She loves to play the martyr. She complains she's got to do everything herself, but when anyone offers to help her, she turns them down.''

"So why was she bugging you?''

"I've got to do the set-up since they'll be using some food service equipment for the PTA bake sale.''

"You get paid for this extra work?''

"Of course not, I'm salaried.''

Of course not. It probably had never even occurred to her these people were taking advantage of her. He listened as she prattled on about her day, finding his task oddly soothing. He poked at the flesh around the wound. She had a compact hand, strong and soft. Warm. The skin was satin. A healthy pink. The only ugliness marring the perfection was the cuts and the stubbly marks of sutures.

"The cuts are healing well,'' he said, interrupting her monologue with the oddly scrambled distractedness of his own mind.

"Oh, well, yes. Thank you.'' Beth cleared her throat and looked around the room. "Eve would love what you're doing with the house. She'd wanted to spruce it up for years, but never had the time. She had a hard time parting with it. It's been in her family since it was built. Her father put in the bay window just a few months before he died in a tractor accident.''

"Umm.'' He continued with his task of wrapping a fresh bandage, going slowly, taking his time. He wanted it done right, so it would hold all day tomorrow…in case she had another emergency.

"All set," he said, smoothing out the last bit of tape, reluctant for some reason to let go of the small hand.

She fidgeted, examined the finer points of his bandaging job and smiled nervously. "Thanks."

Logan needed something to do other than reach for the strand of curly blond hair that had worked its way out of her ponytail's red-and-white scrunchie, so he moved away, rolling the remainder of the gauze.

"I guess we'd better get going." Beth launched herself off the countertop a bit too heartily, and stumbled.

Instinctively Logan extended his arms and caught her. Body landed against body. As if lightning had struck, they both froze. Firm, rounded hips filled his hands. The erotic pressure of breasts flattened against his chest. Blond hair with the muted scent of mint teased the five-o'clock shadow under his chin. How long had it been since he'd held a woman? Since he'd had sex? Tension strung his body tight. Hunger, heavy and insistent, came awake with a savage roar of blood. All he could hear was the persistent pounding of his pulse.

Beth's head tilted back. Her mouth parted. Her breath seemed to have been snipped midinhalation. Watching her eyes darken was like witnessing the birth of a black hole. He wanted to get lost in the impassioned depth of those eyes. Her mouth was another beacon calling to him, as if putting his lips against hers could provide a new breath of life. Impulsively he pressed her closer, spreading the warmth of her breasts, her pelvis, her thigh against his, wanting more, yet fearing the strong current of need reeling through him like a spring tornado.

There she was, a woman with a woman's needs written so plainly in the seductive blue of her eyes. And here he was, against all odds, a man still able to feel hunger for a woman. But she wasn't the type to keep things on a surface level. She struck him as the kind of woman who needed pretty words, a lot of cuddling and the promise of happily-ever-after.

He wasn't ready for a woman's tender warmth and all the complications that went with it, for the responsibility of another child's welfare. And she would never be ready to deal with the cold blackness Sam's death had left inside him.

Yet he couldn't seem to let go, and Beth couldn't seem to push him away.

*Beep, beep, beep,* went the timer.

Saved by the buzzer.

A ragged breath rattled out of him. He released her, swiveled and reached for the knob on the stove, shutting off the noise. She skittered away.

As he opened the oven door, a wave of heat and the shepherd's pie's enticing aroma of mashed potatoes, meat and gravy wafted over him. Jamie's giggles tinkled through the kitchen like wind chimes. The dog's barks added a happy melody to the joyful chaos. Even Beth's fussing over the boy and dog created a pleasant counterpoint.

God, if he closed his eyes, it would all feel so normal.

Warmth and child and dog and food and woman.

So normal.

For a moment, for an hour, was it so wrong?

He took the casserole out of the oven, rested it on the stove's surface. He held on to the glass dish's transparent knobs, felt the heat burn his fingers through the dishcloth's terry material.

Before he could stop himself, the word spilled out of his mouth. "Stay."

## Chapter Seven

"Stay."

Logan said the word more like a command than an invitation, but Beth sensed a note of something—longing?—in his voice.

He turned around, terry cloth towel still in hand. The lines of his body were stiff. The strength in his hands was visible in the hard hold he had on the towel. Nice hands. They'd felt good on her. Maybe too good. They'd sent a series of delicious little shivers up and down her spine. She could feel them still, tickling her skin like an itch she couldn't quite scratch.

And when he'd looked at her with those deep, dark eyes so intense and hungry, she'd tingled from the sudden heat that reawakened sensations she thought had died with her husband.

She knew that with Jim dead for five years there was nothing wrong in seeking a new relationship. But she couldn't help it. Even thinking of another man in that way made her feel as if she was betraying her vows. She'd loved Jim with all her heart. How could she possibly love anyone else as deeply?

She swallowed hard, trying to make sense of the disappointment churning in her stomach. "Stay?"

"For dinner." With a rough, almost nervous gesture, Logan pointed to the casserole on the stove behind him. "There's more than enough for all of us."

"You don't have chairs or a table," she said, feeling like an idiot as soon as she'd spoken. What did it matter about chairs or a table? He was reaching out, and she was making the attempt difficult for him. Why? Because of their awkward embrace—which really hadn't been an embrace at all but Logan stopping her from falling flat on her face. Was it his fault she'd made more of it than there was just because she was missing Jim, because it was the holidays, and the holidays always seemed to find her a little lonely?

"Picnic!" Jamie shouted. "Remember, Mom? Like we did when the power went out last time."

"Good idea, sport. I've got a tablecloth somewhere in here."

Logan set about rummaging through the boxes and came up with a red-and-white-checkered oilcloth, the kind used on picnic tables. For a fleeting moment a sad look pained his face as he looked at the cloth. Was he remembering his wife, his daughter and the good times they had shared?

With all that sadness filling him up, Logan wasn't looking for a relationship, either. Hadn't he planned on hibernating? Better, easier, for them both to keep this on the simple plane of neighborliness. He's a project, she reminded herself, not a prospect. And she needed to encourage her project's sociability.

With a grand flutter that delighted Jamie and Max, Logan spread the cloth on the floor.

Logan rifled through the packing carton once more and handed Jamie a stack of paper plates and plastic utensils. "Here, sport, why don't you set the table?"

Jamie, dogged by Max, placed four plates and three sets of utensils around the cloth.

"Is that what you've been using? Paper and plastic?" Beth asked, laughing. Keep the situation light, she told herself. Make him enjoy this dinner so that going out into the community will be the next logical step. She put her coat on top of Jamie's on the small window seat and sat cross-legged at the cloth's edge, relieved to have a reason to stay. Jamie and Max joined her.

"Saves time. Besides, tomorrow I won't have a sink." He took the casserole dish and set it in the middle of the cloth.

"Why not?"

Another trip to the packing carton produced a serving spoon. He washed it, then handed it to Beth. "I have to take it out in order to renovate the counter."

Beth dug into the shepherd's pie and served Jamie. Max licked her chops and thumped her tail with each move of the spoon. The turkey base was topped with a layer of corn, then another of mashed potatoes. That should be enough vegetables for one day. So what if there wasn't a salad or something green to accompany the main dish? No one was going to die of a vitamin deficiency. Besides, there was more going on here than a meal. This was a small step in implementing her plan to have Logan smiling by Christmas.

"What are you putting up instead?" Beth asked, pleased to hear Logan willing to talk for a change.

"The counter's in good shape. I'm just going to cover it with tile."

"Sounds pretty."

"Durable."

"What's your color scheme?" She piled Logan's plate with a double serving.

"I haven't decided yet."

"Something bright. Especially since there's no natural light in that corner of the kitchen." She smiled. "I know, I know. That doesn't go with your jailhouse theme though."

"I just might surprise you."

And a glance at him told her he just might. There were definitely layers worth exploring beneath that bearish exterior. Deep down, beneath all the protective armor around his heart, was a sensitive, passionate man. She was sure of it. Only a man who could love someone fully could have been hurt so profoundly.

"What about Max?" Jamie complained as Beth served herself.

Logan got up and came back with a serving of kibbles for Max. She took one sniff and crowded Jamie once more, watching every mouthful in hope some would fall her way.

As they ate, Logan seemed to relax a bit. He listened to the conversation Jamie and she kept alive. He distractedly petted the dog once and gently shooed her away from his plate a few times. And if she didn't know better, Beth might have thought he was trying to stretch out the evening with his slow, measured bites.

"Coffee?" Logan asked, after their meal.

There was that silent plea again, not in his voice so much as in his eyes. Yet she was willing to bet that if she asked him what he truly wanted, he would have no answer. Or maybe she was just projecting her own disjointed feelings onto him. She didn't want the evening to end and didn't quite know how to rationalize the longing.

"No, thanks. I won't be able to sleep if I have coffee this late. Jamie, stop running around. Why don't you put these dishes in the garbage?"

Jamie stopped sliding after a panting Max and did as he was asked with minimum grumbling. Beth put what little was left of the casserole in the fridge. It really wasn't enough for a lunch unless she could convince him to make a sandwich to go along with it, or some soup. It's not your problem, she told herself. She shut the fridge door firmly, then didn't quite know what to do. So she wiped the table-cloth clean, then bent to pick it up and refold it.

"Let me help you." Logan took one end and led the folding operation. "What's with you and food, anyway?"

"What do you mean?" She was much too aware of the piercing quality of his gaze tonight. What was he seeing? Was it pleasing? *Come on, Beth, what does it matter? It's not like you're interested or anything.*

"Your life seems to revolve around feeding people."

She shrugged. "Old habit."

"Tell me about it."

The genuine interest in his eyes made her throat feel parched.

"There's not much to the story. My father was Rock-ville's general practitioner for years. My mother was his nurse. They always got home late. I hated eating dinner right before going to bed. So, sometime during seventh grade, I got into the habit of making dinner for my parents."

"They were too busy for their child?"

She frowned at the pointedness of the question. "No, they loved me, and I knew they loved me. And we did spend a lot of time together."

"But…"

He walked his end of the cloth to hers. Her body seemed to hum at his closeness. His gaze was intent, concerned, as if she were still a child in danger of neglect. What had happened to him? The question went round and round in her mind, yet she couldn't bring herself to ask it out loud for fear of shattering the small bit of progress she was making with him.

"But, I was a bit lonely all alone after school, and cooking made me feel useful and needed and creative. I was good at it, and I enjoyed it."

"Experimenting even then?"

Beth thought she saw the beginnings of a grin at one end of his mouth, and she felt enormously pleased. Having him smile as genuinely as he had in the picture she'd seen of him and his daughter didn't seem quite as daunting a task now.

"Even then," she agreed, smiling widely. She'd often experimented with recipes and come up with delicious variations. That eventually led to the dream of owning her own gourmet catering business. But her plans had to be put on hold after Jim's death. Soon, she'd have enough saved to try to make a go of it.

"Where are your parents now?" he asked, taking the cloth from her hands. Their fingers touched, zinging something needful inside her. She tried to shove her hands in the pockets of her corduroy pants, but the bandage made the task awkward, so she stuck her thumbs in the belt loops.

She shrugged. Searching for something else she could do, she spotted the almost empty water bottle and reached for it. She turned the cap one way, then the other, and finally took the last gulp of water. "They died. A long time ago. On a Doctors Without Borders mission. Plane crash."

"I'm sorry."

"What about you?"

Logan was quiet while he put the cloth back into the packing carton. Would he ever trust her—anyone?—enough to open up?

"I never knew my father," he said as if he were chewing gravel. "My mother died a long time ago, too."

Had he ever known any kind of happiness? Then she recalled the picture of him and his daughter at the skating rink. Yes, he'd loved that child, and she's brought him a great measure of happiness.

A detail. It wasn't much, but he had shared *something*. It was a start. She tossed the empty bottle in the garbage bag. Now she had nothing to do again and felt on edge. She heard Jamie and Max sliding up and down the hallway. "Jamie, stop running and come back in here." She turned to Logan. "We should get going. Jamie needs a bath to-night."

She was reaching for her coat when there was a crash in the hallway. Jamie cried out. There was a sickening second of silence, then loud, angry sobs.

Before she could react, a white-faced Logan raced into the hallway. Jamie was in a tumble of dog and drop cloth.

"Don't move!" Logan ordered brusquely. He rushed at the boy, crouching beside him.

Jamie tried to untangle himself from the drop cloth.

Logan pushed him down again. "Don't move!"

Max cowered in the corner, head bent, tail between her legs.

Logan's movements were frantic as he patted her son up and down. From Jamie's cries, Beth knew he wasn't badly hurt, and Logan's overreaction seemed out of place.

"Where does it hurt?" Logan demanded.

"Mo-om!"

Logan held Jamie's face between his hands. "Where does it hurt, Jamie?"

"Logan?"

"Blood." His hand shook as he showed her the evidence—a smear on one finger. "Call 911."

"Mo-om." Jamie's voice trembled as he looked at her. She reached for him, and he climbed into her lap, fear now mingling with his tears. She held him and rocked him.

"He's hurt. The boy's hurt." Logan's voice tore at her with its pained gruffness. The haunted look in his eyes stabbed her with its fierceness. In the starkness of the bright hall light, his features were gaunt, carved with unwarranted guilt and despair.

"No, Logan, look," she said soothingly, understanding that Logan needed reassuring as much as Jamie. "He's fine. Jamie's fine. He just split his lip when he fell." She looked down at her son. "Tell Mr. Ward what happened, Jamie."

Jamie sniffed and swiped at his cut lip. "Me and Max were seeing how fast we could slide on the floor, and Max, she cut across, and I tripped over her and bit my lip."

"Does it hurt anywhere else?" Beth asked.

He shook his head.

She looked up at Logan once more. "He's fine, Logan. He's not hurt."

Logan nodded and slowly got up, tension still strung tight in each of his movements. "Go. Now."

Beth set her son on his feet. "Go get your coat, Jamie."

"But, Mom, I'm not finished playing with Max."

"Max will be here another day."

"Mo-om." He was whining now.

"Now, Jamie."

Kicking at the drop cloth, he headed toward the kitchen.

Beth got up and reached to touch Logan's shoulder. "What are you running away from?"

As if even a simple touch was more than he could bear, he shrugged her hand away. "Nothing. I'm sorry about Jamie getting hurt."

"He's fine."

"He could have been seriously hurt."

She tried to make light of a situation that had taken much too much importance in Logan's eyes. "Don't worry about it. He's a magnet for trouble."

"How can you be so casual about this?" Logan was frowning, his whole face contorted with the strong emotions he was trying so hard to hold in.

"Because he's a six-year-old boy, and six-year-old boys get bruises and scratches all the time. It's part of growing up."

"Of course," he said casually, but there was not a trace of life left in his voice.

A lump formed in her throat. Whatever progress she'd made over the meal had been wiped clean by Jamie's fall. "I'm the one who's sorry. I never meant to add to your burden."

Jamie reappeared, his coat half on, half off. His boots clomped on the hardwood floor. "Can I come play with Max tomorrow?"

Without a second's hesitation, Logan said, "No."

Beth zipped Jamie's coat. "Tomorrow's our library day, remember?"

"But, Mo-om."

"One more word out of you and you won't get to see Max for a good long time."

He opened his mouth, then shut it. With careful shepherding, Beth finally got herself and Jamie out the door and Max to stay inside.

"It's not your fault," she said, reaching for the mittens in her coat pocket.

With the light at his back, Logan's body was a silhouette, hard as rock and unyielding. She could see nothing of his face but the exaggerated play of sharp light and dark shadow on his cheek as his jaw tightened. The wind whipped at her hair, burrowed itself in the loosened collar of her coat. She shivered.

As she turned away, her mind buzzed with questions, her body bubbled with a host of strange feelings. If she let him, he would bury himself deeper in his guilt and sorrow.

Jamie kicked at the snow. "Why can't I play with Max?"

"Because it's late." She reached for her son and hugged him close. Glancing back over her shoulder, she saw Logan still looking out at them. After them, she corrected herself. If a dragon were to suddenly materialize from the ether between his door and hers, she had no doubt he would leap into battle to protect them.

A lazy smile curled her lips, and a renewed sense of security almost banished her tension. He wanted her to give up on him—that had been clear from his curt dismissal. But how could she, when dragon-slaying knights were in such short supply these days?

Logan watched Beth go, until her front door closed behind her and the lights went on one by one in her house. He hadn't asked her to come over, hadn't asked her to feed him. As a matter of fact, he'd done everything he could to discourage her unwanted attention. But she didn't seem to understand the meaning of *no*.

So how could it be his fault her kid got hurt?

Because he'd gone and asked her to stay for dinner.

He should have known better, should have known nothing good would come of it.

To make matters worse, he'd allowed one impulse to

lead to another. He should never have touched her, never have allowed her female desires to awaken his own dormant male needs. Now they plagued him like sirens calling to a lost sailor.

He shut the door, stopping shy of a slam. It was just as well. He'd wanted quiet. He'd wanted solitude. Now he would have them both. He wouldn't have to endure her perpetual cheerfulness, her eye-hurting brightness, her emotion-provoking presence. He could work and purge and forget in the isolation he craved.

So why was anger eating him alive?

He stepped into the kitchen and saw Beth's smile, heard her laughter, felt her touch and cursed a blue streak. Swiveling on his heels, a shaking Max at his heels, he headed for the cellar. There he set a cupboard door on a saw horse, donned a mask and fitted the sander with paper—all under Max's watchful gaze as she sat on one step with her front paws on another. The machine's noise couldn't quite cover the stampede of his thoughts, but it did dull them to a mindless buzz. He worked until he could no longer feel his hands, then stumbled into bed with his dusty clothes still on.

The nightmares came in full vivid colors. Samantha, Jamie, dead and dying. Julia, Beth, tears of accusation wet in their eyes. The vignettes twisted one into the other, black, purple and red. Heat. Longing. Beth. He wrapped himself around her, aroused and ravenous, feeding on her, in her, until he awoke, sheets tangled around his legs, sweaty, arms empty and aching.

He swiped a hand across his face and padded to the shower where the icy water did nothing to dispel his desire. The coffee he brewed tasted bitter and jangled his already-raw nerves. He looked at the clock on the stove, then reached for the phone.

\* \* \*

The phone rang. No, no, no. Not this morning. I don't have time, Beth thought as she rushed to put Jamie's lunch together. She hadn't slept well last night, tossing and turning, worrying about that grouchy neighbor of hers. She should leave him alone, logic told her, let him stew in his own misery. But she couldn't get the image of his once-wonderful smile out of her mind. He didn't belong to the world of the dead any more than she had five years ago. Launching the tuna sandwich into a bag with one hand, she reached for the phone with the other.

"Hello."

"Thursday."

There was no need to ask who was on the other end. She knew only one person so terse, only one person whose voice made her heart leap treacherously. Logan. "Thursday?"

"Your stitches need to come out."

Was this a simple reminder or something else? "I was going to stop by the clinic after work."

"I'll drive you."

Out of guilt for what had happened to Jamie? "That's not necessary."

"Your hands might be a little sore after."

"I'm sure I'll be fine."

There was a long pause.

"I need to go into town, anyway."

And suddenly she realized why Logan was being so insistent. He needed to know that his assessment of her healing was correct, that he had caused no permanent harm. Someone he'd once loved had been hurt, he'd felt responsible and was paying penance even now. That was why he'd sought hibernation. If he saw no one, then he could not be responsible for anyone's pain. After the incident with Jamie last night, she was as certain of that as she was that Logan's remorse was undeserved.

Last night's indoor picnic might have backfired, but now that she understood why, she would be better prepared in the future. His errands and his need to drive her to the clinic were the perfect distractions to get him out of his self-imposed hibernation and into the world of the living.

At this point she had to grasp on to anything she could if she was going to make him smile by Christmas.

"Okay, then. I accept."

If he thought Beth would never darken his doorstep again after he'd ordered her to leave, Logan had been sorely mistaken. Like a bad case of food poisoning, she'd shown up again that very afternoon, casserole in hand, son tagging along. She must have had a talk with Jamie because he behaved more like a boy in a church than a rambunctious six-year-old. Polite, well-behaved, and frankly obnoxious with his formal address and reserved play with Max.

Before he knew it, Logan was dragging a card table and four folding chairs Beth had insisted she was going to give to Goodwill from her cellar to his kitchen. Of course, it couldn't stay bare because of the small stain in one corner, so she'd also talked him into covering it with the red-and-white tablecloth and into unearthing his stainless utensils and stoneware place settings. She'd added a bouquet of yellow and purple silk pansies in a white glass vase to the center, even after he'd told her they'd just get covered with dust.

"Dust wipes clean," she'd said and beamed at the result of her effort.

But they hadn't stayed for dinner, and he hadn't asked, and instead of enjoying a review of Beth's day, he'd stared at Max's inane grin across the table while eating his dinner. Max had been a little short on conversation.

An evening of sanding cupboard frames hadn't eased the knot of restlessness knitting itself into each one of his muscles, nor had a fitful night of sleep. Not when he woke up hungry for Beth—her taste and her touch and the sound of her voice.

On Wednesday Beth sorted the screws and hinges on his counter into empty coffee cans she'd brought along while she rambled on about the town's trouble with the ruined Christmas decorations. After the countertops were cleared, she fussed at him while he hefted the sink out of its hole and into the garage. She'd almost made him drop the thing with all of her fluttering. Then she'd mentioned an emergency meeting set up by the Beautification Committee and had made an early exit, leaving him mildly irritated. Okay, so the irritation had been slightly more than mild. He'd been downright bothered. Bothered enough to finish the priming coat on the cupboard frames and on the walls.

After he'd taken her to have her stitches removed on Thursday, she'd resolutely voted against being driven home before she helped him pick out tile. First they'd had to stop at the coffee shop along the common, to talk about his design plan for the kitchen. She couldn't make an uninformed decision, she'd said. Warm cup of French-vanilla coffee in hand, she'd somehow wormed out of his plans to paint the cupboards and the walls white, to bleach the floor's maple boards, to tile the counter and backsplash in white with a blue accent border.

Logan frowned as he picked up a sunny-yellow tile from the box. How in the hell had he ended up with that when he'd gone in with a blue-and-white design in mind? It was the incessant chatter, he decided. She'd confused him until he'd done as she wanted just to shut her up.

But as he added a placer between the two tiles on the counter, he had to admit that the soft yellow did give the space warmth. And though it was only noon, he was already wondering what she would bring over for dinner tonight and how he could talk her into staying for a while.

## Chapter Eight

Beth and Eve were sharing a Saturday-morning coffee and pastry at the Rockville Diner before yet another meeting of the Beautification Committee. At this rate the Christmas decorations would never go up this year. Beth had purposely chosen the last booth so the kitchen noises would help mask their conversation. She'd waited patiently, too, for Eve to broach the subject of Logan, but Eve seemed immune to Beth's subtle prodding and talked of everything but Logan. Finally Beth caved in and tried the direct approach, knowing she'd never hear the end of Eve's victory.

"Okay, you've got chocolate and coffee. Now spill."

Eve pretended to frown and tried to hide her smile with a sip of coffee. "I haven't the foggiest idea what you mean."

"You're not a very good actress."

Eve broke a piece of her giant chocolate-chocolate-chunk muffin and grinned more widely.

Bacon and hash-browns sizzled on the diner's grill behind them. Coffee perked. Dishes clanked. Voices droned around them, spiked now and then with a barked order to or from the cook. Gum-soled shoes squeaked by them as waitresses dressed in jeans and green aprons rushed back and forth. The bell over the door tinkled like a bird's hello with each patron's entrance or exit.

Beth sighed. "You're going to make me beg, aren't you?"

"A slight show of desperation would be appreciated."

Beth shook a finger at her. "The only reason I'm giving in is because I haven't had a chance to do a search of my own. With the school's freezer not working and all those useless emergency meetings, I just haven't had a chance."

"Not to mention having to make sure you get home in time to feed Logan."

"Eve—"

That, of course, was a line of conversation she didn't want to get into. Eve was seeing a prospect where there was only a project. Beth stirred her black coffee. Still…

Innocently Eve took another mouthful of muffin. "How is your project coming along, by the way?"

Beth twirled the mug before her in tight, noisy circles. She'd made the mistake of telling Eve about the incident with Jamie, and Logan's overreaction. "I think I'm seeing progress. He asked us to stay for dinner last night."

Eve's eyebrows rose. "Ooh, now that's encouraging. Did you?"

"No. I don't think he's ready for that yet." Beth split her cranberry muffin in two.

"How long are you going to dangle him on a cord?"

"It's not like that. I just want to be sure that if anything happens he can take it in stride."

Eve cocked her head. "You may be waiting for a long time, then. Christmas is only a couple of weeks away."

"I know. I'll invite him for dinner tonight."

Eve nodded. "Sensible."

"I thought so."

Eve licked the last crumb of chocolate from her finger. "All right, what do you want to know?"

Beth concentrated on the cranberries in her muffin. With the tip of a knife she excavated a round berry from the surrounding cake. "The hero bit."

"Ah, yes." Eve practically chirped. "There's something about a hero, isn't there? A man in uniform seems to ring a certain chord in a woman's heart—"

Beth slanted Eve a narrowed look. "Eve, I swear, I will strangle you any second now."

Eve laughed and folded the muffin's paper cup into ever-smaller triangles. "He saved a busload of elementary school children."

"How, where, what happened?" Silently Beth cursed the eagerness in her voice.

A smile of smug satisfaction curled Eve's lips. She leaned forward. "Well, it seems there was an unexpected ice storm last winter. The kids were being sent home early. According to the paper, the bus driver slammed on the brakes to avoid a car and ended up skidding on a patch of ice, careening down an embankment and into an electric pole. A live wire was dangling right over the engine, threatening to catch the whole thing on fire."

Eve dramatically sipped her coffee.

"And?" Beth urged breathlessly.

"And Logan was the first officer on the scene. Somehow he got the kids out safely, and the driver, too. Then the bus exploded."

"Wow." Beth slumped back in the chair. Having seen

Logan overreact to Jamie's fall, she could imagine how desperately he'd worked to save the frightened children. She frowned. "All of them got out safe?"

"Yes. But that's not all. It turns out the driver had been drinking. He was borderline drunk."

"No. How could that have happened?" Somehow the information didn't fit with Logan's overreaction, though. There must be more to the story.

Eve shrugged. "Logan refused the commendation the city wanted to give him."

"Why?" Beth's frown deepened.

"He said he was just doing his job."

"Hmm." Beth stared at her muffin, picking out one cranberry after another.

"What's wrong, Beth?"

"I don't know." She shrugged. "There's got to be more. If he saved all of the children, then why was he so shaken when Jamie's lip got cut at his house?"

Eve squirmed in her seat. She sipped her coffee much too intently.

Beth tensed and pushed aside the small plate bearing her mutilated muffin. "Eve, what else do you know?"

"It's not that simple, sweetie."

"What's not simple about it? You know. You tell."

Eve peered into her coffee, then, as if coming to a decision, looked up again. "Do you like him?"

Beth was confused at Eve's evasiveness and the sudden determined look in her eyes. "He's rude, ill-tempered and moody."

"But do you like him?" Eve insisted.

Beth deflated. "Oh, Eve, I don't know. There's something about him." She shrugged. "Underneath all that armor, there's a wonderful man. I just know it."

"But…"

"But after Jim…" Beth lifted a hand in a helpless gesture.

"After Jim what?"

"Nothing can compare." How could she explain her fear at losing someone who had meant so much to her? Jim had occupied all of her heart. He'd been the center of her life. He'd been her best friend, her lover, her other half. If she gave part of her heart to someone else, would she forget Jim and all he'd meant to her? He was already fading so fast from her memory. Distractedly, she felt the lump of her wedding ring hanging on a chain beneath her sweater.

And if she couldn't give all of her heart to someone else, then, would it be fair to them? Logan deserved more than a small corner of heart. He needed someone who could love him completely.

Eve reached for one of Beth's hand and squeezed it. "Sweetie, don't shut doors before you even give yourself a chance to walk through them."

Beth shook her head. "It's not that simple. You of all people should understand that. You never loved again after your fiancé was killed."

"And look at me now. I'm an old spinster who's all alone." Eve squeezed Beth's hand again. "I made a foolish mistake."

"So why do you keep saying no to Gus's proposals?"

"Because I'm too old to change my ways. But you're not. You're young. You have a son to think of. You have a whole life ahead of you. And that's why I can't tell you anything more."

"I don't understand."

Eve drained her cup. "It's something you need to hear from him."

"I could look it up myself."

"You could." Eve ticked a nail against the tabletop to

underline her point. "But the papers give only one version of what happened. They don't tell you about the heart. There's a matter of trust involved here, Beth. You should ask him, and he should tell you."

"In a perfect world…" Beth dug through her purse for her wallet. "He's very closed off. I don't think he trusts anyone, not even himself."

"All the more reason to hear his version of the truth, don't you think?"

Confused now, Beth signaled their waitress.

"Nothing's perfect," Eve said, and reached for her coat. "The sooner you get that through your head, the better off you'll be. Jim wasn't perfect, though you've made him out to be a saint with the passing years. And saving yourself for a ghost is pure stupidity."

"Eve!"

"Well, you asked."

"About Logan—not for a lowdown on my shortcomings."

"One is tied with the other in this situation." Eve perched her red rolled brim hat at a jaunty angle on her head. "So what are you feeding him tonight?"

Beth groaned and stuffed her wallet back into her purse. "Brussels sprouts in a cheese sauce and a sweet-potato and black-bean stew."

"Beth! That's not the way to get to that man. He needs meat and potatoes."

"No, what he needs is something out of the ordinary to knock him out of his loop."

Eve laughed and slipped on her red wool coat. "Well, he's getting that, that's for sure."

Leaning forward over the table, Beth whispered, "Oh, no."

"What?"

"Don't look now, but here comes Laura Darlington."

"Good morning, ladies." Laura Darlington's high-pitched voice cleaved through the diner's noise like a freshly sharpened ax.

"Good morning, Laura," Beth and Eve said resignedly in unison.

With her skinny body, oversize glasses and her prematurely white hair cut in a bob, Laura looked like a cross between an owl and a crane. Being dressed in shades of white, brown and gray didn't help the image. And Darlington really was not a good fit for a name. There was nothing darling about the way she meddled with everybody's business or about her sour view of life.

"Are you headed to the meeting?" Laura asked. Something about her body language suggested she had juicy gossip she was dying to share. Or worse—juicy gossip she wanted to extract.

"Beth is. I've got a house to show in—" with a flourish, Eve looked at her watch "—oops, less than ten minutes. Beth, I'll expect a call tomorrow. About that new black-bean stew."

Eve's eyes twinkled with mischief, and her smile had a swallowed-canary quality.

"The stew's really better the second or third day."

Eve roared with laughter. "Stop by after church, anyway. I just bought a new bag of that French vanilla coffee you love."

With a wave Eve made her escape, leaving Beth trapped on the other side of the table. Laura slipped into Eve's chair.

"So, how are things with you?" Laura asked, taking her brown gloves off.

Beth purposefully misinterpreted Laura's prodding. "I think we finally found what was wrong with the freezer.

The new part should be in on Monday. Everything should be set for the middle school concert on Wednesday. The PTA has nothing to worry about.''

"That's great." Laura waited a beat. "Big Bill is almost well enough to come home."

Give a little, hope to get a little back. Did Laura know her tactic was transparent? Did she even care? Beth cringed as she hitched her purse on her shoulder and stood. "I'm so glad to hear that. I've got some chicken noodle soup in the freezer ready for him."

"He'll love that."

Beth gathered her gloves. "We'd better get to the town hall. The meeting starts in a few minutes."

"Oh, yes, you're right."

Beth wound her way around the closely set tables, hoping against hope to lose Laura in the maze. No chance of that with Laura nipping at her heels.

"I still don't know how we're going to get anything done before the Holiday Fair next weekend," Laura said.

"We'll think of something."

The bell's clang over the door sounded like a screech rather than a joyful chirp. The wind, heavy with the scent of snow, was wheeling sooty clouds over the blue sky.

"The town doesn't have that Currier and Ives quality without the red ribbons and pine boughs." Laura took her position at Beth's side on the sidewalk.

Zipping her coat, Beth insisted everything would come together in time for the Holiday Fair. "It'll be the best one yet."

Laura sighed and professed more gloom. "Christmas will be drastically different this year. Remember last year? Even without the snow the town looked like a jewel. And two years ago we had a bonanza year. Snow before Thanksgiving *and* sunshine every single weekend. Never before have we had such bad luck with…everything!''

"It'll just be different, that's all.''

But Laura was well into her own well-worn groove of lament. "And everyone is so depressed about the Super-Mart opening. You know how people are. Got to check it out. And they've got good prices, but really, when you get down to it, they don't have the service. Still, it's tough to sell that line these days. People just look at the price, not what they're getting for the price. Gene has the same problem.''

Gene being Simon Eugene Darlington, Laura's husband, owner of Darlington Motor Company, one of three used car lots in this small town. Only Gene had inherited the business and had no true interest in cars or selling and seemed more content to sit and watch game shows all day rather than drum up business.

Beth had a theory that Laura saw so much negative in others to deal with the disappointment her own life had brought. If everyone else's life was rotten, then hers couldn't be that bad.

In some ways, Beth felt sorry for her, but not today, not when she knew just where Laura would eventually wind up—needling her about Logan.

"Do they really think that's going to help?'' Laura snorted as they passed a giant banner flapping in the wind, proclaiming in bright-red and green, "Wrap It Up Locally!''

"And Roy is too old to put up the tree this year,'' Laura continued. "Especially after his hip surgery last spring.''

Roy Crandall was an old widower who'd done much for the town. His property on the edge of town was gifted to Rockville as conservation land and housed some of the nicest trails in the area. He'd once been part of the selectmen running the town. Now he simply offered the voice of reason as the town attempted to guide its growth.

"He'll outlive us all," Beth said, thinking fondly of Roy's excitement over the Christmas season. Making sure the town glowed with lights and color seemed to give Roy purpose, and seeing all the children's faces as they sat on his knees and surrendered their secret wishes to his Santa, seemed to energize him for the entire year.

"Maybe so, but he can't be out there hacking down trees and climbing up ladders to set the lights. Not with Big Bill out of commission and those two idiots who make up the public works department busy trying to keep up with the water problems."

Not to mention keeping up with the snow removal and all their other duties. "We've got plenty of healthy men in their prime willing to help out."

"Speaking of healthy men…"

Beth silently groaned. She'd walked right into that one.

"…how is that new neighbor of yours?"

Beth speeded her pace. "Very busy."

"You don't say."

Give her a little and get her off your back? "He's remodeling his kitchen."

"Strange place for him to start, don't you think? I mean him being a man. A bachelor at that."

Beth took the steps in front of the town hall two at a time. "Why? The kitchen is the center of any home. I think it makes perfect sense. Everybody's got to eat."

Laura puffed by her side. "So I've heard. All those dinners." Laura tisked. "Do you think it's wise to lead the man on when you have no intention of ever marrying again?"

"Who said?" Beth frowned. Being the subject of grapevine conjecture didn't sit well with her—especially when it rang too close to the truth.

"Well, it's obvious. After having someone like Jim, how could you even think of replacing him? Everybody loved Jim. There was no one quite like him."

Anger rumbled inside her, but Beth reminded herself that she was talking to Laura. The same Laura who'd had her eye on Jim twelve years ago and who'd nearly torn Beth's eyes out when Jim had chosen Beth over her.

"What I do or don't do is really none of anybody's business." Beth swung open the heavy wooden door and zipped through.

"Oh, you're so right. Still, if you keep feeding him, he could get the wrong idea, you know."

"I don't think so. He's not looking for a relationship either."

Laura grabbed on to the tidbit as if it were caviar on a table of chips and dip. "Really, is that so?"

"Yes."

"Now, I wonder why that is." Laura's voice echoed in the stairwell, and even the tread of their racing feet on the stairs couldn't block out the fact Laura was looking very intently at her prey for any signs of weakness.

"How should I know?"

"Well, you go there every day, and I heard Jamie was hurt over there sometime last week."

"Jamie wasn't hurt. He's perfectly fine."

Laura was zeroing in now. Beth could almost feel the sharpness of talons digging into flesh.

"Logan. Such a nice name, don't you think?" Laura practically purred with delight. "Masculine. Strong."

Beth stopped and rounded on Laura who had to check her step in order not to run into her. "Leave him alone, Laura."

Laura's eyebrows arched with astonishment. Her eyes widened. She gave an owlish blink, then started sputtering, "I didn't mean anything by—"

"He doesn't need to be the butt of town gossip."

Without waiting for an excuse or giving an apology, Beth swiveled back and climbed the last two steps. Her face burned. Her heart was pounding. Her tensed muscles quivered. Where had all this fierce protectiveness come from? And how could she have lost her temper like that? Laura's tongue would wag this tidbit all over town, and she'd never hear the end of it.

Beth breathed a sigh of relief when she entered the meeting room and found the rest of the committee already in place. Claudelle Weston was just banging the gavel to open the meeting, putting an end to Laura's pecking. She squeezed in between Claudelle and Roy, forcing Laura to take a spot at the opposite end of the table beside Mildred Wallace and Clementine Brickman.

But as Beth picked up the typewritten agenda sheet and pretended to give it all of her attention, she had to wonder why this conversation with Laura had disturbed her so much, why she was still a little shaky.

Because having someone dissected by Laura was not a fate she would wish on her worst enemy, she rationalized. And Logan had already been hurt enough. It wasn't because she felt she had to protect the privacy he cherished so much, and certainly not because her stomach fluttered every time she saw him.

She frowned and stared at the paper on which she could suddenly see nothing but a blur of black ink on white paper. Roy had to nudge her twice to get her attention, and even then, she could hear nothing he said over the loud drum of her pulse pounding.

No, it couldn't be. Hand on her stomach, she shook her

head to clear it. Could Laura be right? Could she be half falling for her surly neighbor? Could she be leading Logan on?

Mind stuck on fast forward, she reviewed each of her encounters with Logan, then huffed out a breath. He was a project, not a prospect. She was feeding him because he wasn't feeding himself. And she'd have done that even if Jim were alive. As a matter of fact, Jim would have encouraged her. She'd done nothing to make Logan think she was seeking anything more than a neighborly relationship.

"I'm sorry, Roy. For a second there I scared myself, thinking I'd left the house without turning off the oven." The whole room chuckled. "Can you repeat your question?"

An agenda had been set. Donations of boughs, wreaths and ribbons would be sought, and twice this week they would gather volunteers to decorate lampposts, the town hall and the bandstand on the common with hopes Rockville would look festive by the Holiday Fair next Saturday. They would worry about the tree lighting next week.

After picking up Jamie at his friend Bobby's house, Beth made a quick stop at the post office before it closed at one. A yellow slip waited in her box.

"Look, Jamie, there's a package from Grandma and Grandpa Lannigen."

Not being able to deal with their only child's death, Jim's parents had left the area soon after Jim's funeral. They'd been living in Arizona, far from all the reminders of their loss—including her and Jamie. They sent packages on birthdays and at Christmas, but not once had they made the trip up north in the past five years.

Beth lowered the square box to Jamie's height. "What does the sticker say?"

"Don't Open Before Christmas! Awww." Jamie grabbed the box and shook it. He was rewarded by a clanging that sounded suspiciously like Legos. "Can we put in under the tree?"

"We'll see." That could be a mistake. Out of sight would be out of mind. Under the tree might prove to be too big a temptation for her curious son.

Jamie skipped around her as they made their way back to the library where she'd parked her car.

Looking up at her with a wide smile, Jamie rapped on the side of the box. "Knock-knock."

Beth groaned and laughed at the same time. "Who's there?"

"Felix."

"Felix who?"

"Felix-cited all over."

Beth twitched Jamie's nose. "You're still going to have to wait until Christmas."

"Awww."

She unlocked the car and stowed the package on the front seat, then, looking at the library building, she hesitated. Already snowflakes wafted in the air and salted the pavement. She wanted to get home before the brunt of the storm hit. But this curiosity was an itch that needed scratching. "Let's go in for a minute."

"Why? I already got books."

"I just want to look at something real quick." Real quick—before I lose my courage and change my mind.

Jamie started to whine.

"I'll bet Miss Sarah will let you punch cards if you ask nicely."

"Yeah!" He raced ahead.

Her palms were damp as she handed her library card to reserve Internet time. Tension knotted through her as she sat and stared at the screen. Her fingers stuttered on the keys as she typed in commands. Then when the search engine page was up and the cursor blinked waiting for instructions, Beth swallowed the lump in her throat, but could not seem to make her fingers move.

"Need any help, Mrs. L?"

She was startled by the unexpected voice at her shoulder. Chandler Mackenzie, a student she knew from school, was working as an aide shelving books.

"No, thanks, Chandler. I was just getting off."

With a resigned sigh she exited the program. She hated it when Eve was right.

She wasn't ready for marriage or any kind of serious relationship. Someday, maybe. But not now. Still, Logan was becoming a friend, and with friendship came the obligation of trust.

The answers had to come from him—perhaps all he needed was the opportunity.

The sound of his own phone was an alien screech amid the near-silent task of grouting his newly tiled counter. Logan stared at the offending implement on the floor. Who could be calling? He hadn't given anyone his number and was paying for the privilege of keeping it unpublished. He swept the float across the tiles, but curiosity finally made him pick up the receiver.

"Logan, are you there?"

Beth. A simultaneous zing of pleasure and annoyance coursed through him. "How'd you get this number?"

"I have my ways."

He could hear her smile and turned to look out the window at the seafoam-green house across the street. The Christmas lights were shining as brightly as their owner. He imagined her in the kitchen, dressed in red and green or maybe yellow and purple, phone between ear and shoulder, stirring something. As if to prove him right, the soft pinging of the oven timer chimed. A smile twitched at his lips. There was something to be said about predictability. "I'm feeling violated."

"Violated? Really?" There was hesitation in her voice. "You know I can never tell when you're serious and when you're attempting a joke."

"That's me, a man of mystery."

She laughed, and the sound popped through him like soap bubbles from a wand. "Has this man of mystery worked up an appetite?"

He was immediately transported back to his vivid dreams of her and him and the insatiable appetite he'd tried to quell in them. He cleared his throat, and as if she could see him from across the street, he shifted his body away from the window. "I don't recall giving my number to anyone."

She giggled. "Except Gus to call you when the part you ordered came in."

"The kitchen fixture." He should have ordered it online, then he wouldn't have to deal with this unexpected burning hunger. "Is nothing private in this town?"

"Not much. I guess I should have warned you that he's seeing Eve and that Eve is an incorrigible meddler. How about I tell you all about the latest gossip over dinner?"

"I'm not much into gossip." And the thought of seeing her again was a bit too appealing, dangerous even, in this state of mind.

"I made your favorite—brussels sprouts and sweet potato."

A gruff puff of laughter escaped him. Beth and food. Predictable. Tension drained out of him. Besides, his fridge was empty, and he didn't want to attempt a trip into town with all this snow falling. "Well, when you put it like that, how can I refuse?"

## Chapter Nine

The weighty snow had already dropped half a foot of white over the landscape. Even with the dark of evening, the temperatures were rising, turning the flakes into ice pellets. A town snowplow, yellow lights blinking, rumbled by, sealing off the end of his driveway, then Beth's. He'd have to borrow a shovel in case he needed to get out—in an emergency, of course.

The burning welcome of Beth's porch light, the icing of snow on the roof and the colorful bulbs he'd installed made her house appear like a gingerbread creation.

"Can we make one, Daddy? Can we?" Sam had stood mesmerized in a grocery store check-out line by the gumdrop-and-licorice-adorned graham cracker house on the cover of a magazine. "They've got plans and everything." Their effort wouldn't have been mistaken for a work of art, but Sam had beamed with pride at their Christmas table centerpiece. After the accident, he'd smashed the cookie house against the wall and hadn't bothered to pick up the pieces for more than a month.

Hunching his shoulders, he whistled to Max who'd stopped to sniff at a disoriented autumn leaf. She rabbitted up to him. He couldn't quite figure out why he'd let her tag along.

Jamie answered his knock. "Mr. Ward! I got some new hockey cards. Wanna see?"

The boy seemed glad to see him. "Maybe later. I brought Max."

"Really?" Jamie beamed, giving his heart an uncomfortable tug.

"She wanted to play."

"Thanks!"

Max squirmed around Logan's leg, half her body wagging in anticipation. Jamie reached for her. His laughter at Max's canine kisses warbled like a bird's song and a strange satisfaction softened Logan. He shrugged it off.

"Max, come, Max." Jamie lured her toward the living room. "Mom's in the kitchen."

As if she would be anywhere else. His lips twitched as he headed for the kitchen. The aroma of something sweet and spicy greeted him, then warmth enveloped him, and brightness dazzled him, stirring dormant echoes of a nearly forgotten hope.

Places like this really did exist; they weren't just the fiction of needful children's dreams. He suddenly thought of Dorothy in *The Wizard of Oz* as she fervently said "There's no place like home," and regret soughed inside him.

But it was the vision of a dancing Beth that stopped him short and had him leaning against the door frame, arms crossed over his chest, with the uncomfortable captivation of a voyeur. There seemed to be a barrier preventing him from crossing the threshold into that inviting world of kitchen comfort and feminine zest. As if taking that step would alter something vital.

She looked like a candy cane with her fuchsia corduroys and pink sweater with its white stripes and sparkling silver snowflakes. Where did she find clothes in such bright colors? There couldn't be a market for those things.

The radio was turned up and, using a wooden spoon as a microphone, she was singing "Winter Wonderland" along with Elvis, swiveling hips and all. He had a sudden urge to grasp that candy cane of a woman and taste every inch of her. He stuck his hands in his pockets, frowning at the craving gnawing at his gut.

She whipped around, saw him watching her. A spark of surprise and pleasure flickered in her eyes even as her cheeks flamed. Her gestures became the short, snappy ones of the embarrassed as she cut Elvis off midtwang.

"Hey," she said, busying herself stirring a pot, "take your coat off and stay a while. Want something while you wait for dinner?"

*You.* He was enticed by the energy and the softness she exuded, by her unwarranted attraction to him. When she discovered the real Logan Ward, would she still think she wanted him?

Not in a thousand years.

So why had he accepted her invitation tonight? He didn't need the complications, the responsibilities, the obligations. He didn't want to hurt her or Jamie.

A long breath shuddered out of him. He'd come because, no matter how often he told himself it wasn't so, the truth was that he wanted Beth—wanted to lose himself in her softness and warmth...in her vibrancy.

But he couldn't. For all of their sakes, he had to keep this relationship on a neighborly level. His muscles suddenly twitched for something to do. "You got a shovel? I'll clear your drive."

"No need. Ed Barclay plows me out after every storm." She opened the fridge. "Tea, coffee or juice?"

"I'm fine." As fine as he could be given his dueling conscience. He shook off his jacket and hung it on the back of a chair.

A clashing of metal on metal charged from the living room, followed by a childish peal of laughter and an excited bark.

He curbed his urge to check on the boy and silently prodded Beth to go look in on her son. She blithely kept removing produce from the crisper. A sour streak of frustration turned his disposition to vinegar.

Beth wasn't any better a parent than Julia. How many times had he come home to find Samantha alone in a room, the danger of ordinary things all around her? And here was Beth slicing cucumbers without a care while Jamie was getting himself into trouble. "How could you have that radio turned up so loud? What if Jamie had needed you?"

Her hands stopped in the middle of shredding lettuce over a salad bowl. She shot him a questioning glance. "Mother's intuition. He's in the living room, playing with his toy cars. You brought Max. They're having fun. What's the problem?"

"No problem." And she was a meddler, too. If he had any sense, he'd leave right now.

She was right, though. He was being unreasonable. Just because he couldn't trust his instincts anymore didn't mean he had to take it out on her. "Max likes your cooking."

"So you came just to feed Max?" She quirked him a smile as she set the salad bowl on the table.

No, for that smile. "A dog's gotta eat."

"I see. You're afraid you still won't like brussels sprouts

and sweet potatoes.'' Beth's throaty laughter was a caress. ''Why don't you go round everybody up for supper, and we'll find out? Everything's just about ready.''

Yeah, everything was just about ready to push him right off the tightrope he was walking.

There it was again, that look in Logan's eyes, something between hunger and terror. It made her shiver with delight and a dose of doubt of her own. Projecting again, are we, Beth?

She shrugged, squirted soap into the sink and watched the water foment bubbles. Thinking of Logan in that way was dangerous. She wasn't looking for a quick affair and wasn't quite ready for anything else.

Maybe someday. But not right now.

And certainly not this fast. Falling in love with Jim had taken time, but the results—that deep friendship, that enduring love—had been worth the leisurely pace.

Besides, Logan needed to heal the grief deep inside him before he could consider a relationship. He wasn't ready, either.

Still, there was that look in his eyes. And there was something to be said for companionship. She liked having someone to talk to over dinner, hadn't realized how much she'd missed that until Logan sat at her table and asked about her day.

A friend she could use…and so could he. Unconditional friendship—that was the way to make him find his smile once more.

''Where do you want these?'' Logan asked, holding up the red-and-green snowflake placemats.

''Just shake them out and put them back on the table.''

Without being asked, he took the sponge from the dish above the sink and wiped the table. He did the task with the ease of someone who'd had practice, which aroused her curiosity again.

"You've done this before," she said, hoping he'd fill in a detail or two.

He shrugged. The sharpness of the movement spelled *do not enter* more clearly than any sign. Okay, Logan, I'll back off. For now.

He took a clean dishcloth from the linen drawer and joined her at the sink.

"How's your kitchen coming along?" Ease into the hard stuff. Basic Psychology 101. It worked with teenage girls, sullen six-year-olds and bruised adults.

"I've got the priming coat done on the walls and cabinets. Now I've got to decide on paint."

"Still going with plain white?" A bit of humor always helped loosen things. She tried to keep a straight face, but her lips quivered as she slanted him a teasing glance. "Have you considered adding gray stripes? For the prison-cell look."

He frowned a deep, intent glower.

She was used to humor. Eve had a wicked sense of it. Jim had been witty, and constant exposure to his jokes had brought out her own lighter side. Almost everyone she knew enjoyed good repartee. And Logan himself had endured her teasing about his color scheme before.

But he'd worn a strange expression when he'd caught her singing along with Elvis earlier and had kept it on all through dinner. He seemed preoccupied, more distant than usual. She should have realized he wasn't in a playful mood. Her insides pounded at her blunder, and she frantically searched for a way to lighten the mood once again.

Logan took the saucepan from her still hands and wiped it dry. "Don't smile like that."

"Like what?" She scanned the counter for something else and found the Dutch oven.

"It makes me want to kiss you."

His unexpected admission choked her breath. It was one thing to think he might want to kiss her, quite another to have him express the desire.

Her voice squeaked. "I see."

Frowning, she plunged the Dutch oven into the suds and scrubbed hard, afraid that if she stopped he'd see her fingers shaking. "Logan—"

"I don't want to care for you in that way."

"I understand." Beth worked at a piece of stuck-on sweet potato. She didn't want to care for him in that way, either. He was a project, not a prospect. "You confuse me."

Avoiding her gaze, Logan dried the bowl in his hand to perfection. "I'm sorry."

It wasn't that she wasn't attracted. There was something about Logan that did reach out to her and made her want to reach out to him. But was it just her need to heal the wounded or something more?

Jim had often teased her with the fact that only his allergies kept the house from turning into a zoo. While Jim was alive, more often than not, their spare room had been occupied by one lost soul or another. And if they hadn't been so cruelly parted, a brood of children would be trampling these floors. She swallowed her regret.

"I saw the pictures in your wallet," she said, concentrating on the pan in her hands, on her project.

He made no reply. The drip of the faucet, the crank of the water pump beneath them in the cellar, Jamie's faraway voice filled the void with glaring discord.

"What are you hiding from?" Beth swished the soapy water over the already spotless surface of the pot.

"Where does this bowl go?"

"Just leave it on the counter."

He attacked the serving spoons with bone-rattling intensity. She should drop the subject. Everything about the stiff lines of his body, about the stern set of his face told her to. Yet there were also ghosts of pain in his eyes, and she found she could not ignore those.

"You can't outrun demons," she said.

He held up the spoons. "Where do these go?"

"In the jar by the stove."

He rescued the soapy Dutch oven from the water, leaving her hands empty. She pulled the plug and listened to the soapy water gurgle down the drain, then scrubbed the stainless-steel surface free of germs.

"There's a cure, you know."

He grunted and held up the pot.

"In the cupboard behind you."

The kitchen clanged with noise until he found a home for the saucepan, the vegetable steamer and the Dutch oven.

"Logan—"

He slammed the cupboard door. "Drop it, Beth. You don't want to go there."

She reached for the towel hanging on the oven door handle and leaned against the counter to dry her hands. The space between them might as well have been the Grand Canyon for all her ability to reach him. "The cure. It's called living."

He let his head fall forward on his chest. She could feel him counting. When he looked up again, there was a dangerous fire in his eyes. "It must be nice to view the world with rose-colored glasses."

"I'll take my rose-colored glasses over your personal black cloud any day."

"Dreamer."

"Cynic."

He strode to the door, the heels of his boots striking a strident plick-plick on the tiles. She could not let him go on this bitter note.

"Logan."

He paused but didn't look back. She dropped the towel on the countertop, crossed the expanse of tile and put a hand on his shoulder. His muscles stiffened beneath her fingers.

"You're a good man, Logan Ward."

Slowly he turned, leaving her hand adrift like a bird on a thermal. He caught her shoulders and pressed her body roughly against the wall, drawing a gasp of surprise. The cat clock's tail brushed at her ear time and again counting the seconds as he stared at her, his gray eyes volatile—a storm ready to erupt.

He wanted her to be afraid, but she refused to comply and stared right back at him.

He crowded into her, lowered his face, leaving an inch of space between their noses. His restless energy wrapped itself around her in tentacles. The scent of soap and coffee and man spiraled around her on the waves of his checked temper.

He was hurt, angry, and she'd pushed the wrong button. She knew that, on a logical level, but something about the animal ferocity of his gaze stirred an echo of fear, anyway.

"I killed my daughter. That's what you're fishing for, isn't it? All the low-down dirt."

Oh, God. A greasy knot tightened her gut. His guilt cut deeper than she thought. No wonder he sought isolation. He was bleeding with the worst kind of remorse, and he needed her—the world—to believe the worst of him.

"You could never hurt anybody."

She knew that with certainty—knew it by the way he

cared for her after she'd cut her hands, knew it by the sensitivity with which he treated Jamie, knew it by the way he looked after Max, knew it by his selfless action in saving those schoolchildren, knew it by the love shining in his eyes for his daughter in that photograph. Knew it by his soul-deep grief.

"That's where you're wrong, Beth." His voice was low and gritty. "I've hurt everybody I've ever cared for. I will hurt you."

He crushed his hard, unyielding body against hers and plundered her mouth savagely. Her thoughts dervished. Her heart boomed. Her pulse zigzagged. She tasted his guilt, tasted his pain, tasted his grief, and rebuffed with tenderness the ruthlessness he wanted to assert. Seeking to soothe, she reached out to him, circling his neck with her arms.

"Logan," she murmured against his cheek, "stop pretending you're a monster. I don't believe it."

He shuddered and gasped, then reached back, trapped her hands in his and pinned them against the wall. His chest heaved. From grief, from anger? She couldn't tell. "I will hurt you, Beth."

Regret tormented his voice. He tried to move away, but she grasped his thumbs and held onto them. The wound in his eyes slashed her. She leaned forward, feathered her lips against his.

"The only person you're hurting is yourself."

A choked sound of anguish keened from him as he pitched back. Pure agony squalled in his eyes. She'd amplified his hurt, cut him to the bone.

"Logan, please..." She had no idea what she was asking for, only that she desperately needed to undo the damage she'd caused. She reached toward him palm open, begging.

He jerked away from her poisoned offering, turned on his heels and left.

* * *

Relief. That's what he should be feeling. But it wasn't. Logan slathered another brushful of paint onto a cupboard door propped on a sawhorse in the cellar. God knows he'd tried, but nothing could distract him from the tenderness of that kiss. He'd wanted to hurt her, wanted to show her the empty darkness rattling inside him. Instead she'd shown him that part of his soul was still alive.

How often had he kissed her in his dreams? Yet nothing had prepared him for the reality. Her scent was an awakening. Her touch was a quickening. Her taste was salvation. Unwanted sensations had rushed through him in a prickly pain. He'd wanted to let the river of tears trapped in his soul flow onto her capable shoulders.

But the last time he'd given in to that yearning to have and to hold, it had proven to be an illusion. His love hadn't been enough to reach Julia. His love hadn't been enough to save Samantha.

In the real world, wives left, children died, criminals went free.

And hearts were broken.

He slung the paintbrush into the can. Paint splattered onto the drop cloth. Max sat up, batted her tail once and cocked him a nervous grin.

"Don't go getting all in a flap." What was wrong with that mutt?

Max licked her snout and thumped her tail.

"I just need to sweat, and painting isn't cutting it." He needed numbness to forget.

Logan pounded up the stairs, Max at his heels. The kitchen offered no solace. With its yellow-tiled counters, it reminded him of Beth, which made him think of that kiss and had him shuddering with pain and pleasure all over again. Besides, the walls weren't finished, and he didn't have all the right equipment to start on the floor.

"The living room," he told Max. "That faux walnut paneling has got to go."

He snagged a pry bar and cat's claw from his toolbox. Max dogged him to the living room. At the first crack of paneling, Max's head sunk into her shoulders, her tail tucked itself between her legs and she shivered.

Logan threw the broken panel into the middle of the room. She flinched. "What's wrong with you?"

She licked nervously.

He crouched. "Come here."

She hesitated and went to him, hunkered as if she expected a slap for her trouble. He scratched her behind the ear, felt the tension in her little body. "No one's going to hurt you here."

*You could never hurt anybody.* Beth's voice haunted him.

"This has nothing to do with you. I just need to sweat."

He straightened, then attacked the paneling once more. Max watched his every move with a mixture of kicked-puppy and mother-hen intensity, refusing to leave even though being there seemed a trial.

So he talked to his little guardian angel with the crooked halo while he ripped and tore and sweated. Watched her out of the corner of his eye until the edginess relaxed from her shoulders. Finally she lay in the doorway, head on paws.

He wanted to tear the head off whoever had put so much fear into this animal.

*Stop pretending you're a monster. I don't believe it.*

Beth was wrong. There were secrets about him no one knew. "You'd better believe it, Beth. I'm the devil himself."

Better for him. Better for her.

That way there would be no shattered illusions.

*The only person you're hurting is yourself.*

And that's the way he wanted to keep it.

He couldn't love her. He couldn't love anyone.

The pain would be too much.


"School's been canceled again," Beth told Eve over the phone.

She slipped a batch of candied fruit and spice muffins into the oven. Fresh coffee percolated on the counter. Jamie, happy with the unexpected freedom, watched usually forbidden cartoons in the living room.

"I saw it on the news. That's three days in a row I haven't been able to get out. I'm starting to get cabin fever." *Tippety-tap, tippety-tap-tap* went the keys on Eve's keyboard. "I'm down to the last of my paperwork, too. Once I'm done with this letter, I'll have nothing to do. Except get down on my hands and knees and scrub that rotten kitchen floor."

Eve made a shuddering sound, and Beth laughed.

For more than a week the weather had played Ping-Pong, dumping a mixture of rain, sleet and snow over Rockville. Because of the hazardous driving conditions, even the Holiday Fair to be held last Saturday had been postponed. Today a glaze of ice frosted everything in sight and bowed the limbs of the maples in her yard.

"Don't you dare go out there and try to drive on that stuff," Beth said as she capped the flour canister and pushed it back in its place against the wall.

"I'm stir crazy, not insane. Have you talked to Logan yet?"

"No. He needs—"

"A swift kick in the rear. I've never seen a more stubborn man. A week of moping is more than enough."

Beth put the candied fruit and raisins back into the pantry. "Eve, it's not like that. He's really hurt, and if he's pushed, he's just going to retreat even more."

"How's he going to know you're available if you don't tell him?"

"I'm not available." At least not in the way Eve wanted her to be. Beth frowned, then gathered measuring cups, measuring spoons and bowls and placed them in the sink.

"You know what I mean. He should know he can count on you."

"That may be a tough sell." After that disastrous display of ill-timed self-righteousness, he knew he could count on her to add to his misery. She'd deliberated over an apology and had finally decided that giving him space would be the best thing she could do for him. For her, too.

She'd missed him, though, missed talking to him over a meal, missed cooking for him. But she wouldn't admit *that* to Eve.

*Tippety-tap, tippety-tap-tap.* "Wish I'd been a fly on the wall."

Beth chuckled as she pried the cotton out of a new jar of vitamins. She set two smiley-shaped tablets at Jamie's place along with a glass of orange juice. "Good thing you weren't. You'd have been swatted flat. Jamie loves a good fly hunt."

The typing stopped abruptly. "How are you going to get that man to smile in time for Christmas if you won't even talk to him?"

"I don't know."

"You're too nice, Beth." Eve's chair squeaked. "That's the problem. You won't stand up for anything you need or want. You're so afraid of putting anybody out. How long did it take me to convince you I *wanted* to take care of Jamie in the morning? That it wasn't an imposition?"

"Eve—"

"No, don't you 'Eve' me. You're being a fool. Do you think Jim would want you staying at home, taking care of everybody but yourself?"

"That's not the way it is." Beth had never heard a stern word come out of Eve's mouth, and her friend's uncharacteristic anger strung a clothesline of tension down Beth's spine.

"Really? When was the last time you went on a date I haven't pushed on you?"

Beth took two bowls out of the cupboard, searched for spoons in the drawer. She didn't want to date. All that meaningless small talk, trying to impress a stranger with her worth. All the little flaws that had to be camouflaged. Going through the dating game as a teenager had been bad enough. Now as an adult, just the thought made her shudder. And she had Jamie to consider. He would—had to— come first in any decision. "Dating sucks."

"That's what I thought. Jim wanted you to go on, Beth. He made you promise."

She had to remember not to confide so much to Eve. She didn't like having her own words used as ammunition against her. "He made me promise not to cry."

"And you haven't. Not one tear. That's not normal, you know."

Beth opened the pantry and scanned the contents, but couldn't seem to locate the cereal. "I'm honoring his last request."

"But he didn't mean it literally, sweetie. He meant he wanted you to rejoice in the time you had together and find someone else to share the rest of your life."

Had he? Jim was a generous husband. He'd meant for her to be happy. For Jamie's sake, so his childhood would be filled with happy memories and not the sadness of loss. But had this man, who'd once confided he couldn't stand the thought she might one day want to leave him, meant he wanted her to marry again? "I don't know."

Eve sighed. "You can be exasperating at times."

"Me? You're the one who's being pushy."

"Well, someone's got to be. You don't have any family to take care of you." Her voice softened. "I'm trying to save you the heartache of learning this lesson too late. Like me. I just want to see you happy again."

Beth closed the pantry and strode to the fridge. "I am happy. I'm content. I've got Jamie, a terrific job, friends and great plans for the future."

"But no one to share them with."

"Eve…"

"Logan is a good man. You two have a lot in common. I know you could make each other happy."

Beth seized a half gallon of milk from the fridge and thumped the plastic jug on the table. "He says he killed his daughter."

Nine slow bongs from the grandfather clock in Eve's living room filled the long silence between them. "What do you think?"

Beth sunk into a chair. "I don't think he could. It's the pain talking."

"Exactly. That's why you need to draw him out again."

Beth toyed with the poinsettia place mat. "He won't talk about his past. Maybe if you gave me a hint as to what happened to him."

"It's not my place. It needs to come from him."

"Then we're at an impasse." Beth rose abruptly and served herself a mug of coffee. He wouldn't talk, and she couldn't make him. Not when so much confusion stirred her mind with more speed than a blender on high.

"Maybe you're just using Jim as an excuse to stay exactly where you are. Safer that way."

Beth cracked her cup against the countertop. "Don't get Jim mixed up in this."

"Oh, but, sweetie, he is. And the reason for your habit of keeping so busy taking care of everybody else's trouble is so you won't have to feel that empty corner of your heart."

"You're wrong. My life is fine the way it is." And she had a feeling Logan thought his was, too. She took down her recipe file and thumbed through it.

"He came into Gus's store a couple of days ago. Bought some paint and tape."

"Did he now." That was a good sign, wasn't it? He couldn't be mired in the depths of depression if he was working on his house. Which just went to prove he didn't need her meddling.

She tabbed past the soups and stews, past the fish and poultry, past the breads, and didn't slow down until she got to the desserts. What did it matter if he never smiled again?

Then a picture of him and his daughter flashed through her mind. She bit her lower lip and shuffled through the dessert recipes. It didn't matter. Not one bit.

"Yellow, brown, green and white. What do you suppose he's going to do with that?"

"Since when is Gus such a gossip? At this rate he'll give Laura Darlington a run for her money." Chocolate caramel bars. She lifted the card from its slot. Did she have any walnuts left?

"You should check out Logan's plans for the paint."

"He's a big boy. He knows he should have good ventilation while he's working. There's a fine line between helping and meddling, and I don't want to cross it." Not when she'd already dipped more than a toe on the other side and had found such a bewildering reaction.

He'd wanted to scare her, wanted her to think the worst

of him. But that hurtful kiss had swiftly changed to something potent. Before he'd pushed away from her, he'd responded to her tenderness with the ardent male hunger she'd spied in his eyes earlier that evening. It had lasted only a moment, but the moment had taken her breath away, melted her bones, and flooded her heart with a river of warmth—and confusion.

She ripped open the pantry door and searched through the shelves. Surely she had some chocolate chips somewhere.

"You could bake him a casserole. When was the last time you fed him?"

Feed a man, starve his grief?

The lights cut off. Beth put a hand over the speaker. "Jamie, are you okay?"

"The TV's not working," he called from the living room.

"The power's gone out. Why don't you come in here and have some breakfast?"

"What if *Dragon Knights* comes back on?"

"Then you can go back."

"Okay."

"Beth, are you there? The electricity just went out."

"Here, too. Are you going to be all right?"

"I'll walk over to Gus's."

"You'll do no such thing." Jamie shuffled in, dragging his stuffed panda by one paw. He slipped into his chair and reached for the chewable vitamins. Beth held up two boxes of cereal, and Jamie pointed to his selection. "It's much too icy out there. I don't want you to fall and hurt yourself. You've got wood?"

"Gus brought a stack a few weeks ago. You might want to check on Logan. He's not used to winters like these."

"He can take care of himself."

"And you can take care of yourself. I guess I'm the only one who needs somebody else to keep her warm when the power goes out. I'm going to Gus's."

Eve was a stubborn old mule. She would head out in this weather just to prove she could and end up breaking a leg or a hip when she fell on the ice.

"Tell you what," Beth said, "you call Gus and make sure he comes to you, and I'll call Logan. Deal?"

Beth could hear the smile in Eve's voice. "Deal."

Was Eve right? Had she been hiding behind Jim's memory, behind her busyness in order to keep the promise she'd made to a dying man?

Looking back over the past five years, she chewed on a mouthful of cereal. No, she wasn't hiding. She simply wasn't looking. Relief slunk through her.

For the past week she'd feared she was half in love with Logan, but Eve's pointed probing made her face what she'd been afraid to look at.

Logan wasn't becoming a prospect; he was still just a project. She wasn't looking for a husband. The dating rules didn't apply.

Only an hour ago the thought of seeing him again would have spiked panic in her blood. But now a strange kind of anticipation licked at her. She *would* make him smile before Christmas.

First she owed him an apology, then he needed a quick introduction to Winter Storm Survival 101.

## Chapter Ten

Logan had no idea what he was doing in Beth's entryway. When the power had gone out, his first thought had been for her and Jamie. Before he knew it, he was heading to her house. He'd just about convinced himself he'd have done the same thing for any neighbor, when Beth opened the door.

Her voice held no rancor, her eyes no spikes of hatred. If anything, she seemed glad to see him, and the notion cracked the wall of objections he'd expected to have to batter in order to assess their degree of safety. And now he was being peppered by questions and ushered toward the living room as if he'd been expected. Jamie greeted him brightly, asked about Max, then went back to his handheld electronic game.

"Do you have any wood?" Beth asked as she crouched beside the glass-fronted wood stove fitted into the fireplace.

"Acres of it."

She looked at him over her shoulder and smiled. Smoke poured from the stove's opening and wet logs sizzled. "You made a joke! I'm so proud of you."

The compliment warmed him more than it should have. He almost smiled. It felt good to see her again—too good. No, not her, her home. The bone-thawing warmth and the baked-in aroma of welcome here was a childhood fantasy.

Beth herself was a grown man's fantasy with her sparkle, softness and sweet curves. But he'd found a way to deal with that. After the house was finished, he would put it on the market and head farther north.

"Eve hardly ever used her fireplace," Beth prattled on. "Don't know what shape it's in. You might want to have it swept."

"You want some help with that?" he asked, reaching for the long match in her hand.

"Let me give it one more shot. The tarp got blown off the woodpile, and all the logs are icy. Every winter I promise myself I'll build a woodshed and every summer I forget—till the next winter. Ordering a cord or two of wood should be something you put on your fall to-do list."

He crouched beside her and swallowed a chuckle when she crossed the fingers of one hand, then touched the flame to the balled-up newspapers with the other. The whole thing smoked and fizzled out in less than five minutes. "Do you have any kindling?"

"Just this little bit." She handed him three sticks, a strip of birch bark and a fresh match.

He reached for the newspaper on the coffee table.

"No, that's this week's *Rockville Register*. I haven't read it yet. Here."

She leaned across him to a pile of yellowing newspaper on the other side of the hearth. When she straightened, he almost reached for her, almost succumbed to the sudden yearning to kiss her, taste the sweetness of her mouth once again.

He concentrated on the task of lighting the wet logs while Beth chattered about the storm damage, about Eve, about the postponed Holiday Fair. She bustled as she spoke, straightening, getting out hurricane lamps and placing them in strategic spots around the room. Then she turned on a battery-operated radio and tuned in the news.

"...lines are down from Concord to Nashua. Public Service of New Hampshire estimates it may take up to three days to get service back to every affected household. Crews are working twenty-four hours a day, and they've put out a plea for patience.

"Sunshine, where's the sunshine is the question on everyone's mind this morning. According to our meteorologist, Joe Luckhardt, it's a day away. Folks, if you don't have to go out, stay home! That's the word from the state police who've seen more accidents than they care to. We'll be back in a minute with the complete list of closings, the traffic report and the latest news."

Beth turned down the volume. "I'll bet you don't have any bottled water or candles or batteries or food. You've got an electric stove, too. Mine's gas. So unless you've got a camp stove or a barbecue, I don't see how you're going to eat. That settles it. After you get that fire started, you can go get Max and spend the day."

The thought pleased him more than it should.


Beth made a game out of retrieving Max. She dressed Jamie in layers, then they headed out the door, slipping and sliding down the drive, pretending to skate. Ice pellets pelted them and pinged on the crust of ice covering the snow.

Jamie spun circles around her and Logan, calling shots

as if he were an announcer at a hockey game. "He shoots! He scores! The crowd goes crazy!" Arms raised, brandishing an imaginary stick, he cheered at his phantom hat trick. "See, Mom, I'm ready for real hockey."

"You sure are. A couple more years and that Mite league is all yours."

"Aw, Mom."

Max did not have to be invited twice to join into the games. With all their zigzagging, Max and Jamie covered twice the territory she and Logan did.

Logan kept a unerring eye on Jamie, frowning as deeply as The Grinch Jamie had once compared him to. On impulse, Beth reached through the crusty layer and scooped a handful of soggy snow. She launched it at the middle of Logan's black ski jacket and hit her target dead-on.

Logan stopped in his tracks and looked at her over his shoulder. He cocked his head sideways. A grin crooked one side of his mouth. "You shouldn't have done that."

She dipped for more ammunition but wasn't fast enough. Logan's missile hit her on the shoulder. Jamie howled with laughter. She screeched and launched another shot of her own. Jamie joined the melee, and soon slushy snowballs and laughter were flying all around. She thought she even heard a few rusty chuckles coming from Logan.

They were soaking wet by the time they reached the house.

Beth sent Jamie upstairs. "Off with your wet clothes and into dry ones. Then we'll have hot chocolate."

With the towel Beth handed him, Logan dried Max by the fire. Then Beth offered him a pair of Jim's sweatpants.

Upstairs, as she reached for the handle to slide the closet door open, her throat went dry, her hand shook. How long had it been since she'd opened Jim's closet?

Five years. The last time had been the day she'd picked

out his newly cleaned uniform for his funeral. The tears that had choked her then threatened to rise again. Pain, broken-bone sharp, sliced at her.

"Don't cry for me, Beth," Jim had said. "I want you to laugh, always laugh. Your smile, that's what I like best about you. Smile for me, love, please." She'd tried because he'd asked. How could you refuse a dying man anything? But the trying had almost killed her. "When you think of me, smile. Promise me, Beth. Promise me you'll smile. Always."

A hand went to her lips. They trembled beneath her fingers. Tears burned her eyes, but she fought them. She forced a smile, felt it wobble and fall. "I'm trying, Jim, I'm trying."

She closed her eyes and slid the closet door open. Beneath the staleness of dust and years, she could still discern the wind-fresh scent that had been Jim's. His favorite gray sweatshirt found its way into her hands. She buried her face in the soft material and inhaled the past.

When she opened her eyes, the closet's contents seemed to rush at her, each piece of clothing blossoming into memories. The red sweater he'd worn the day Jamie was born so she could focus on him and not the pain. His favorite jeans, white at the knees from so many wearings. The plaid shirt he'd worn while showing her how to use the new wood stove. And when the fire had burned hot, he'd taken it off and shown her the real pleasure of making love by the fireplace.

"Beth?"

Crushing the gray sweatshirt against her chest, she looked up to find Logan. "I miss him."

Worry creased his forehead, but he didn't say anything.

"Here." She blindly handed him the sweatshirt and searched the upper shelf for the matching pants. A pile of sweaters tumbled onto her. With a strangled cry, she tried to stop the avalanche, but could do no better than to snag a sweater or two from the fall. The sleeve of one, the hem of another caught in her fists. The garments unfurled and hung lifeless from her hands.

She tried to picture Jim wearing the black sweater with the gray flecks, the moss-colored one, and could conjure only a misty photograph, blurred at the edges, devoid of color. She swallowed convulsively, staying the tears.

"Mom? Where do you want this stuff?"

She couldn't take her gaze off the sweaters, couldn't stop the frantic search for details.

"Mom. Are you okay?"

She tried to talk, tried to reassure her son, but nothing could squeak past the knot in her chest, past the tightness in her throat.

"Your mom's fine, sport. She just dropped all those sweaters. Hey, why don't you go check on Max for me? She's all alone in the living room, and I don't want her to get in trouble. I'll help your mom with the sweaters."

"Okay."

Jamie's footsteps pounded down the stairs.

"Beth?"

Firm hands turned her around. She was crushed in a gentle hug, sweaters and all. "It's okay."

She looked up at those dark-gray eyes, at the concern and the discomfort etched in Logan's face. Shaking her head, she tried to explain, but all that came out was a throttled sob. And once that sob had worked its way into existence, it seemed to break a path for all the others.

Gently Logan pressed her head against his chest, murmured soft words with no meaning into her ear. Her chest heaved. Her throat rasped with anguish. Hot, salty tears gushed. Sobs tore from her like sheets being rent into rags.

"I promised."

"Promised what?" Logan's voice was soft against her ear, his body strong against her sorrow, his arms protective against her open wound.

"Not to cry."

He brushed a kiss against the top of her head. "Some promises have to be broken."

Trying to stop the flood of tears, she sniffed. "He's fading. Every day it's a little harder to remember what he looked liked, how he laughed, the sound of his voice."

Logan's body stilled. His breaths rasped against her ear.

"I thought it was just me." He tightened his hug. His throat convulsed against the side of her head. One hand slid up to her ponytail, still wet from their outing. He raked his fingers through the tangled mass. "I braided Sam's hair every morning, and I can't quite remember how soft her hair was or just what shade of brown it was. Even when I look at pictures, it's like there are pieces of her missing."

"I'm so afraid to forget."

"Most of the time, I'm afraid to remember. What if…"

A note of understanding chimed through her. Sometimes it was as hard to remember as it was to think you were forgetting. "The picture in your wallet. The one where you're smiling at the little girl. I just wanted to make you smile like that. I never meant to hurt you."

She could feel him moving away, receding like the tide, dragging a reluctant half pull at the shore. Dropping the sweaters still clenched in her fist, she hung on to his hands. He closed his eyes. The lines of pain, scored into his face, deepened. "My daughter. Samantha. She died two years ago."

She felt no triumph in the fact her intuition had been right, that he was a man grieving with his very soul. "How?"

He turned away, raked a hand through his hair, then faced her once more. "I don't want to talk about it."

"Okay." She wanted to hold him the way he'd held her, help dampen his sorrow, but sensed he wouldn't welcome the sentimentality. So she tucked back her own grief and sought to regain the fragile balance and lightness of their morning snowball fight.

"We make quite a pair, don't we?" Beth wiped the drying tracks of tears with the back of her hands. "You want to cry and you can't. I promised I never would, and I spend half my time trying to figure out ways to keep that promise."

She bent down and started picking up the sweaters, piling them in her arms without refolding them. She stuffed them back on the top shelf, found the sweatpants and slid the closet door closed.

"Here." She handed him the pants. He accepted them awkwardly. "You can change in here if you like. Hang your wet things in the bathroom. I'd better go check on Jamie. It's way too quiet down there. How does soup sound for lunch?"

A hush fraught with static crackled between them. Soon the intensity of his unwavering gaze had her blushing.

"Soup sounds perfect."

"Good."

At least he wasn't running away this time. That was progress.

Halfway down the stairs she stopped and looked up. On the wall at the head of the stairs hung a family portrait. Jim, her and Jamie. Their first as a family. Jamie was only a few months old.

Jim's voice came to her. "We had a good run, didn't we, love?"

"The best."

"I loved you with all my heart."

"I love you, too."

"It's time to let go."

A surge of panic prickled her chest. "I can't. What if you disappear completely?"

"I'll still be there in your heart. Always."

"What if I forget?"

"You won't."

As she watched the photograph, it blurred in a pool of fresh tears. Heart heavy, she made her way down the stairs wishing she could truly believe she could move on and that love would survive.

While he'd held her as she'd cried, Logan had felt close to Beth, closer than he'd ever felt to anyone. If anyone could understand what he was going through, it was her. Yet when she'd asked about Samantha, he couldn't bring himself to tell her the whole ugly truth.

He'd pushed her away, felt her hang on and breathed a silent sigh of relief when she'd transformed herself into her usual cheery self—today a green-and-white elf with dangling mistletoe earrings.

Logan couldn't sit still, couldn't confront the thoughts spinning around his mind. So while Beth heated soup, he oiled the squeaky drawer in her kitchen. While she played board games with Jamie, he split firewood into kindling. While she played Go Fish and Crazy Eights with Jamie, he filled the inside wood box and stacked logs in her garage.

After dinner Jamie brought out a 3-D puzzle of a medieval castle and asked Logan for help. Logan could think of no polite way to push the boy away, so he took a position on the opposite side of the coffee table. Jamie separated the pieces into piles. Snuggled against the boy, Max watched the operation with interest.

"Knights protect the castle." Jamie snapped portions of a wall together. The pieces were fat and squishy, easy for small fingers to handle. "See these holes here. They shoot arrows from those."

"You don't say."

"It takes a long time for a boy to be a knight. First he has to be a page, then a squire. He's got to learn all about the armor and the weapons and the horses. And how to fight."

Growing a boy into a man still took a long time. In those rebel teenage years, he'd needed the influence of a good man in his life. If his mother hadn't chosen to ship him to his grandfather's for school vacations, Logan often wondered how differently his life would have turned out.

Dallas Ward had given him hope when the world had sought to take it away. Dallas had made him believe in the system, in the wisdom of the law. Because of Dallas he'd believed he could make a difference in the world. At least for a while.

Would Jamie find a Dallas of his own? Would Beth allow herself to welcome another man in her life to play that role? He pushed too hard on a piece and crumbled part of the tower he was building. The answers to those questions were none of his business.

"How come you know so much about knights?" Logan squared off the watch tower.

"I watch *Dragon Knights.*"

"What's that?"

"A show on TV. They got knights and dragons and bad guys and wicked-good fights. I like the red knight the best."

"How come?"

"His horse is the fastest. He looks like a streak of fire when he runs. I'm going to have a red horse, too."

Jamie handed him the entrance tower he'd completed, then tried to fit the cardboard peak to the top of the tower. The tabs refused to go into the slots. "You hold this end, and I'll hold that end."

Working together, finger against finger, they got the tower cap on. Jamie's giggle of pleasure, his smile, tugged a string of regret. Sam had loved building things, too. Her room had been filled with popsicle-stick houses of all sorts—for crickets and frogs and the imaginary fairies and pixies that visited her in the night.

"I thought you were into hockey."

"That's for winter. In summer I'm going to ride."

A little speed demon heading for sure trouble. Did Beth know about these daredevil yearnings? Did she know they could take away her child in a second?

Logan glanced toward the stairs. She was up there, rounding up sleeping bags and pillows, turning the adult inconvenience of a power outage into an adventure for a child. With a mother like Beth, no matter what circumstances brought, Jamie would turn out all right.

"Can I put a log on the fire?" Jamie asked, eyes dancing with excitement.

Logan's first instinct was to say no, but the memory of his grandfather and all he'd taught him still walked the edges of his mind. How old had he been when Dallas had taught him to light the Franklin stove? Six? Seven? Dallas had no patience for fools, but he'd had an ocean of it for the awkward boy Logan had been. Learning that simple skill had instilled him with a confidence he couldn't explain—even today. "Only if you listen real carefully when I tell you how."

Eyes rounded with anticipation, Jamie nodded.

"The number-one rule is the stove is hot so you only touch the handle. Got that?"

Jamie fiddled with Max's ear as he nodded again.

"What's the number-one rule?"

"Touch only the handle."

"Number-two rule is nice and easy."

"Nice and easy."

Logan parked Max out of the way. The dog had a knack for getting right in the middle of things. He picked out a small log, handed it to Jamie, accordioned the safety screen away, then positioned himself at Jamie's side ready to guide and shield.

"Open the door how?"

"Nice and easy." Tongue sticking out, Jamie turned the handle and opened the door. A wave of heat blasted at them. "Wow, that's hot."

"Sure is. Fire isn't a toy. You've got to be real careful." Taking Jamie's hands in his, he guided the boy's actions, placing his own arms close to the danger of the stove's hot sides. Coals greedily sparked the fresh wood, shooting flames all around it.

"I did it! I did it!"

Jamie's hands shot out with the excitement of the moment. Heart hammering, Logan foresaw the path the small hand would take. "No!"

He grabbed Jamie's hand in his fist. His knuckles singed against the door. He drew the hand trapped in his fist away from the heat, crushed the boy against his chest. Jamie let out a frightened squeak.

Heart thundered against heart.

Stupid, stupid to have let a child get so close to the fire. What was he thinking? That he could be Jamie's Dallas? Stupid. Irresponsible. Slowly he loosened his hold on Jamie. "What's the number-two rule, sport?"

"Nice and easy."

"That's right. You almost got burned. Now close the door, how?"

"Nice and easy."

"You got it, sport. Good job."

Jamie glowed with pride. His arms snaked around Logan's neck, and he gave him a hug. "Thanks, Mr. Ward!"

Arms loaded with bed fixings, Beth returned to the living room. "What's going on here?"

Would her smile be so bright if she knew he'd almost caused her son to be burned?

"Mr. Ward showed me how to put a log on the fire."

"Wow. Guess what? Time for bed, young man."

"Aw, do I have to?"

"It's late. The more you whine, the less time I'll have for storytelling. Come on, let's go get your pj's and pick out a book."

Ten minutes later they came back, Jamie in his pajamas clutching a panda, Beth armed with half a dozen books. After she'd read him stories about a Christmas bear, Greek heroes, green eggs and ham, a dragon or two and a round of knock-knock jokes, Jamie finally nodded off.

Logan itched to leave, to return to the cold grimness of his house, but he couldn't seem to make himself get up. He reached for the small pad and the pen by the telephone on the end table and started sketching ideas and notes of his plans for the house.

"Listen to this," Beth said, reading the newspaper by the glow of a hurricane lamp on an end table. She sat on the floor, her back against the sofa. Jamie slept by the stove, an arm draped over Max who didn't seem to mind in the least.

"An employee at Gus Leonard's Country Store found a pair of wreaths in the storage space in the attic. The wreaths date back to the store's opening thirty-five years ago. They were fashioned by Alice Leonard, Gus's beloved wife. They were seen every year until Alice's death ten years ago. Gus has generously given them to the Beautification Committee who will use them to decorate the town hall doors.

"Isn't that great?"

"Mmm." The walls seemed to be closing in. Ice ticked against the windows. His muscles wound tighter and tighter.

"Look at these pictures. Aren't they wonderful?"

She handed him a section of paper showing black-and-white photographs of Christmases past. New England charm and tradition were preserved in each one. There were bright lights and faces. Snow and sleds. Greenery garnished with ribbons and bows on lampposts and the band shell. He could almost hear the voices of the children's chorus dressed as angels, their excitement as they surrounded a Santa distributing presents from a large pouch, the high decibels of their games at a long-ago party.

"It says here donations are piling in. Looks like we'll be able to have our old-fashioned Christmas after all. Next week is going to be crazy. I hope the weather decides to calm down for a while."

They spent the rest of the evening in companionable silence. Every now and then Beth would change positions. She moved from floor to rocking chair to the opposite end of the couch, switched from the newspaper to a recipe book, which she read as avidly as a novel. It wasn't long before she was dozing and the book fell to the floor.

*101 Casseroles for Busy Cooks.* Logan smiled as he put the book on the end table. A hundred and one more nights of Beth's cooking to look forward to.

Logan unzipped one of the sleeping bags she'd brought down, and draped it over her. Somehow she ended up with her head against his shoulder. He started to extricate himself only to have her snuggle closer. So he relaxed. She would move soon enough. Even in sleep he was willing to bet she didn't stay still very long.

Peace reigned in this room. Warmth poured from the hearth. Surrounded by night, in the soft glow of light, it seemed to be a world of its own. Jamie and Max slept by the fire, a Rockwell portrait of innocence. Beth dozed in his arms, completing the picture of contentment he'd grown up longing for. He should have fallen asleep in a blink. But he couldn't.

Feelings crowded him. Satisfaction. Anger. Desire. Confusion. Mostly what kept him wide awake was an itchy need to grab on to this fantasy of family come to life. But how could he hold on to it and not hurt Jamie, not hurt Beth?

He couldn't stay. Not forever. That much was clear. Happily-ever-after just wasn't in his cards—not with all his baggage.

This time he knew ahead of time the fantasy wasn't a forever thing. So he was in control. He would call the shots. And when spring came, he could walk away without a scar.

He felt Beth shift in his arms, felt her hand creep around his waist, her head nestle deeper into the crook of his shoulder. He placed his cheek against the top of her head, inhaled the subtle scent of peppermint and woman. Heat, heaviness, hunger invaded his body.

Beth wasn't free of her past, either, he reminded himself. But in her case there should be no guilt. She hadn't stood helplessly while the one she loved was mowed by a drunk kid. She'd been there, supported, eased her husband's crossover into the next world.

She was a vital woman who had much to give the world. She'd made a worthy life for herself since her husband's death. But she hadn't made room for another man. She deserved someone who could give her that happily-ever-after, not someone who would break her heart.

Who was he to hurt her?

And Jamie deserved a man who would teach him to be a good man. Logan wasn't the one to do that, either. Not when every move would have him on edge wondering when the next truck would hop a curb. He couldn't afford to become attached to the boy.

Who was he to injure another child?

Yet he couldn't seem to let go of the fantasy of family come to life.

They would talk, he decided. Tomorrow. She, too, would know the score ahead of time.

The prospect sent a lightning bolt of fear through him. To talk meant opening up, telling her the truth of what happened, showing her there were limits that couldn't be breached. He would have to take the chance that, like Julia, after she knew the real him, she might turn away.

## Chapter Eleven

Waking up nestled against Logan's body had felt much too comfortable. Given the small confines of the sofa, Beth should have felt cramped. But she hadn't. Her curves seemed to fit just right against Logan's hard planes. Her arm draped just fine over his chest. Her leg slipped just perfectly between his. No wonder her dreams had bordered on the erotic.

Beth tried to rid herself of the rapturous images floating in her mind by making coffee. From the gallon jug on the counter she poured water into the bottom section of the percolator, then counted scoops of ground beans and added an extra one. Strong coffee should wake her up. She placed the contraption on the stove to perk, sure she could now go on with her day—until the images came back.

Huffing out a breath, Beth raked fingers through her sleep-tangled hair. She'd been on a beach. The moon was full and hot like the sun, but it was night, of that she was sure because the stars, a diamond field of them, were out. The wash of warm ocean water lapped over her and her faceless lover, keeping pace with the rhythm of their love-making.

Her body tingled even now at the memory of that slow, deliberate seduction, of kisses deep and caresses soft, of body moving against body, of the need building then cresting, of the explosion of sensations that made her feel as if she were part of the stars.

She groaned. *What is wrong with you? You're acting like a teenage girl who's never slept beside a man.* She went to the pantry but didn't really see any of the goods lined up on the shelves. Her mind was too full of Logan and the feel of his body next to hers. *It has been a while,* she rationalized.

Frowning, she opened the fridge, remembered to conserve the waning cold and shut the door once again. What should she make for breakfast? She had to use up the supplies in the refrigerator before they spoiled. That's it, concentrate on important things.

Logan stirred in the living room. The sleeping bag they'd shared rustled. His feet hit the floor. The wood stove door creaked. The coals crackled when he added another log. Then his footsteps padded down the hallway. Her pulse scampered. And the sight of him, face smooth in sleep, came back to her, splashing the erotic dream into her consciousness all over again. Heat flushed her face. Her movements around the kitchen became jerky.

*Stop that!* She swiveled, took out a skillet and slapped it onto the stove. Chiding herself did not help.

Along with the remembered pleasure came a measure of guilt she wasn't quite sure how to handle. Jim was dead; it wasn't wrong to want another man. But not now, not during the Christmas holidays, which had been so special to Jim, not while he was fading from her memory.

Still, the yearning was there, making her pop crazily like corn kernels in hot oil as she searched the pantry again. Bread. Where had she put the bread?

"Good morning," Logan said.

She caught her small sound of surprise and turned to face him. He looked much too handsome with his disheveled hair, his bare feet and his shirt not quite buttoned all the way. There was a tension buzzing around him, too, as he leaned against the kitchen door frame—like a spring storm approaching, fraying nerves and setting off flickers of expectations even though the sky was still blue and the storm was hours away.

"Good morning!" She cursed the overbrightness of her voice and turned back to the stove. "Want coffee?"

She didn't wait for an answer but poured him some. As she pivoted to hand him the mug, she found him there ready to take it. His fingers curled over hers, hugging them against the warmth of the cup. Her heart thundered. Her throat went dry.

"Since that first day you came over with the casserole," he said. His voice was butter soft against her skin. "I wake up with the taste of you on my mind."

The storm she'd sensed brewed in his eyes—much closer than she'd thought. She cleared her throat. "Oh…"

The aroma of coffee smoldered between them, strong and rich. Would the thought of sex come to her every time she had a cup of that dark brew from now on?

"How do eggs sound for breakfast?" Her voice squeaked. She tried to slip her fingers from the mug, but he tightened his grip.

"Does that frighten you?"

She knew he wasn't talking about eggs. "It petrifies me."

He leaned forward, kissed her. A gentle possession that spoke of intent. A shiver of delight rolled through her, leaving her weak-kneed and wanting.

He pressed into her. "Was that so bad?"

She inched back. "Oh, no, it was, um, very…nice."

Without taking his heated gaze from her, he plunked the coffee mug on the counter, trapped her between the sink and his hips. Her hands had nowhere to go but on his chest, holding him back. His hands circled her waist, setting off alarm and desire in equal measures. Then they traveled up, stirring an avalanche of sensations. She swallowed hard. Her fingers dug into his chest. To push him away or to pull him closer? "Wait!"

He said nothing, but his darkened gaze questioned. His fingers were splayed over her ribs, his thumbs rested against her breasts, making them ache, making it hard for her to think. What exactly was she objecting to?

"I—I'm not very good at this sort of thing," she said, searching for an explanation, looking intently at the plaid pattern of black, gray and white on his shirt.

"Neither am I."

"I don't…I'm not…"

Not quite sure what she wanted to say, she lifted her face, meaning to talk directly to him. He took it as an invitation and kissed her again. The slow, seductive kiss of her dreams. Her thoughts spun. Her pulse galloped. Her heart would surely jump right out of her chest if it kept up that pounding pace. She reached for his shoulders, fisted the soft fabric of his shirt around her fingers and hung on to keep herself from slinking bonelessly to the floor. His hunger fired hers until she was lost in a soup of stirred needs. A helpless sound mewled through her.

He pulled away slowly, rested his forehead on hers, skimmed his wonderful hands up and down her sides, making her shiver all over. His breath was as ragged as her own and puffed in heated bursts against her mouth. "There's something between us, Beth."

"Logan, I…"

"We understand each other. You're not ready for a husband, and I'm not ready for a wife. We both know happily-ever-after doesn't exist."

"I…"

"But we're both ready to feel alive again."

Alive? Yes, alive, that was the overwhelming feeling prickling through her—aliveness.

"I don't know." It was part plea, part apology.

He dipped his head again, touched his lips to hers, sent her senses spinning, her mind reeling, her body melting against his. It shouldn't be so easy to muddle her.

"It feels right," he rasped against her ear. "I want you, Beth. I want you like I haven't wanted anything in a long time."

His confession brought a host of confusion. She'd wanted him to find his heart again, had wanted him to smile, to feel alive. But was she ready to give away part of herself to reach her goal?

"I think you want me, too."

She groaned. "Yes, but…"

His thumbs caressing her sides were making it hard to concentrate. "Logan…I'm afraid."

"I know. So am I," he assured her. "We'll take it slow."

"Yes, slow." A wave of relief swept through her, but before she could analyze what she might have agreed to, Jamie's footsteps and the click of Max's nails echoed in the hallway.

Beth sprang away from Logan, blushing as guiltily as the time the principal had caught her and Jim necking outside the gym in high school. She swiveled to the stove, could make no sense of the dials, lifted the skillet and put it down again. "An omelette maybe. I've got to use up the cheese before it goes bad."

"Sounds good," Logan said, reaching for his abandoned mug of coffee.

"Good morning, sleepyhead," she said to Jamie as he walked into the kitchen. "How did you sleep?"

Max trotted over to Logan, sat in front of him, thumping her tail, and looked up at him expectantly.

"I wish Max could stay over every night." Jamie sleepily wiped at his eyes and sank into a chair.

Beth smiled at the cozy picture Jamie and Max had made sleeping by the fire and wished she'd caught the moment on film for Jamie's album. "Yeah, Max is a good dog."

"Knock-knock," Jamie said, resting his head on an upraised arm.

Beth reached inside the fridge for the carton of eggs. "Who's there?"

"Juno."

"Juno who?" Beth grasped a bowl from the cupboard.

"Juno what time it is?"

Logan crouched beside the dog and scratched her ear. "It's time for Max to go outside and take care of business."

"Woof!" Max agreed.

"Want to take her, sport?"

The sleepy eyes filled with anticipation. "Can I?"

"Sure. Why don't you get dressed, and we'll take her out?"

Jamie ran up the stairs. Max bounded after him.

"Beth?"

She heard Logan rise and advance toward her. The egg

she was trying to crack against the side of the bowl crumpled in her grip. Bits and pieces of shell slid into the bowl along with the white and the yolk. Slimy egg white gooed her palm.

"Do you want Monterey Jack or cheddar in your omelette?" she asked, discarding the shattered shell and reaching for another egg.

He caught her by the waist, stilled her with his hands. Her breath caught in her throat. She felt his smile against the side of her face. Her heart knocked hard once. She cracked two more eggs into the bowl.

"Cheddar." His imitation of laughter rumbled in his chest, against her back. "I'm in the mood for cheddar this morning."

She smiled, too. Slow, they would take it slow. "Cheddar it is."

"I need a favor," Beth said, even before Logan had opened the door all the way. Her mouth was agape, ready to apologize for her request and promise repayment, only to discover that Logan was half-naked with suds slathering part of his face and chest. He wore a displeased scowl, but Beth couldn't help laughing. "What happened to you?"

"A slight disagreement with the mutt about the necessity for a bath."

"Oh." She swallowed another wave of giggles. That was good. That was excellent. If he was giving Max a bath, surely that meant he planned on keeping her. He said he was ready to feel alive again. Giving Max a bath was living proof. "Who won?"

He grinned and wiped suds from his chest with a lazy swipe of hand. "I'm not sure."

"Where's Max now?"

"Hiding behind a box."

"Still soapy?"

"No, most of it's on me."

She ogled his chest. "You wear it well, too."

Pure devilment registered on his face when he noticed her appreciative inspection. One hand slid to the button of his jeans. "Want to see the rest?"

She blushed and stammered. "Uh, no, not right now. I..." The sudden image of Logan naked leaped to her mind, and she forgot why she was here. More evidence that her ordered life was quickly slipping into pure bedlam.

She'd spent the past five days in a state of total distraction. Dinners were stretched to their limits. Touches were snuck under the table. Kisses were stolen while doing dishes, lingered over in the front doorway. She was late twice to a Beautification Committee meeting. Since age twelve, she'd never messed up a recipe, but in the past few days she'd managed to burn a batch of pancakes, turn a skillet of chicken breasts into a charred mess and forget the sugar in a pan of brownies. Sleep was becoming a stranger. Even Jamie had noticed her distractedness and asked if she was all right.

She was afraid she was taking a fast slide into incompetence.

That fact became clear this morning, when after she loaded her car with her Holiday Fair goodies, she discovered she'd left the lights on all night, and the battery was dead.

"I, uh..." she tried again, but her brain refused to engage.

"Need a favor?" Logan, ever so helpful, reached for her and made whatever thought she might have regained fly out the door. "Happy to oblige, ma'am."

"Yes, a favor." She sampled the side of his neck and drank in his scent. "My car won't start. The battery's dead.'' She waved vaguely in the direction of her house. ''Cookies. Boxes of them. I've got to get them to St. Mary's for the Holiday Fair.''

''You want me to drive.'' He nibbled her earlobe, sending shocks of pleasure down to her stomach.

''Yes, that's it. Please.'' But the please wasn't politeness, it was unadulterated begging. She tilted her head up, and he was glad to indulge her with a deep, dark kiss.

''I can't stay,'' she whispered, trying to push away from him, enjoying the heated feel of his skin under her palms. ''Jamie's by himself. He's supposed to be looking for his boots.''

He let her go, but she was pleased by the apparent reluctance of his hands leaving her hips. ''I'll pick you up in ten minutes. As soon as I dry the mutt and get some clothes on.''

Her gaze followed the hard planes of his chest, took in the definition of biceps, the enticing flatness of stomach. ''Pity.''

''Yeah?''

''Yeah.'' She took a backward step out the door.

He hung onto the doorknob. ''Beth?''

''Mmm.''

''Soon.''

He wasn't talking about the car ride, not with eyes that hungry. She swallowed hard thinking soon wouldn't be soon enough, thinking soon would be too soon, thinking she was going crazy. Her heart was pounding. Her palms were sweaty. There was a queasy anticipation tap-dancing in her stomach. And she spilled her half-formed thought. ''Jamie's spending the night at Eve's.''

''Is he?''

The raw hunger in Logan's eyes turned ravenous.

''Secret hush-hush mission. I'm guessing Christmas

shopping in the morning.'' She tucked a stray strand of hair behind her ear.

"All night?"

She gulped. "After the Holiday Fair. After the tree-lighting ceremony."

"But all night." His hand snaked out, cupped the nape of her neck, and she was forced to look deep into those smoky eyes.

"All night."

This close, she couldn't miss the leap of the pulse at his neck, the small flick of his tongue over his lips, the croakiness of a dry throat in his voice. "Stay?"

The wind had arrived last night, scouring the sky clean of clouds. The air was crisp and cold. The sky eye-hurting blue. But Beth felt only heat prickling her skin, saw only the dark desire gleaming in her neighbor's eyes. "Logan…"

"I'll make dinner."

"You will?" She was touched. No one had made dinner for her since she was twelve.

A teasing half smile turned his harsh face into the picture of temptation. "Real stuff. Steak and potatoes."

"You don't like my casseroles?"

"I like them fine. But once in a while a man needs real food."

"Steak and potatoes." Her mouth quirked into a smile.

"Steak and potatoes."

"I'll bring dessert." A meal. They'd shared dozens of them already. She was making much too big a deal out of his offer to cook for her.

"I was hoping you'd be dessert." The gruffness of his voice had her shaking and quivering like whipped cream.

"Oh." Her throat was working overtime. Her body felt on fire. Her brain ceased to function.

"Beth?"

"Mmm?"

"Say yes."

The thump of her heart was a mule kick. She was treading on dangerous ground, heading into risky territory. She was sliding headlong down a perilous hill and going way too fast. But she couldn't seem to stop herself. After so many years of doing without, she'd thought herself incapable of feeling those melty, delicious sensations, had thought her skin incapable of pining ever again for a man's touch. And here they were, all those yearnings, directed at a man who'd made it clear he wasn't offering a future, had nothing to give but a broken heart.

And she was no better. She'd loved Jim, and he'd left her, torn her heart right out of her chest and taken it with him to his grave. She'd sworn she'd never go through that pain again, had been glad to bury her sexuality along with her husband. She'd never love that deeply again. Of that much she was sure.

She looked into Logan's eyes, saw the vulnerability of his offer exposed in the soft gray of his eyes. They were a matched pair, broken by life, trying to muddle through.

"Yes, Logan."

With a last kiss that promised much, he sent her on her way. "Jamie's waiting."

She wasn't sure how she got home, but she was pretty sure her feet hadn't touched the ground.

Although the Holiday Fair wasn't slated to start until ten, traffic was already clogging the common. According to Beth, there were twelve venues to visit, not counting the Rotary Club Christmas-tree sale and the free hot chocolate and apple cider that would be handed out—both on the common. Horse-drawn hayrides were planned to go to and from each fair venue and various choirs were to wander around entertaining shoppers.

To Logan it all added up to a mess he didn't want to be caught in.

Dropping Jamie off at his friend Bobby's had required a minor miracle and careful maneuvering. Beth's directions needed careful attention. And his temper was slowly simmering. The last place he wanted to be was in the middle of all this merriment.

"The weather's perfect, too," Beth chirped. "It's going to be the best fair ever. Turn here. The church parking lot is on your left."

He grumbled an answer.

She was dressed like a Christmas tree—green pants, green sweater adorned with a decorated tree, white turtleneck, lightbulb earrings and a lightbulb necklace. Her ponytail bounced a bubbly rhythm as she talked nonstop. He couldn't wait to slip those earring off her lobes, to peel away the layers of brightness and taste all that soft skin below—to shut her up with a kiss and feel her quivering beneath him.

She'd said yes. He couldn't believe she'd said yes.

He had a feeling this day was going to drag on forever. He half feared she was going to change her mind, half feared she wouldn't. A day was too long to wait and worry…anticipate.

When they reached St. Mary's of the Angels church, it became clear he couldn't effect the quick escape he'd planned on. Beth's booth wasn't ready, so he helped her set up the table. Her teenage assistant, Sasha Blake, hadn't shown up, so he helped Beth carry her boxes of cookies inside.

When Sasha, pierced and dyed, and Eve finally showed up, Logan thought he might be able to slip away.

Then the kid caught his eye. Twelve, maybe thirteen, trying to look older. A biker or a skateboarder, Logan guessed by the shoes he wore. The army-green cargo pants, the black coat two sizes too big, and the expression of nonchalance that was anything but, added to the impression. The kid was up to something. He kept looking at the booth where two girls were setting up Christmas stockings on wooden trees.

When he thought no one would see him, the kid reached to the table of beaded jewelry and snagged a teal necklace from the velour tablecloth.

None of your business, Ward, he told himself. You're not on duty here.

Before he could do anything either way, a woman came panting in.

"Beth! Beth! You've got to help! The tree fell, and Roy is trying to fix the mess by himself. You're on the committee. Talk some sense into him."

"Oh, no." Without a thought to her boxed cookies, she rounded the table and followed the panting woman. Over her shoulder she said, "Logan." Then ran out the door.

A murmured roar waved through the room and everyone rushed out to witness the disaster. The boy tried to join the flow of the crowd, but Logan accosted him.

"You gonna pay for that?"

"What?"

"The necklace you slipped in your pocket."

The boy sneered at him. "Who the hell are you?"

Logan crowded into him. "I'm the meanest son of a gun you'll ever meet. You don't want to mess with me."

"Yeah? What are you going to do?"

Voice low and slow, he drawled out his threat. "I'll embarrass the hell out of you."

The boy's lip curled. "Oh, yeah?"

Logan flashed a bit of metal from his pocket. "I'll drag you out in handcuffs and make sure we go right by your girlfriend."

"Jerk. I don't have a girlfriend."

"So who're you stealing the necklace for?"

"None of your business." The boy tried to shoulder his way past Logan and was met with steel resistance.

"My guess is the little red-haired girl over there by the Christmas stockings."

Shock lit the boy's eyes. He leaned back against the wall, pretending he didn't care.

"The choice is yours. You can put it back, or we can take this up at the police station."

The boy threw the necklace back on the table.

Logan eased off. "Tell you what, you keep an eye on things, make sure nothing walks away, and I'll buy the necklace for you."

A flash of eagerness gleamed across the boy's eyes, then he shrugged and shuffled his feet. "Sure, whatever you say."

He's not a bad kid, Logan thought as he headed out the door. He just needed a reminder of what was right. The thought had Logan frowning, but he wasn't sure why.

Outside, Beth was on the common, along with what seemed like half the town. An old man, shoulders bent with age, was trying to straighten a ladder by a crooked tree. His white hair and beard were carefully trimmed to Santa perfection. His round glasses gave the image more weight. His black work pants were held up with suspenders, and a thermal Henley top was visible over the top button of his red flannel shirt.

"Roy, please, be reasonable," Beth begged.

"It's tradition."

"But Roy, Big Bill isn't here to help you this year."

"I've been doing this for near-on fifty years. Seems to me I know how by now."

"Look, everyone wants to help."

"You think I'm too feeble?"

Logan groaned. Talking wasn't going to help. He'd seen Roys before, and the only thing that was going to get things done was to give the man an out. People like Roy were too stubborn to give in when it meant losing face.

"How are you holding up that tree?" Logan asked as he sidled between Beth and the old man.

"It's on a stand."

"Nails or screws?"

"Screws."

Logan crouched and reached beneath the lower branches. "Hold it in place, will you? I'm going to tighten these screws a bit."

The old man pushed on the trunk.

"Is it straight?" Logan asked. "Hey, Beth." He jerked his chin, inviting her closer. "Come hold the tree so Roy can take a gander and tell me if it's straight."

A smiling Beth obliged. "Of course."

"How's it looking, Roy?"

"To your left a bit. No, not that much. Okay, that's good."

Logan tightened the screws.

"Thanks," Beth whispered, using the tree's branches as cover so Roy wouldn't see her.

Logan grunted. He didn't need thanks. What he needed was to have his head examined. What the hell was he doing here? *A doormat, Ward. That's what you are, a friggin' doormat.*

Logan straightened and admired the tree with Roy. "Fifty years," he said and whistled. "Guess you're the expert, then."

"Nobody else knows the tricks," Roy agreed, pulling on his beard.

Logan reached for a string of lights in one of the boxes on the benches. "Where do you start?"

The old man joined him at the boxes. "The trick is to use different sized bulbs. I use the smaller ones up top, the bigger ones near the bottom."

"This one first?" Logan asked, taking hold of a string.

"For the top third, then I switch to these."

"I'm no artist. You'll have to tell me where they go."

Logan climbed the ladder and allowed Roy to impart his wisdom and expertise. He caught a flash of Beth's smile, of her wave, and silently swore.

Here he was, putting up another set of damned Christmas lights when all he'd wanted to do was go home and work on his house.

But it didn't seem so bad this time. Even Roy's harping flowed over him.

He would be going home with Beth.

Soon.

She'd said yes. He still couldn't believe she'd said yes.

As Roy passed him up another length of lights, Logan started whistling. He was halfway through the tune before he realized it was one of those nauseating elevator ditties—"You Light up My Life."

## Chapter Twelve

"There's only one reason a man obeys so meekly," Laura Darlington said as she arranged her crocheted pot holders in the booth next to Beth's. The brown cowl of her sweater lent her an overstuffed look. She leaned across the table, neck craned, eyes owl wide in her round glasses, mouth beaked in accusation. "You're being intimate with him!"

A steady pace of fairgoers trampled through the church basement looking and comparing, hoping to find a treasure. Laura's insinuation had a few of them lingering at her table, pretending interest in her gaudy potholders, but like dogs to some inaudible whistle, their ears were trained to the conversation.

The heat of a blush fired Beth's skin. Why did her embarrassment have to be so obvious? She wasn't sleeping with the man...she was just *thinking* about it. "Really,

Laura, don't let your unhappiness color everything you think you see."

"Well, I—" Laura sputtered and blinked. "I'm perfectly happy, thank you. I'm just worried at the example you're setting for the children who look up to you."

"What example would that be?"

Before Laura could answer, Eve chimed in. "Beth, you're turning red."

"I'm working. I always get hot when I'm working." Beth pointedly looked at Laura. The plate of white-chocolate cranberry cookies in front of Beth overflowed. Several cookies fell onto the red-and-gold tablecloth and Beth was forced to put some back in the box.

Mischief twinkled in Eve's eyes as she whispered, "Oh, we'll definitely have to have a heart-to-heart soon."

"Well, why else would he follow you like a lamb and take care of Roy?" Laura shook a skinny finger at her.

"Because he's a good man." That much was true. Beneath all the armor he wore, there was a tender heart, a gentle spirit, a strong sense of honor. He'd handled Roy just right and possibly saved him from an unfortunate accident. Roy was obstinate enough to have carried on with his self-imposed task no matter what.

"In my experience," Laura said, "men don't comply unless they're after something."

"Maybe your experience is limited." Beth sorted through the boxes. Where were the Russian teacakes and the shortbreads?

"You've been late, distracted," Laura continued. "Mrs. Bronski said you even started on the wrong menu yesterday. You were making Thursday's lunch all over again."

Mrs. Bronski talked too much. "I switched days because of a delivery problem." One she hadn't discovered until after her unfortunate blunder, but she wasn't going to admit that. She found the Russian teacakes and displayed them on a green plate.

Logan *was* on her mind much too much lately. His kisses, his touches lingered long after he'd left. He was slowly driving her crazy as she wavered between guilt and guilty pleasure.

Laura tisked. "The signs of a woman who's got her mind on a man, if you ask me."

"I don't believe anyone has." Beth dusted powdered sugar from her fingers and put the top back on the box of Russian tea cakes.

"Everybody knows—"

"Everybody is wrong. There's nothing going on."

The proclamation came out much too loudly. Half the crowd in the room turned to stare at her. Some tittered, some blushed, some disapproved.

She wasn't having sex. Not yet. Maybe not ever. The thought petrified her as much as it excited her. And Jim, her gentle Jim, was caught in the middle of her seesaw. Was it betrayal? Was it simply life being lived?

"Not that it's any of your business." Beth crouched to stow the box of Russian tea cakes under the table and wished she could stay there, away from the stares and the conjecture. Geez, she couldn't even think about doing anything without having to take the whole town's reaction into consideration. She'd never given this small-town fact or a second thought before. Now it bothered her.

Eve joined her beneath the table. She had butterscotch on her breath.

"Have you been eating the goodies?" Beth asked.

"Taste testing. The butterscotch sandies are perfect, by the way. And I'm glad."

"About the sandies?" Beth sorted through the boxes.

"About you and Logan."

"There's nothing going on." Beth let out a small growl of frustration as she fussed at the boxes, making sure each label was clearly visible, but not actually seeing any of them. "Just because Laura isn't getting any doesn't mean everyone else is."

"If you say so."

"Eve—" Beth made the mistake of looking at her friend and seeing the amused expression on her face.

"Jamie's staying overnight."

Feeling heat creep into her cheeks, Beth turned away. She was not going to give Eve the satisfaction of knowing she'd already imagined all that could happen. "Jamie's really looking forward to it. Whatever the big hush-hush plan you two have cooked up."

"Can't say, or it wouldn't be a surprise. But I think you should take full advantage of the free time." Eve reached an arm around Beth's shoulders and squeezed. "Cook the man a real meal. Lambchops or steak or chicken. Something he can sink his teeth into. I haven't got the faintest idea why you've been stuffing him with casseroles."

Beth didn't have a clue, either. At first it had seemed the easiest way to give him a balanced meal. Now? It was habit. It was connection. It was…care in a glass dish? "He likes them."

"Try real food. Then, after you've fed him, seduce him. Give yourself permission to be a woman instead of a caretaker, for a change."

"Eve! You're as bad as Laura."

"I am not. I care about you. She's just jealous."

Beth knocked over two boxes as she reached for the shortbreads, which turned out to be lemon stars. "And you should speak. You keep brushing Gus off."

"I turn down his marriage proposals, not his bed," she said, slanting Beth a meaningful gaze, then threw her hands up. "Okay, I'll shut up. You're too young to wrap yourself in a cocoon, that's all I meant. I just want the best for you."

"Then let me do things my way."

Eve backed off. "Okay, you're right. Did you make any of those chocolate caramel pecan bars?"

"In the box right by Sasha's feet."

Sasha's upside-down, blue-dyed hair appeared. "What are you two doing down here?"

"Eve's being a busybody, and I'm trying to find the shortbreads."

"They're already on the table."

"I'm buying the whole box of these pecan bars." Eve riffled through her purse and brought out her wallet. "I'm going to run them home real quick so you don't sell them by mistake."

Sasha crouched in the spot Eve vacated and played with the ring that pierced her eyebrow. "He's not really your boyfriend, is he?"

Beth sighed. Laura had the knack of turning a snowball into an avalanche. "No, why do you ask?"

Sasha shrugged. "Nick Barlow said his dad saw you two kissing."

Nick Barlow, son of Mark Barlow the mailman. "And when did he see that?"

"The day the power came back on."

Wednesday. Her front door. In bright daylight. She'd thought she was safe because Jamie was happily watching *Dragon Knights*. She thought she'd heard a car, too, but it didn't seem to matter when she was melting in Logan's arms. "Oh."

"It would ruin everything."

Beth rocked on her heels and faced Sasha. The crowd's noise buzzed all around them, but they were sheltered by the drape of the tablecloth. "What do you mean?"

"You'd get all goo-goo-eyed and forget—" Sasha shrugged again and started retreating.

With a hand on Sasha's arm, Beth pulled her back. "You can always talk to me. I'll always listen."

"Sure."

But her eyes said she wasn't convinced. The girl who, with her short razor-cut, blue-dyed hair, her slashed black clothes and her pierced nose and eyebrows, was so desperately trying to convince the world she wasn't worth loving needed reassurance.

"Have I missed a lunch?" Beth asked.

"No."

"Have I ever sent you away?"

"No."

"Do you still have my phone number?"

"Yes."

"If you need me, you know where you can find me. Kissing or not kissing a man isn't going to change that."

Sasha puffed a small sigh of relief.

"Hello?" a voice came from above the table. "How much for the gingerbread men?"

Sasha started to rise, and Beth touched her arm once more. "I'm so glad you could come and help me today."

"Me, too."

It was good to see Sasha smile. She'd already shed too many tears in her short life.

The ripples of a pond, Beth mused. She'd thought her decision a private one, one that would affect only her. She was beginning to see it could swash outward and touch others in unexpected ways—Jamie, Sasha...even Laura. A new heaviness preoccupied her as she manned her booth. What right did she have to disturb their world only to please herself?

The day sped by. Laura took occasional potshots at Beth.

Beth did her best to ignore them. Eve and Sasha ran interference. And when the crowd finally thinned, when the cookie boxes were empty, Logan reappeared, and her heart seemed to sing.

She wanted to run to him, throw herself into his arms, burrow her head into his shoulder and be held while she tried to sort the dilemma weighing her heart.

But she didn't. She simply smiled.

Silently he helped her clean up. Silently he walked with her to pick up Jamie at Bobby's house. Silently he sipped a cup of hot cider while the crowd gathered on the common for the tree-lighting ceremony.

Dusk blanketed the sky. Stars appeared. The wind picked up bite. And the pitter-pat of uneasiness marched louder and louder with each beat of her pulse. Something was wrong, but what?

She tried to keep the mood light, but sensed armor plates of steel going up one by one as Logan hunkered farther and farther from the crowd. She took his hand. He pulled it away.

"Logan?"

He shook his head. "Watch your show, Beth."

"We can go."

In the fading light, in the hard darkness of his eyes, she could read nothing. But she sensed his distress. He hated Christmas—the noise, the bustle, the brightness. She'd placed him in an awkward position when she'd asked him for a ride this morning. His sense of duty wouldn't let him leave her stranded. "Eve can drive me home, if you'd rather—"

"I'm fine." He jerked his chin toward the street. "The parade's starting."

An antique fire engine honked its way up the common. Santa Claus, sitting proudly on its high seat, waved at the crowd. Church bells chimed a welcome. A children's choir sang "O, Christmas Tree." Microphone in hand, Mildred Wallace stepped up on the bandshell and introduced, then thanked, each sponsor in turn.

"Now the moment we've all been waiting for," Mildred said. She patted the curl of her flip hairdo, smiling and nodding at the crowd. "Is everyone ready?"

"Yes."

Mildred cupped her ear. "I can't hear you."

"Yes!"

"Okay, here we go. Help me count. Five…"

"Four."

"Three."

"Two."

"One!"

There was a hushed moment of expectancy as the crowd held its breath, then the tree blazed to life, the bright-red bulbs shaming the stars into oblivion. Oohs and aahs of appreciation rippled through the crowd. The choir broke into a rendition of "Joyful Noise."

"For someone who hates Christmas, you did a wonderful job with the lights."

Beth turned, but Logan wasn't there. His hunched figure was fast disappearing into the night.

Her heart seemed to drop to her feet. Panic plucked a frantic beat. She should have known this would be too much for him. All the children, their happy shouts, their eyes wide with wonder would remind him of his loss.

"Oh, no. Dear God, no." Her hand flew to her throat. She swallowed hard. Her sudden insight had the blood draining from her face, leaving her cold and queasy. His daughter had died during the holidays. And Beth had brought him here to witness a reminder of his dead daughter.

Torn, she glanced from Logan to Jamie.

Eve caught her eye and took Jamie's hand firmly into her own. "I've got him. Go."

*Sam, Sam, Sam.* Logan tried to flee from the pain, but it hunted him down, latched on to him, biting, gnawing, eating him alive.

"Logan. Wait!"

He couldn't wait. He couldn't slow down. He couldn't give the memories a chance to catch up, to choke him.

She'd been there tonight, his beautiful Samantha, in every child. He'd heard her laughter, seen the sparkle in her eyes, felt her ghost bouncing up and down by his side. And he'd been nearly swallowed up in her imagined wonderment. "Daddy, oh, look, Daddy!"

She'd loved Christmas. Everything about it. The colors. The noise. The whole messy excitement of it all.

"Slow down," Beth said.

He threw his coat open, welcomed the stab of wind. Gulping big bites of frigid night air, he threw himself into the rhythm of his frenzied strides.

"Where are you going?"

Anywhere. Nowhere. It didn't matter. Away, that was all that was important. Away from the crowd, from the noise, from the joy—away from all the memories of his beloved daughter.

"Logan, talk to me."

"Go away." He wanted, needed to be alone.

"I'm staying." She shoved her hands in the pockets of her damned fuchsia coat and matched him stride for ground-eating stride. Her labored breaths became a companion as she puffed beside him, the swish of her coat a soothing balm, the crunch of her footsteps a grounding metronome.

It wasn't until he'd walked half a mile that he realized he was heading home. Six miles. Beth wasn't dressed for the long, cold walk. And she was stubborn enough to stick by his side. "How do I get back to the church parking lot?"

"This way."

She led him around the side streets, avoiding the common, her silent presence an unexpected comfort. He reached for her with one arm, pinning her to his side—a human crutch for his shattering spirit.

*Sam, Sam, Sam.*

When they reached his car, Beth got in. He found he couldn't tell her to get out. They drove in silence to his cold, dark house.

Before he could shut the engine, she reached for the keys and drilled him with a determined gaze. "I'm coming in."

He put his hand over hers, meaning to reclaim his keys. "Beth—"

"No, when your heart's breaking, you need someone there with you."

"Beth—"

"I've been there, Logan. I won't leave you alone. Not tonight."

There was no pity in her eyes, only simple strength. The kind a friend lent a friend. The engine's rumble jittered Beth's hand against his. His throat constricted. Suddenly he didn't want to be alone. He didn't want to fight the specter of Sam's ghost, of his guilt, on his own. He would ask Beth about her day and let her inexhaustible babble lull him back into the safety of not feeling. He would paint, and she would talk…and Sam's ghost would fade back into the dark hollow of his chest.

But once they were inside the house, Max greeted them with exuberant barks. In them he heard the echo of Sam's voice. *One more time, Daddy. Just one more.* And he knew he could never escape the pain. Not wanting Beth to witness his descent into hell, he pushed her away. "Go."

"I'm staying." Her voice was gentle but firm. The feel of her arms wrapping around his waist, of her small hands clutching the shirt beneath his coat undid him.

He crushed her against him, pressing her head against his hardened heart. A rush of dread quivered through his body. When she left he would be alone. Again. There would be nothing between him and the soul-shredding claws of grief.

*Stay. Please stay.*

But he could not ask for what he didn't deserve.

So he bent to kiss her. A kiss. One last kiss. Fight a ghost with the memory of another dead dream. He wouldn't wait until spring. Tomorrow he would leave. Before he hurt her.

But one kiss wasn't enough. Not when she opened to him so willingly, not when she claimed his darkness as her own, not when she breathed so much warmth into his cold body.

"Beth." It was a curse. It was prayer.

He wanted more. He needed more. He was going to eat her alive. And when he was through, they would both be damned.

"I'm not afraid," Beth whispered against Logan's dark kiss. He wanted her to be frightened by his grief, by the pain and guilt eating him bit by bit. If she left, he could blame himself and let himself fall into the dark pit of despair. She knew; she'd been there. She knew what it was like to want to die, to have to live, knew what it was like to hurt down to the very nucleus of each and every cell of her being. "I won't let you fall."

She took in the darkness he offered her, swallowed it

whole, and tendered him back the goodness of his own heart.

"Beth." Her name was a hard rasp in her ears, heavy with pain, with need. Her body shook in a long-forgotten echo from deep inside her, inciting a small gasp of surprise, a small stab of fear. Not of him; of herself. Of her readiness to give of herself to this man who could not love her, might never love her.

Logan stilled in her arms. His hands gripped her shoulders, ready to push her away. The uncertain storm in his eyes touched her more deeply than any caress. She reached up, skimmed his jaw with the tips of her fingers. "Let me love you, Logan."

He stood there for a long time, searching her face, allowing her space to retreat. Then, without breaking the intense hold of his gaze, he nodded. "I've got to see to Max."

Max had seemed to sense her master's dark mood, and her exuberant welcome had soon faded. She'd slunk to the corner where she now shivered. Logan went to her, reassured her, then let her out while he filled her bowls with kibbles and fresh water.

The kitchen took Beth by surprise. He'd added a chair rail and painted the lower section the color of ripe wheat. The upper section was white with an ivy border. The cabinets were the same golden color as the lower walls, but in the center panels, he'd painted a white trellis design with the illusion of ivy growing through the slats. The whole effect was one of warmth and hominess. "I like what you've done."

He didn't answer, but brushed past her as Max pawed the front door. Moments later the dog followed her master uncertainly back into the kitchen, accepted the chew bone he offered her and settled on her bed with a snuffle. Her liquid brown eyes darted from master to intruder as if she sensed and feared the tension growing between them.

Without a word, Logan took Beth's hand and led her up the cold, dark stairs. She swallowed hard as a fresh crop of doubt sprouted with each step she took. But one look at his drawn face, at his tense body, settled her apprehension. He needed to be held, to be loved, to be accepted—darkness and all.

The scent of loneliness filled his bedroom. The mournful slap of maple branches against the side of the house echoed the sense of forlornness. Shafts of moonlight pierced through the slats of the blinds, hatching the night-grayed sheets of the unmade bed with bars of soft silver. A box spring, a mattress, the shoved-aside mound of a dark comforter, the slept-in sheets were all pushed against one wall. An opened duffel bag sagged across the top of a packing carton. A pair of running shoes and a pair of snakeskin boots were the only occupants of the closet.

He had no plans of staying, she realized with a start. He was a man in transition. But she'd known that on a gut level from the first day. Disappointment curled in her stomach. She brushed it away.

She was a woman in transition, too, finding a way across the past into the future. It was time, past time. No one would be hurt by this night of passion. She would be helping him abate the burden of his grief. He would ease her into that last step of reclaiming her womanhood.

What she did, what she didn't do, wasn't anybody's business but her own. Life would go on as it always had. And the ripples of this night would affect only her, only him.

With fingers that weren't quite steady, she undid the buttons of his shirt. His breath rasped inward. His nostrils flared. The muscle of his jaw tightened. The dark hunger of his unflinching gaze sped her pulse, heated her blood.

Her hands slid across his chest, pushing aside the denim of his shirt, admiring the hard pectorals beneath the smooth skin. It had been so long since she'd touched a man in this way, let a man touch her, that she felt awkward. To hide her sudden shyness, she placed her ear against his chest, heard the thunder of his heart. The powerful sound awoke something deep inside her. Like honey from a freshly cut comb, desire spiraled, thick and warm.

His touch was unsteady, too, as if this was an experience with which he was out of practice. And his hesitation gave her courage. She tilted her head up and pressed a kiss against his lips. Warmth and the heady taste of cider and desire greeted her. The tension in him shifted from guardedness to the potent sensuality of leashed male power. That honeyed ribbon of need inside her turned to surprising urgency, and a moan shivered up her throat.

His hands reached for the scrunchie holding her hair in a ponytail. His fingers raked the strands free. Delight serpentined down her spine. He framed her face with his hands and looked at her with eyes of silver smoke. "I want you. Tell me you want me."

"I want you." No question, no hesitation. It felt right to be here with him in this black and gray world of night and moonlight, to leave the ghost of her loss at the door and give rein to her own physical desires.

With trembling hands, they undressed each other, scattering clothes on the bare wood planks. On legs that were rubbery, she followed his lead to the bed. He sat on the mattress, pulled her into his lap. He devoured her mouth, her throat, her collarbone. His touch fired her skin, enlivening long-dormant nerves. Her breasts ached for his attention, but he skimmed past them to her arms and ended at the scar bisecting her palm.

"I hurt you," he said, kissing the scars tenderly. "I never meant to."

"I hurt myself." Her throat was dry, her body shivery. She wanted, needed more of him. "Kiss me again."

He did—in teasing nips and whispers while his hands cupped her breasts and his thumbs drew tormenting circles around her nipples. A raw sound of needy protest rasped at her throat. It was too much; it wasn't enough. "Please."

She had no idea what the plea meant, except that the intensity of the feelings building inside her couldn't go on much longer.

He leaned back against the pillows, drawing her down with him, a willing prisoner of his consuming gaze.

Her wedding ring on a chain, the symbol of her infidelity, sprang from the valley between her breasts and dangled between them. It twirled on the chain, glinting in the moonlight. Gasping, she reached up, cupped it in one hand, closed her eyes. What am I doing? She thought of Jim, but could not bring forth a vivid picture of him. He was fading as she was waking. And something inside her keened.

"Look at me." Logan gently pried her fingers loose, watching her, waiting.

Her thoughts were a tornado, throwing up debris of the past, mixing it with the present, confusing the future. As she hung on to Logan's shoulders, the gold ring spun between them, a pendulum, and she waited, breath held until it spoke its verdict. Up and down, yes. Back and forth, no. But it just wheeled in a dizzy circle.

She closed her eyes again. The ache in her heart played a heavy counterpoint to the need still singing in her blood. The decision was up to her. Jim was dead. He couldn't absolve her or condemn her.

When she opened her eyes, Logan's gaze, dark with desire, creased with worry, met hers. He cared. He would never hurt her. She had made the right choice.

He shifted so that they both lay on their sides, eye to eye, bodies joined by her hands on his shoulders, his on her waist.

''He's between us,'' Logan said.

The look in his eyes told her he would stop now, let her back out. He would wrap up his need, his bleeding grief to save her from regret.

The static of expectation built energy. It crinkled along her skin, raising the fine hairs at the back of her neck until the sharp stab of lightning exploded into the thunder of understanding.

Her husband was dead, but she was alive. And though Logan's heart was breaking over his daughter's death, he was alive, too. They needed each other, if not forever, then for tonight.

She sat up, reached for the chain's clasp, and gently set the ring aside.

Logan moved his hands hungrily over Beth's body, feeding his senses with the feel of her skin. He took her mouth and drank in her taste, let the sweet scent of her swirl madly with the disjointed thoughts crowding his mind.

Even without knowing all the details, she understood. About Sam. About him. And she still wanted him. She wasn't scared of the darkness eating him alive, of the pain chipping slowly at his soul. It was in her, too, this core-deep hurt. She understood.

Her body flowed with his, melding, melting, soft, so soft. She wasn't a ghost haunting him. She was real. She was here. She was his.

Distantly he was aware of the shaking of his body, of the hunger so strong it fought him for control. He needed this to last. Needed the ghosts to stay at bay for a while. Her gentle touch, her hot kisses, the purr of pleasure low in her throat were a comfort, a torture.

Her stomach trembled under the slide of his palm, and masculine satisfaction fed his hunger. A throbbing urgency sizzled through him.

Make it last, make it last.

But logic no longer held any ground. His body obeyed a primal instinct too powerful to deny.

He found her center, hot and wet, felt her shudder against his intimate caress. And he needed her acceptance with a desperation he couldn't understand. "Tell me you want me."

"I want you." Her voice was a breathy whisper filled with a need as urgent as his own. Her eyes were stars dancing in the moonlight for him. Her hands shivered against his nape, drawing him to her. "Logan. Please."

He took her plea into his mouth, savored its taste as he pushed himself between her thighs. She wrapped her legs around him, capturing him. She was alive against him, her body a sensuous invitation, her moans an erotic song.

Silky flesh moved into silky flesh. His pleasure was an exquisite torture. Heat slicked his skin. He was driven to stake, to conquer, but forced himself to slow down.

When she arched against him, hunger turned into pure greed. More. He needed more. "Look at me."

Her eyes opened. He watched her face soften with every one of his thrusts, felt the tension coil strand by strand in her body, reveled in the demanding curl of her fingers into the muscles of his shoulders. He took her faster, higher until her eyes glazed, until her mouth opened for a long, shuddering moan, until her body quaked with pleasure, then melted into a boneless mass of satisfaction.

Holding on to her, he surrendered to the mad fever coursing through his body and spilled himself into her with a guttural growl. He couldn't let her go, so he eased himself sideways and held her tighter, burying his face in her hair while breath found his lungs once more.

The feel of her palm against the hard beat of his heart, head nestled into his shoulder, body molded against his, was thick with comfort. It was heaven, it was…home.

A strange sadness wove into the threads of his satisfaction and had him swallowing thickly. He pressed a kiss against the sweet scent of Beth's hair. Her sigh of contentment reverberated against his heart.

"No regrets?" he asked, skimming his hands tentatively over the skin of her curvy side.

"Life's too short for regrets." She snuggled closer. "Logan…talk to me."

Her soft whisper trooped an army of goose bumps all over his body. Cold replaced the wild heat of mating, shattering the comfort of escape.

He started to leave, but she hung on to him. "Talk to me. Tell me about Samantha. I want to know that part of you."

She was asking for an intimacy he couldn't give, an intimacy that would drive her away.

"I can't love you, Beth."

"I'm not asking for love." Her hand caressed his jaw. Her lips gently grazed his chest. Her head tilted up, and she looked at him with those starry eyes so bright and sure. "Do you believe in the value of human worth?"

"Of course."

"Then every life matters—even yours."

He started to deny her claim, but she put a finger against his lips. "No one wanted me to talk about Jim. It was too painful for them. But I needed to talk, and I'm glad Eve was there to listen. Let me be there for you, Logan. Talk to me.''

Falling back against the pillow, he closed his eyes, saw the parade of the memories he'd tried to outrun returning one by one.

In the darkness, with Beth, warm in his arms, a willing listener, would it be so bad to give voice to his ghost?

## Chapter Thirteen

"It was Christmas," Logan said. His cold body felt nothing, not the sheets beneath him, not the woman in his arms, not the pain so intent on slicing him open. The memories charged at him, bloody warriors leading a coup. He saw them all clearly on the screen of his mind, watched them from a psychic distance. To do anything else would be to invite disaster.

"Sam died when a drunk kid changing a CD in his truck drove over the curb and plowed into her. She was learning to ride the new two-wheeler she'd gotten for Christmas."

He'd been running behind her all afternoon, impressed by her determination to show off for her friends the next day.

"One more time, Daddy! Just one more."

"One more and that's it. Daddy's getting tired."

He had run beside her, holding the vinyl seat with nothing more than the tips of his fingers while she found her balance.

Then he had let her go.

Hands braced on knees, catching his breath, he had watched her triumph. Long, brown hair flying from under her purple helmet, she'd been so happy. Her grin with its missing front teeth, her laughter had been forever imprinted in his mind.

"Look at me, Daddy. I'm doing it! I'm doing it!"

He'd watched her, pride swelling his chest, and he'd missed the pickup truck cresting the hill farther up the street. Pride had quickly turned to horror. By the time the truck had jumped the curb, he'd been flying helplessly toward her. "Samantha!"

But it had been too late. All he'd been able to do was hold her broken and bleeding body while he'd waited for the ambulance.

"My wife blamed me. She hadn't wanted Sam, had never given her much care, but she blamed me." Their marriage, already brittle, had fallen apart. They'd divorced. She'd gone back to her parents.

"I kept working, trusting in the system to make things right for Sam." But the system had betrayed him. "The kid, a judge's son, got away with a slap on the wrist."

Logan lost faith in law and justice. He couldn't work with kids anymore on the special school projects he'd kept doing while waiting for the trial. The noise, the people, the memories drove him crazy. He couldn't stand to see children play, to hear them laugh. He wasn't making a difference, anyway. Half of the kids he tried to save from gangs ended up killed or mutilated. So he handed in his resignation and left.

"If I hadn't let her go, Sam would still be here." He couldn't forgive himself any more than his ex-wife had.

"One day you'll begin to live again," Beth said. Her hand was warm against his heart as if she were holding it in place for him.

"No." He was glad she hadn't tried to talk him out of his blame.

"There's no other choice." She hugged him tighter, and her soft strength was a comfort. "Samantha's death is a tragedy, but if you let everything around you die, you're just compounding the disaster."

How could he ever be happy again when Sam would never know happiness? How could he ever be happy knowing he'd prayed for her death as she lay like a broken doll on her hospital bed?

He was glad for the cover of night, for the fact Beth couldn't see his face, that he couldn't see hers. His throat was tight, his lips parched. It hurt to speak. "I was relieved when she died."

A shiver ran through Beth. Disgust? He tried to move away, but she clung to him, as if she needed someone to hang on to as much as he did.

"How long did Samantha live after the accident?" Beth asked.

"Nearly a month."

"Jim, too." Her hand slipped from his chest. He stopped the slide and held her hand in place with his own. "A month of racking pain while the cancer ate him alive. I felt awful because I was relieved when he died."

"No more suffering." She wasn't disgusted by his admission. She'd felt it, too, the tearing apart of seeing a loved one die, wanting the suffering to end, needing them to live. She understood.

"Yes." Her tears plopped onto his chest. He wiped her cheek with a thumb, kissed the top of her head. "Then I felt guilty."

"Ashamed." He could still feel it now, the heavy weight of shame. The admission wasn't so hard, knowing it was shared.

"Angry." Her hand fisted against his ribs, her body echoed the remembered anger. "How could he leave me like that?"

"I was her father. She was in my care. I should have saved her." He'd been responsible for Sam's welfare, and he'd failed her.

"I should have seen. I should have sensed. I should have known."

No, he wanted to say, you couldn't have. But he knew words couldn't take away the burden. It was there, an invisible appendage forever a part of them. "I would have given anything to take her place."

"If I forget him, how will Jamie ever know his father?"

He ached for her, for her loss, for her fear, yet felt an uncommon peace envelop him. He wasn't alone. She understood.

Like shipwrecked survivors at sea, they turned to each other, seeking comfort and courage. And when the storm ebbed, a tiny ray of hope flickered in Logan's heart.

For the first time in years he slept without nightmares.


"The ice is ready," Jamie announced when Logan opened the front door a week later. It was a glorious winter day with clear skies and no wind. The kind of day that would give a boy red cheeks but allow him to play outside for hours. "Wanna come skating?"

The picture of his grandfather holding his hand as he balanced on skates for the first time flashed through Logan's mind. Dallas had had unbounded patience with an awkward boy, and Logan had returned the favor with wholehearted devotion.

"I've got too much work to do." Sharing stolen moments with Beth was one thing—they both knew it was temporary—but being with Jamie was still hard. The boy didn't understand the rules grown-ups lived by. And even though Jamie tugged at his heart, there was no sense wishing for things that could never happen.

He could not be for Jamie what Dallas had been for him—not even until spring. It would hurt too much when he had to leave. He had to keep their interactions to a minimum, but Jamie had a way of asking questions that required tough answers, of demanding attention in a thousand small ways.

Jamie swiped a blue mitten beneath his nose. "Yeah, Mom's busy, too."

Max trotted behind him and, spying Jamie, began a whole-body wag. Logan slanted a leg across the door so she couldn't run out. She whined. "Don't you have any friends?"

Jamie shrugged carelessly. "They're all busy."

"What about Bobby?"

"He's at a hockey game watching his brother. Can I watch you?"

Hope shone bright in those hazel eyes and cut Logan to the quick. "Too dangerous. I'm using a saw."

"Oh." The pout nearly had Logan giving in. What could it hurt to have him watch? "What're you making?"

"A present. For your mom." Idiotic, really, to waste time on such a project. But he'd seen the walnut and the maple at Gus's store, and it had reminded him of the muffins Beth was so fond of making.

"What is it?"

"Can't tell you or it wouldn't be a surprise."

"Yeah, that's what Mom says, too."

"You go on home," he told Jamie when he felt himself

weakening again. "I don't want to catch you on that ice, you hear?" Not with that pond half on his land.

"Yeah, I hear." Jamie kicked at the snow at the edge of the porch. "Can Max come out and play?"

Max squirmed even harder against his leg at the mention of her name. He planned to leave Max behind when he moved; she might as well get used to her new master. "Sure. Take her to your house."

Logan released his leg, and Max shot out. Boy and dog started bounding down the path. "Wait, take her leash."

The last thing he needed was to have the stupid mutt hit by a car. He showed Jamie how to fit the leash in the collar, how to control the unruly dog, then went back to the cellar.

In the jaws of a set of clamps were the light and dark pieces of maple and walnut he'd glued together. Once he shaped the piece, he still had hours of sanding to get the cutting board as smooth as he wanted. Giving a small smile he lifted the piece from the clamps, then transferred a muffin pattern to the wood with a pencil. A muffin to celebrate Beth's breakfast experiments. He hoped he would have enough time to oil the piece before Christmas in two days.

He was thinking of Beth, of seeing her later in the afternoon, of holding her, of getting lost in her. A small regret nagged him at the thought that he would have to leave the warmth of her bed to return to his own cold house before Jamie awoke. But in this game, no child would be a victim. He switched the saw off.

As he lifted his safety glasses, he heard a noise that didn't sound right. Barking. Max. What was the mutt up to?

The sound reached him again. Not right. Too close. Hadn't he told the kid to go home?

The next bark seemed to reach inside his heart and squeeze it tight. Something was wrong. Jamie. Nausea billowed. He dropped the wooden muffin and shot up the stairs. He flung the front door open and ran out without a coat.

"Max! Where are you?"

Her frantic barks came to him from the bottom of the hill. She strained and tugged. Her leash was caught beneath a bright green lump on the snow. Ice clogged Logan's veins.

*Jamie.*

Logan staggered, feeling as if his guts were being torn apart. *No, please, not Jamie.*

Heart pounding, he forced himself forward, then raced for the unmoving boy. *God, no. Not again.*

"Jamie!"

Beth cut and sliced vegetables for a stew, holding the telephone in the crook of her neck. She concentrated on each movement of the knife to keep her mind from straying to Logan. Eve was not making the task easy by insisting she air her feelings as if they were laundry. Beth wasn't exactly sure what those feelings were, except that they were jumbled, and she was confused.

She was slowly, surely falling in love. In love? No, that was crazy. She couldn't be in love. Not with Logan. But the tender bruise on her heart ached, denying her claim. How could she feel so much for Logan when she'd been so in love with Jim?

"I'm not going to leave you alone until you tell me what's going on," Eve said. "I'm worried about you."

"I'm fine." Then she sighed and felt it sweep all through her body. Tears swam up, and she swiped them away. *I am not going to cry over this.*

Maybe sharing wouldn't be so bad—she kept telling Logan so. She ought to listen to her own advice. "I think I'm in love, Eve."

"That's wonderful!"

"I don't want to love him." She added oil to the Dutch oven and turned on the burner beneath the pot.

"Why not?"

"He's going to leave." The meat sizzled, seeming to hiss a warning: you knew it, you knew it. And she had, even before she'd made the mistake of giving him her heart as well as her comfort. Sooner than later he would leave.

"You don't know that."

"I can feel it." Beth stirred the chunks of lamb around the pot. The moving-cartons still unpacked in his house shouted transiency. And the kitchen with its country garden was not a decor Logan would have chosen for himself. He was marking time.

"Talk to him."

"I don't want to pressure him." He already felt too much self-imposed stress. He couldn't forgive himself for watching his daughter die and not being able to do anything about it, and he continued to punish himself with what-ifs and if-onlys. Being cheated out of the grace of closure that the court case could have given him hadn't helped his healing process. She was no prize, either, asking him to share her with her dead husband's fast-fading ghost. "He's already been hurt so much."

"All the more reason for you to talk to him."

Beth dumped the cut-up vegetables into the pot and churned the mixture. "Eve…"

"Beth, he needs to know what's in your heart."

"You don't understand." Beth thwacked the wooden spoon against the counter and unsnapped the cover from the container of broth. Her movement was jerky, and broth sloshed over the side onto her hand. "If I tell him I love him, I'll send him running."

And that scared her as much as Jim fading from her memory.

"Or make him realize he's got something to live for, for a change...."

Eve went on, but something in Beth came to high alert. The first sharp bark sent her to the window above the sink. Nothing. No Jamie. No dog. She frowned, reached for a cloth and wiped her hands dry. Jamie had told her Logan had let Max come out and play.

"I told him to stay where I could see him," she said distractedly.

"What?"

"He's going to get an earful when I catch up with him." But her anger was soft-boiled, fast frittering into concern. A tingling of premonition skittered down her spine.

"Eve, I've got to go." She dropped the phone, launched the cloth on the counter and ran.

As she opened the back door, a blast of cold stole her breath.

"Jamie! Where are you?"

There was no answer, except Max's barks around the front. Frantic, frenzied barks as if the animal were hurt.

"James Andrew Lannigen. Answer me!"

Great. Logan had finally gotten attached to the dog, and her son's carelessness had led Max to injury. She marched around the house ready to read Jamie the riot act. But something about Max's barks had a quality of urgency.

*Hurry, hurry, hurry.*

Suddenly her heart wanted to burst. Her breath choked through the narrowed opening of her lungs. She sped around the corner, jittery with adrenaline. Her gaze darted wildly, trying to locate any movement. Panic rose, sticky and thick, setting her whole body shaking. ''Jamie!''

Movement. Not Jamie. Logan.

Logan was racing toward the fence at the bottom of the hill. Her gaze dashed ahead. There beside a fence post was a frantic Max barking and leaping, fighting some unseen demon around the unmoving lump of her son's bright-green coat and red sledding saucer. Her heart gave a sickening thud.

''Jamie!'' He wasn't talking. He wasn't moving. *No, please, not Jamie. Don't take him, too!*

On stocking feet, Beth slipped and slid her way across the street.

''Jamie, wake up, wake up,'' Logan shouted as he assessed the small body.

''What's wrong with him?'' He's going to be all right. He has to be all right. She skidded to a halt, dropped to her knees and reached for her baby.

Logan's hand held hers at bay. ''Don't move him. He hit his head on the fence post.''

''Jamie,'' she choked out. So pale, so pale. ''Jamie, Mommy's here. Talk to me, sweetheart.''

He looked as if he were asleep in the snow. A sob hitched in her chest.

''There's no blood,'' she said, pressing a fist against her mouth. ''There's no blood. How come he's not moving?''

Helplessness rolled through her, weighing her down.

Logan moved the red knit cap aside, and Beth gasped at the swelling bruise on her son's forehead.

''Help him. Logan, please. Help him.''

Beth's terror tore at Logan. Her skin was whiter than the snow. Her eyes were saucer-round with fear. Her body shuddered. But he could not take her in his arms. Not after sending her son away, not after leaving him outside unsupervised. And now the boy was hurt. On his land. On the rail he'd put up to keep the boy from trespassing. If he hadn't, Jamie would have safely sledded into the opening.

She wouldn't thank him for this deed.

Don't think. Don't feel. Jamie's alive. He's breathing. Keep him that way.

Logan pulled the sweater off his body and wrapped it around Jamie to stave off shock. "Look at me, Beth."

She lifted her gaze. The strain of worry and fear etched her face. His chest hurt at the sight, his hands fisted at Jamie's side, but he forced himself to speak in a slow, even way.

"Don't move him, Beth. Keep him warm. I'm going to call for help. I'm going to bring back some blankets."

He had to drag Max away. She fought him every step of the way, barking and squirming. "Jamie's going to be all right."

But he didn't believe it. Neither did Max. She kept barking and whining, scratching at the door even after he locked her in the laundry room.

It wasn't long before the sound of sirens pierced the air. But even as the shrieks came nearer, Beth's voice never wavered in her encouragement. She never left her son's side as they loaded the small body into the ambulance. When the emergency technician suggested she follow in her car, she ignored him.

"It's against company policy," the technician insisted, holding her back.

Beth keened and tried to claw her way past the technician.

"Are you going to sit here and argue with a mother?" Logan said. "Or are you going to take care of that kid?"

"It's comp—"

Logan got in the technician's face. Beth took the opening

and lunged into the ambulance. "She's going. Deal with it."

Without another word the technician climbed in and closed the door.

The ambulance's shrieks faded away, but not the dead look of Jamie's face, not the devastation etched in Beth's features. Not the guilt in his own heart.

She shouldn't be alone. But the last person she needed was him.

He couldn't go. He couldn't watch another child die. He couldn't watch another woman turn away from him in blame.

He would call Eve.


The cloth Beth had thrown on the counter landed next to the stove. A corner brushed the burning gas hissing beneath the pot of stew. The fibers burst into flames, which consumed the cloth. Still hungry, the fire latched on to the oven mitt then jumped onto the curtains, licked at the wallpaper and devoured the walls.

## Chapter Fourteen

Logan and Eve stood side by side at the end of the drive while the firemen stowed their gear into the truck. The flashing red-and-white lights bled stark shadows into the snow. The stench of fire and smoke filled the air, leaving an acrid taste in Logan's mouth.

After the fire engine growled away, an eerie hush settled over the scene. Stars shone through the house's broken silhouette against the frosty evening sky, giving Beth's home a surreal appearance.

Nothing was left but a burnt shell.

A parade of memories trampled through his mind. Beth's smiles. Jamie's laughter. The scent of home. The taste of peace. The warm, woolly feeling of contentment.

All gone now with the house.

He steeled himself against the soft emotions seeping through his guard. If he were to survive, he could not let himself drown in those sticky feelings.

"She wanted me to get Jamie's bear and some books," Eve said. Her bottom lip trembled. Tears shone in her eyes.

Beth probably hadn't even thought of herself when she'd sent Eve on this errand. She'd run out of the house without a coat, without shoes and more than likely hadn't even yet noticed. "She needs shoes and a coat."

"I know."

Jamie hadn't regained consciousness yet as his little body fought the trauma to his brain. The doctors wouldn't promise anything, but expected the best.

Logan reached into his pocket and handed Eve a clean handkerchief. "I didn't see the flames until they were coming out the roof."

Eve dabbed the handkerchief against her eyes. "I'm not blaming you."

"I know." But he was blaming himself. So many things he could have done differently. He closed his eyes against the guilt.

"She needs you."

He shook his head. "I can't."

"You have to."

"I'm leaving." Because he couldn't help himself, he looked at the house once more, felt the tug of regret.

"She's lost everything." Eve slanted him a glance. "Losing you, too, would finish her off."

"She's better off without me." What could he bring her but more pain?

Eve's features crimped. "You're a fool."

"No argument there." He'd been a fool to think he could have a scrap of peace—even for a while. "I hurt her."

"She needs you."

"I put the fence rail back up. If I hadn't—"

"Jamie would have found another way to get into trouble. It's his nature. Why do you think Beth keeps an extra-large tool kit filled with bandages? After Jim died, she could have kept him on a short leash, but she didn't want her fears to affect Jamie's enjoyment of life.''

Logan said nothing, just kept staring at the house's blackened frame. At another dream gone up in smoke.

''Do you love her?'' Eve asked, her voice softening.

Love? What was love? These jumbled, painful feelings tearing him apart? ''I don't know. I'm not sure what love feels like anymore.''

''You know, or you wouldn't be feeling so bad.'' She placed a glove-covered hand on his arm and squeezed. ''Go to her.''

He had no right to go to her, no right to hold her, no right to dry her tears. Not when he'd caused them. He would never forget the devastation in her eyes at the sight of her unmoving son, the image of her clawing her way into that ambulance to be at Jamie's side. Why would she ever want to see him again?

''She'll send me away.''

''That's what you want, isn't it?'' Eve wheeled on him, eyes glaring. ''Then you wouldn't have to face the fact that you love her, that you want to live again. No, you're just too damn busy feeling sorry for yourself to see past your own nose.'' She scoffed. ''Dying for your daughter! What kind of memorial is that?''

''A deserving one.'' His jaw tensed, and he ground his back teeth in a tight circle. Eve didn't understand. How could she?

''Dying for the dead hasn't worked for anyone else. What makes you think you're so special?''

His fingers curled into fists, but knowing Eve was speaking out of her own pain, he bit back his hurtful retort and drew short, sharp breaths to steady himself. The bitter scent of smoke filling his lungs only served to make his anger boil hotter.

"No matter how many times you kill yourself, it's not going to bring your sweet child back."

"You think I don't know that!"

The disappointed look on Eve's face echoed the failure pinging inside him.

"I thought you were a hero, Logan Ward."

He sneered. "A hero? Whatever gave you *that* idea?"

"Poor judgment, obviously." Heated breath steamed from her mouth. "It's easier to feel guilty than to feel sad, you know."

"That's where you're wrong. There's nothing easy about guilt." Not when it ate at you so slowly, so insidiously. Not when it killed you bit by bit. Not when it shoved your failings in your face and forced you to look at them time and again.

"Then try acting from your heart for a change." She shoved both her hands into his chest. He didn't try to dodge the blow; he just let it rock him on his heels. "Beth wouldn't turn you away, and you know it. She loves you. She needs you. And she can't ask for help any more than you can. If you can't see that, then you're a bigger fool than I thought."

With that she strode away, leaving him alone with the moan of the wind sighing through the burnt shell of Beth's home. As he stared at the house, it began to blur.

Her house was gone. Everything in it.

No, not everything. Beth looked down at her son, so tiny and pale against the hospital sheets. She rubbed his hand to let him know she was here, to keep her connection with him. If she let go, would he just slip away from her?

She tried to imagine life without Jamie, without the

memories of Jim, which the house had held. She thought of all the joy she'd had within those walls, all the joy she'd planned for the future. She thought of the pictures gone forever. The books. The recipes. Gone. All gone.

"Things," she said. "Just things."

She watched her son's chest rise and fall, breathed with him. He was alive, and the doctors expected him to awaken as soon as the swelling went down. The machine monitoring the pressure in his brain was already showing improvement.

But the waiting…the waiting was killing her.

If she closed her eyes she was back in another sterile room, ripe with the scent of death, fraught with the clicks and clacks of machinery keeping the body alive while the spirit faded. She was holding another hand, feeling it grow cold.

He was gone.

Jim and all the reminders of him that had kept him alive in her mind were lost forever in the rubble of their home.

But Jamie was alive, and Jamie needed her. So she swallowed her fear, stroked her baby's hair and murmured a litany of sweet nothings so he would know he wasn't alone.

"Here," Eve said as she entered the room juggling cups of coffee and cracker packages from a vending machine.

"I don't want anything, thanks." Her throat was too narrow to swallow spit let alone anything with substance.

"You've got to keep your strength up." Eve forced a cup of coffee into Beth's hand. "You won't do Jamie any good passed out on the floor."

Eve ripped open a pack of peanut butter and wholewheat crackers and handed one to Beth. "Here."

"I'm not hungry."

"Eat it, anyway. You look like a ghost."

She felt like a paper doll, flat and mindless.

"Go on, eat."

Beth nibbled at the cracker because it was easier to comply with Eve's request than to fight her. The dry crumbs stuck in her throat, making her choke. Eve thumped on Beth's back and guided the cup of coffee to her lips. The lukewarm coffee washed away the cracker but not the deadness slowly numbing her limbs.

"You need to rest, sweetie." Eve tucked a strand of hair behind her ear—the way her mother used to when Beth was feeling down, and Beth felt a fresh wave of loss buffet through her. She needed her mother's soft hands and gentle words. But her mother was gone, too. So she leaned against Eve's hand, accepted the caress and choked back her ready tears.

"I can't rest. What if he wakes up and I'm not here?"

"Then I'll be here." Eve wrapped an arm around Beth's shoulders. "And if I'm not here, then someone else will be. You're part of a community, Beth. We won't let you go through this alone."

Tears blurred her vision. "I need to stay."

"Okay, then I'll stay with you."

"Thank you."

Eve parked herself in a chair next to Beth and read newspaper articles about the success of the Holiday Fair and tree-lighting ceremony. She cajoled the nurse into providing an extra pillow and blanket for Beth. She carried on a distracting chatter that kept Beth from slipping into self-pity.

"…and when Jamie is ready to come home, you'll stay with me. You two can have the upstairs rooms. I've already asked Gus to move my things to the downstairs room."

"I couldn't impose."

"Nonsense. You're family. Don't you know that by now? I love you as if you were my own daughter. And

Jamie is the grandson I'll never have." She leaned forward and whispered, "Why else would they let me stay if I wasn't family?"

Despite everything, Beth found herself smiling. "You are a treasure, Eve."

She let Eve tuck the blanket closer around her. Still holding Jamie's hand, Beth leaned her head against the stiff hospital pillow, careful not to disturb any of the tubes tending to her son. "Why won't you marry Gus?"

"Fear."

"Fear?"

Eve sighed, settled more heavily in the chair and chewed half a cracker. "When you've had two fiancés die on you, it kind of makes you gun-shy. And I really like Gus. I don't want anything to happen to him."

"Two? I thought only one." The steady rhythm of the machinery tending to Jamie was lulling her into drowsiness.

"First there was Ethan. He swept me off my feet the very first time I saw him. Oh, he was so handsome. Jet-black hair. Built like a Greek god. And that smile! Why just one look at it would make me dizzy. We had such plans." She covered her frown with a sip of coffee. "He died three days before we were to be married. Car/moose accident while he was driving down from his family's farm in Maine."

Eve sighed and popped the rest of the cracker in her mouth. Her unfocused gaze was aimed at the ceiling as if she were viewing a movie on the white surface. "Then there was Stan. Sweet-talking Stan. He was on the fast track to success. He could sell reading glasses to the blind if he put his mind to it. And he had his mind set on selling me the idea of marriage. He was going to take care of me and Mother." Eve drained her coffee cup and stared at the bottom as if more would magically appear. "He was shot by his own brother when he was mistaken for a burglar. He'd come home a day early from a business trip.''

''What bad luck you've had.''

Eve clucked and shook her head. ''Horrible luck. It hardened my heart, that's what it did. You and Jamie, you made the difference. It was after you two came into my life that I allowed myself to love again.'' She gave Beth a watery smile. ''I waited too long. I missed out on so much.''

''You're still young.'' Beth stifled the pang of regret the thought of Logan brought. ''Gus loves you.''

''You're right. He makes me feel young.'' Eve laughed. ''I just might have to make an honest man out of him. Life really is too short.''

And fragile, so fragile. Beth drew Jamie's hand closer and kissed the soft little-boy skin. She was having to learn that lesson much too often.

Just like Eve. Just like Logan.

Frowning, Beth plucked at a thread dangling from the pillowcase, giving it all her attention. She licked her lips and tried twice to speak before she found her voice. ''Has Logan left?''

''Not yet.'' Eve cleared her throat. ''He should be here.''

''No.'' Beth shook her head. ''He told me about his daughter. Being here would be watching her die all over again.'' She couldn't do that to him no matter how much she wanted his arms around her, his shoulder to cry on.

''Call him. Tell him you need him.''

''It would just scare him.''

''Stubborn fools. The two of you.'' Eve noisily crumpled her cracker wrapper and stuffed it in the empty cup of coffee. ''It would be easier, wouldn't it? If he left? Then you wouldn't have to face the fact you love him.''

Beth pulled on the thread, watched the seam unravel. ''Jim—''

"Will always be a part of you. Just like Ethan and Stan are a part of me. It took me too long to understand that." Eve placed a hand on Beth's knee. "Do you want him to leave?"

"No." What had started off as mutual support had turned into something deeper. At least for her. And the descent into that forbidden place had been so fast and so smooth she'd barely noticed. Now it was too late. Clutching Jamie's hand, Beth closed her eyes and pretended to sleep. She didn't want anyone to know how much Logan's departure would hurt.

Sleep evaded Logan all night. He packed his tools. He stacked boxes. He filled garbage bags. Max dogged him every step of the way, silently watching him with those worried eyes. Blanking his mind and staying busy had done nothing more than keep the ghosts at his heels rather than right in front of him. At dawn he could no longer fight them.

He needed to see Beth one more time before he left.

Nausea billowed as he entered the hospital. His skin grew cold and clammy as he jabbed the elevator button. When the doors opened on Jamie's floor, his body was too tense to move. It wasn't until the doors started closing again that he swallowed and pushed himself forward. He felt like an arthritic old man as he searched for Jamie's room.

Eve was asleep in a chair next to Jamie. A nurse was checking the boy's machinery. His heart started racing as he avoided looking at the small still figure on the bed. He'd expected Beth there, a sentinel guarding her young, but she was nowhere to be seen. Panic thrummed through him. Something was wrong. Where was she?

His fingers dug into the door's frame. "Where's Mrs. Lannigen?"

"Visitors aren't allowed," the nurse said.

"I'm not a visitor. Where's Mrs. Lannigen?"

With a narrowed gaze, the nurse eyed him up and down, then relented. "She went to the chapel."

He rode the elevator to the first floor, then paused at the chapel's door unable to go inside. Taped music reverberated through the room. A chaplain led a hymn he didn't recognize. Half a dozen voices rose to sing, quiet at first, then growing. His gaze was drawn in by a familiar sound.

Beth's voice.

She knelt in the front pew, hands knotted in prayer, eyes closed, singing. The sound was sweet and joyful. How could that be? The sound of her voice wasn't sad at all. After all she'd lost, how could she still have hope?

The service ended. The chapel emptied. Only Beth remained, kneeling in the front pew, head bent in supplication.

"It doesn't work, you know," he said. His voice echoed in the small chamber.

In the heartbeat of silence, her shoulder stiffened, and he flinched as if she'd slapped him.

"What?" Her voice was a strangled whisper, and it wrenched his heart.

"Prayer. He doesn't answer to pleas or bargains." He should know. He'd tried often enough to bargain his life for Sam's. None of his implorations had been heard.

"I'm not asking for either."

"Then what?"

She looked at him then, and his chest swelled at the sight of her fortitude. "Strength."

A sudden flash of anger barreled through him—at her for her acceptance, at himself for offering challenge rather than comfort. "Strength? You're just going to wait and take whatever happens?"

"What else can I do?"

"He might die. Don't you care?"

She pitched sideways. He felt like a heel. I'm sorry, Beth, I'm sorry. But the words would not croak through his constricted throat, and his body refused to enter the sanctuary that had repudiated his appeals when he'd prayed for a miracle for his daughter.

"Jamie's not dead yet," she said, the pain in her eyes a knife to his heart. "As long as there's an ounce of life left in him, I'm not going to give up hope."

"Hope," he scoffed. He'd had a mountain of it while he'd sat by Sam's bedside. He'd fed on it every day, for all those weeks. And it was cruelly shattered by the pain on his child's face, until it had completely faded away.

Instead of begging for her recovery, like a coward, he'd started pleading for her release.

"What if he dies?" How could Beth endure it? How could she think of going on?

She swayed as she stood and placed her hands on her chest. "Then I'll have to use both hands to hold my heart in and keep it from breaking into a million pieces." Her breath staggered. "And somehow, I'll have to find the courage to go on—for Jamie, for Jim."

Logan swore. He wanted to punch the wall, to kick out the door. He wanted to crush her in his arms, to consume her grief. Instead he lashed out at her goodness. "Your Pollyanna attitude isn't going to save you from the pain."

"No, it won't," she agreed. "Jim told me that he had the easy part in dying. Going on, living a good life, that was the hard part. He was right. Jim loved life so much. Lived every second of it. I have to make myself keep on living to honor him. To do any less would say that his life had no meaning."

"You can't really believe that. Not now."

"Yes, I do." An almost beatific smile appeared on her face, as if a sudden insight had filled her with peace. "'You are more than the sum of your parts. You belong to a community and must feed it with your hope and service.' That was my father's philosophy. He lived it every day of his life. He died living it. My work isn't as important as his, but it serves a purpose."

"You'll go on cooking as if nothing happened."

"I'll go on cooking *because* everything happened. If you didn't feel the same way, you wouldn't have risked your own life to save that busload of kids last winter."

He froze, and in the stillness, he heard the hard knocking of his heart. How did she know about the accident? The city had wanted to crown him a hero for his effort, but he knew there was nothing heroic about his thoughts that day. "That's where you're wrong, Beth. Those kids saved themselves. I just opened the door. But the driver was pinned beneath the steering wheel."

Logan scraped a hand through his hair, stared at the cross at the front of the chapel. *Have mercy on me.* "I smelled liquor on his breath."

He swallowed hard and looked at Beth, ready to see condemnation in her eyes. "I wanted to kill him. I wanted to leave him in there and watch him fry."

She didn't flinch. She didn't turn away. She came toward him, placed a hand against his cheek. "But you didn't."

The lump in his stomach started to rise. He had to get away. Stumbling back he said, "I want Jamie to have Max. I'll leave her with Gus."

"Stay."

He shook his head. Something had changed. It ticked inside him like a bomb counting down to detonation. "I can't."

He pivoted, shoved his fists into his coat pockets and

hunched forward, intent on plowing his way out the door before he burst.

"Logan."

He stopped, rocked back on his heels like a disoriented boxer. "What?"

"I love you."

He knew then he'd waited too long to leave. Those words cut him, and it took everything he had to keep one foot moving in front of the other.

She was right, her work had purpose. She fed people with her compassion and her generosity. She could light up a room with just her smile. With her casseroles and her chatter and her wide-open heart, she'd brought him back to life.

What had he given her in return but heartache?

Blindly he bolted to his car. *Beth.*

Something tore inside him as his tires screeched out of the parking lot.

He made it all the way home before he exploded.

## Chapter Fifteen

Logan roared.

The sound exploded out of him, reverberated down the empty hallway of his house, sending Max creeping back into the kitchen with her head scrunched down low between her shoulders and her tail tucked tight between her legs.

All the anger he'd stored for the past two years tornadoed out of him, leveling everything in his path.

He shoved the tower of boxes he'd stacked in the hallway in readiness to flee, toppling them into the living room. The top one burst open, spilling its contents. He kicked at the papers, shooting them into frenzied flight.

He balled, he ripped, he tore. Copies of court case documents, newspaper articles, collected records—the innuendoes, the lies, the truth. They became snow around him, and still he couldn't stop.

Samantha's Raggedy Ann doll collided with the wall, crumpled upside down, turning her red smile into a scowl.

The popsicle-stick cricket cage, painted purple, splintered against the half-torn paneling. The treasured lumps of quartz from Sam's bedside cracked dents into the floorboards. He destroyed everything from the box.

Even the frame.

He hurled the pink porcelain rectangle, sending Sam flying across the room.

"No!"

He threw himself forward, tried to catch the frame in flight, but the porcelain shattered against the wall, showering his hands with shards of glass and pottery. Blood beaded along his fingers.

"Sam. Sam. Sam."

Brushing away the splinters, he streaked red over his daughter's smiling face, bolting him back in time to the accident. He slumped against the wall, shoulder digging into the sheetrock as if it could hold him up. One second she'd been grinning with pride, the next she'd been lying bloody in his arms.

"Samantha!"

The cry came from deep in his soul and tore out of him in a desolate lament. He pressed the photograph against his heart. Slinking against the wall, he collapsed in a heap on the floor.

"Samantha." The whisper contained a plea.

He'd been a cop. A tough cop in a tougher beat. Dry-eyed, emotionless, pain-free. That was the face that was expected of him. At first people asked, "How's it going?" And he knew he was supposed to say "fine" to relieve their discomfort so they could go on with their day. He wasn't supposed to show how empty he was feeling, how dark and cold his heart was, how the hurt was cutting him raw.

But when Samantha died, she'd taken more than her life

to the grave. She'd taken his legacy, his family, his future. Everything he'd dreamed of. All that was left was the cancer of guilt. Even running away to the peace of his childhood had not diminished its growth.

"Samantha." Her name was nothing more than a dry rasp of breath.

Holding on tight to the photograph, he closed his eyes and rocked back and forth.

The picture against his heart had been taken at a birthday party a month before her death. He saw it all again so clearly. The kids screeching with delight on the ice. The scent of sugar cloying beside him at the table decked out with chocolate cake, Dr. Pepper and party favors in neon-pink bags. His back against the wall, he had kept a watchful eye.

Sam had skated to him, tiptoed into the sitting area and swung her leg onto a bench. "My boot is loose."

"Sit. I'll tighten the laces for you."

He pressed the blade against the tough denim of his jeans.

"How come you and Mom don't laugh?" she asked, watching Allison's parents waltz by her on the ice. They were having as much fun as the kids.

"I don't know, princess. I don't think many adults laugh."

"Allison's parents do. Mr. Miller, he dances with Mrs. Miller in the kitchen every night when he comes home from work, and they laugh then, too."

What could he say? Sam was getting older now, old enough to sense that all wasn't right between her parents. How long could they realistically keep up the charade?

"I wish you and Mom would dance in the kitchen."

"You do, huh." He tied the laces in a double knot and released her foot.

"Then maybe you would laugh."

He tweaked the end of her nose, and she grimaced. "Your mother would think it's silly."

Samantha glanced wistfully at Mr. Miller dipping Mrs. Miller on the ice. "When I get married, my husband, he's going to be handsome like you, Daddy, but he's going to like dancing in the kitchen like Allison's dad."

Samantha's voice reverberated in his mind, fading to a silence so profound he thought he could elude the storm quickening low in his gut.

His daughter would never have a husband, she would never dance in the kitchen.

Then it came.

A hard point of lightning directly in his heart, splitting it open. Thunder reported in shudders through his chest. Waves of choked sobs swelled from low in his belly and crested high into his throat.

Guilt, love, hate, anger, sadness hit him all at once.

"Sam!"

Max sidled up to him and whined pitifully as she licked at the tiny wounds covering his hands.

Then he lost it.

Despair, thorny and viscous, exploded out of him in harsh rolls. He cried for hours holding the scratched photograph of his daughter against his chest with one hand, the dog tight against his side with the other. He cried until his soul was empty.

"Mom?"

Beth could not contain her smile. It had graced her face for an hour now and showed no sign of fading. Jamie had woken up, crying for her. The doctors had checked him over from head to toe and declared him in excellent condition. As far as they could see, Jamie had suffered no damage from his trauma. They were going to keep him for a couple of days, run some tests—just to be sure. But in her heart Beth already knew that Jamie was back to his old self—two parts angel, one part urchin.

His miraculous recovery was the best Christmas present she'd ever received.

"What, sweetheart?" Her son was snuggled in her arms on the hospital bed. Not even dynamite could pry him from her. She kissed the top of his head and hugged him a little bit tighter—just to be on the safe side.

"Will Santa know where I am?"

Santa. In the chaos of the past few days, she'd forgotten all about their Christmas Eve ritual of cookies and carrots, of hope and expectation. Santa would be making his rounds, but he wouldn't find Jamie's house. How to explain to a six-year-old that Santa wasn't real, that their house was nothing but rubble, that all the presents had gone up in smoke?

"I'm sure there'll be presents under the tree when the doctors say you can go home." Eve. She would get Eve to find skates for Jamie. Surely Gus could set aside a pair until she could pay him back.

"Skates and a stick. I wrote Santa my size and everything."

"I know, sweetheart." She'd smiled at the note, at Jamie's fervent assurances that he'd been a good boy. She'd pasted the crayoned letter on an album page she'd planned to add to his book when he no longer believed in Santa.

That, too, was forever lost.

"Where's Mr. Ward?" Jamie asked, turning his sweet face to hers.

Beth's heart gave a heavy lurch. The smile she'd thought permanent faded a bit. "Probably at his house."

"Oh." His fingers twiddled with the decorative fringe on her sweater. "Max, is she okay?"

"Of course, sweetheart." She stroked his hair. How like Jamie to worry about the dog. "Max is fine. She's a hero, you know. She called us after you got hurt."

"I want to see her."

"I don't think dogs are allowed at the hospital."

He pouted. "When can I go home?"

"When the doctors say you're 100 percent A-OK."

"I feel fine. See."

Jamie tried to sit up, but she only let him stray half an arm's length away. "Hey, knock-knock."

He tried not to smile and failed. "Who's there?"

"Gladys."

"Gladys who?"

Beth tickled him gently. "Gladys can be you're feeling better."

Jamie laughed, then snuggled into her arms once more, lifting his head up until their gazes locked. The florid bruise on his forehead reminded her how close she'd come to losing him.

"I want to go home, Mom. I want to sleep in my bed so Santa can find me. I got to leave him some cookies that we made and carrots for the reindeers." His fist scrunched her sweater. "Please, Mom, call Mr. Ward and tell him to come get us. He's my friend. He'll come."

In spite of her happiness at Jamie's recovery, a part of her wanted to cry. How to tell this precious little boy with so much trust in his heart that his home was gone and that Logan might have already fled and left them behind?

He remembered that Christmas. Sam had plowed through her pile of presents in record time. She'd been standing in front of him, waiting impatiently while he adjusted the straps of her new bicycle helmet. Purple—her favorite color.

"Do you think my Christmas angel friend liked the present we got her?"

"What did the card on the tree say?"

"It said she wanted some paint and some paper because she likes to draw."

"And what did you pick out?"

"Some watercolors, two paintbrushes and a big pad of watercolor paper."

"Then I think she's a very happy girl. I'll bet she's sitting in her house painting a picture this very minute."

"I'm so glad."

He fitted the helmet onto Sam's head, and she smiled up at him. "I just love Christmas. Don't you, Daddy?"

"I love *you,* princess."

She had flung herself in his arms, helmet, elbow and knee pads and all. "Oh, Daddy, you're so silly."

Something shrill pecked at his brain. He brushed it away with the wave of a hand, but the sound persisted.

The phone.

He tried ignoring it, but it beat a sharp tattoo, adding a jagged insult to his already pounding head. He pushed himself off the floor, padded to the kitchen and ripped the offending instrument from its cradle. "What?"

"Logan?"

Beth. His heart chattered like castanets. "Is everything okay? Jamie—"

"Is fine. Tired and achy, but awake."

His sigh was heavy with relief.

"He's asking for you."

"For me?" The receiver felt heavy in Logan's hands.

"He wants you to rescue us from the hospital." She

paused and he thought he heard her gulp. "Please, Logan..."

"Beth..." The kitchen started spinning around him.

"It's okay."

In the background he heard Jamie's voice. "Mommy, tell him we got to get home before Santa leaves the North Pole."

His mind whirled. Adrenaline surged through him, making him light-headed. He didn't know what to say, what to feel. He closed his eyes and clutched the phone tighter. "Oh, God, Beth."

"I'm sorry, Logan. I shouldn't have called."

Before he could say anything, she hung up.

He looked down at the picture of Sam still clenched in his hand. Like Jamie, she'd believed in Santa Claus. She'd loved Christmas. Everything about it. The colors. The bustle. The giving. Especially the giving.

She'd once asked him why Santa didn't make it to every house, why there were so many drives for presents for poor kids. He'd had no ready answer for her, but she'd come up with her own.

"I'll bet it's because they don't believe in their hearts." And she'd made it her mission to make everyone believe.

She'd spent hours making presents for everyone she knew and insisted on participating in every Christmas drive she heard of—the mitten drive at school, the food drive at church, the book drive at the library, Toys for Tots, the angel tree at the mall. She'd saved her allowance for months and gladly spent it on strangers.

His whole body shook. His hands grew ice cold.

"I just love Christmas," Sam had said. "Don't you, Daddy?"

Maybe his daughter had been wiser than he.

Maybe instead of running away, he should have been running to.

Maybe it wasn't too late.

In that moment something warm and light swelled through him. His heart, dead for so long, suddenly burst with life.

He glanced at the clock on the stove. "Come on, Max. It's late. If we're going to pull this off, we've got a lot of work to do."

Max thumped her tail against the floor. "Woof!"

He made it to town in record time. neither the falling snow nor slippery roads were going to stop him. He had a plan and not much time to put it together. Thoughts and ideas swirled in a dizzying twister. It had to work. It had to.

He screeched into the parking lot. Leaving the car running, he raced to Gus's store only to be stopped by a locked door.

Pounding on the glass door, he yelled, "Gus, open up! Open up! It's an emergency!"

All that got him was the attention of the local police.

## Chapter Sixteen

The holding cell at Rockville's police station was a tiny room that looked more like a meat locker than a typical barred cage. Logan pummeled the solid locked door with the tiny window until his fists were bruised. He cursed. He paced.

Time. It was running out, and those fools wouldn't listen. He had to get out. He just had to.

He was about to start another round of pounding when a key scraped the lock, and the door clicked open. Gus appeared in the doorway. An officer slanted his bulk between Logan and Gus, ready to slam the door closed between the two should the need arise.

"Gus," Logan croaked with relief. "I knew you'd come. I told them you would."

Gus's white hair was spiked as if he'd been roused out of bed. His clothes looked thrown on in a hurry. But the bushy eyebrows over the glasses framed clear-blue eyes that were not amused. "What the hell's going on here? What were you doing trying to break into my store?"

Logan grabbed the old man's shoulder and started shaking him. The officer jabbed him back. "Back off."

Not knowing what to do with himself, Logan stumbled back, stuffed his hands in his jeans pocket and paced the small room.

"Jamie. Beth. Christmas," Logan sputtered. "It's almost midnight. We've got to hurry."

"You're not making any sense."

Of course he wasn't. He was halfway out of his mind. He had to do this. He had to. For Beth. For Jamie. For Sam. Gulping in air, Logan tried to calm down, stood in one spot and faced Gus. "Jamie's awake. He thinks Santa's not going to know where he is. Beth's house. It's gone. The skates. I have to get him skates."

"Well, why didn't you call me instead of breaking in?"

"I thought you might still be there. I didn't know where you lived. I was desperate." He'd had only one thing on his mind—giving Beth and Jamie a Christmas they wouldn't forget, one Sam would be proud of.

Gus turned to the officer. "No charges. I'm taking him with me."

"Gus—"

"Beth deserves a Christmas, too. If she wants him, who are we to argue? We're stopping at the store, then we'd appreciate an escort to the hospital."

Reluctantly the officer nodded. "For Beth."

Lights flashing, they raced to Gus's store. Gus dragged the door open and switched on the lights. "What do you need?"

Looking around the store, Logan suddenly felt overwhelmed. He puffed out a long breath. "Everything. I need everything. A tree, a few lights, skates for Jamie, something for Beth—''

"Okay, okay, I get the gist." Gus threw up his hands. "You get the tree and trimmings over there. I'll find the skates."

Logan sprinted down the aisles, loaded his arms with a three-foot potted spruce, a string of lights, a package of wooden ornaments. Then he saw her. The angel with the long brown hair and smiled. "Sam."

Sam would be with them, too.

Calm descended over him.

Everything would be all right.

Gus came teetering his way weighted down with boxes, a tube of bright-red wrapping paper and a roll of tape. "Ready?"

As he looked out into the night, at the snow falling, a sense of peace settled over his broken heart, healing him. "Yeah, I'm ready."

As the elevator doors opened, the nurse on duty looked up from her station.

Arms overloaded, Logan plowed past the nurse's desk—dog, tree, presents and all. Behind him trailed the two cops who'd arrested him, Gus, Eve, Sasha, Bobby and his family, half the lunch ladies from the middle school, kids and parents Beth had touched over the years with her kindness. How they'd all come to join the police caravan, Logan didn't know, but they all braved the night and the snow to let Jamie know Santa hadn't forgotten him, to let Beth know how much they cared for her.

"Hey! You can't come in here. Visiting hours are over." Face pinched, the nurse skittered around the desk and trotted behind him.

"We're not visitors. We're Santa's helpers."

"Dogs aren't allowed in this building."

"She's not a dog. She's a hero." Max licked his cheek. Logan smiled down at her. The red bow around her collar jiggled. She swiped his coat with her tail.

"Security! Someone call security!"

"Good idea." Logan threw back his head and laughed. He couldn't remember when he'd felt this good, this alive. "The more the merrier."

At the door of Jamie's room he stopped and looked at Beth. She and Jamie lay side by side on the bed. Her arm and head were bent protectively over her son. Both their eyes were closed. His heart was suddenly filled with overwhelming happiness. They were alive. They were healthy. And he loved them. His chest felt too small, and his vision started to blur.

"Beth."

She blinked awake, and her eyes rounded with surprise. "Logan?"

"Yeah, Logan." He smiled—a wide, open-from-the-heart smile and moved aside to show the troop waiting impatiently behind him. "And company. Merry Christmas, Beth."

"You don't know the trouble he's caused to give you and Jamie a Christmas," Gus said. "He tried to break into my store, he did."

"No!" Beth's hand covered her mouth.

"Sure did." But Gus didn't sound mad at all. His gray mustache was twitching with delight.

"Got arrested for his trouble," Eve chimed in.

"Logan?" Beth looked at him wide-eyed with disbelief.

"Mr. Ward! Mr. Ward! You brought Max."

At the sound of her name, Max squirmed in his arms. He placed her at the foot of the bed, and she scampered up to Jamie, dousing his face with canine kisses.

Awkwardly Jamie tried to scramble out of bed only to be settled back down by his mother. "I knew you'd come. I told Mom you'd take us home."

Then the room filled with people and noise. Like a hive, they buzzed, surrounding Beth and Jamie with cheer and good wishes. "Surprise!" "Merry Christmas, Beth!" "Are you surprised?" "So glad you're feeling better, Jamie." "Merry Christmas!" "Merry Christmas!"

Beth took it all in, openmouthed and silent. Tears were running down her cheeks.

Bobby bounced on Jamie's bed. Logan orchestrated putting up the tree. Sasha and Bobby's mother decorated the tree. The lunch ladies noisily wrapped the boxes in the hallway.

Then the room lights were dimmed, and the tree lights dazzled on. "Merry Christmas, everyone!"

"Wow!" Jamie said.

"For you." Logan handed Jamie his presents—skates, a mask and a stick.

"Skates! Just like I wanted. The mask is so cool!" He turned to his mother. "Mom, you gotta take me skating now."

"Soon, Jamie, soon." Her voice was choked as she reached for her son.

She looked up at Logan and mouthed, Thank you.

"We're not done yet." He took the box Gus handed him and placed it on Beth's lap.

She alternately batted at the tears sliding down her cheeks and ripped at the paper over the box of pots and pans. "Oh!"

"I know they're not the kind you like—"

"They're perfect." She hugged the box to her chest. "Thank you."

"Why is she crying?" a small voice asked.

"She's happy," an older one answered.

Logan reached inside his jacket and brought out a small package. Beth scooted to the edge of the bed and accepted the box. Jamie was busy trying on his mask with Bobby's help. "I'm sorry, Beth, about everything. I tried to save—" he lowered his voice "—the house, but it was too late."

"I know."

Her hands shook as she brought out the frame from the box. Jim. The picture of Jim that had been sitting on the mantel in the living room.

"The frame was melted," Logan said, "but the picture was intact."

Beth launched herself at him, sobbing into his shoulder. Her heart overflowed. First the miracle of Jamie's recovery. Now Logan here, for her, and on his face, the sight she'd never thought she'd see—a real smile.

"Did I do something wrong?"

"Oh, no." Her lips quivered and her vision blurred again. "You did everything right. I don't know what to say."

His fingers weren't quite steady as he held her by the waist. The frown creasing his forehead made her suck her breath in. In his eyes she saw uncertainty. Her hands tensed on his shoulder.

"Say you'll marry me."

Shock made her gasp. Of all the things she'd expected him to say, this was the last. "Marry you?"

"Yes, please, Beth. I need you. I love you. You gave me back my life, and I want to share it with you and Jamie." He swallowed hard. "Sam, she loved Christmas. Everything about it. The lights. The colors. The whole Santa scene. But mostly she loved the giving, Beth. I'd forgotten that. It took Jamie's accident to make me remember. She wanted to make people believe, to make them smile. I want to see her every day in other people's smiles.''

''Oh, Logan.'' Joy spilled out of her in a mixture of laughter and tears. She clutched her hands around his nape and brought his face down to hers. She kissed him with heart and soul and finally understood she'd lost nothing and gained everything.

Jim wasn't in the rooms of the house they'd shared. He wasn't in the photographs, in the clothes, in the details of her memory. He was in Jamie's eyes. He was in the people whose lives he'd touched. The essence of the man he'd been lived on in her heart. She would never forget him.

Having loved a good man like Jim only made loving someone else a more precious gift. One she was finally ready to accept.

''What did you get, Mom?''

She leaned back from her embrace, looked at Logan straight in the eyes and smiled. ''A family. I got a family.''

As he pulled her against him, she felt his body shudder, his breath whoosh out, his love melt around her.

''Yuck, mushy stuff,'' Bobby said and pulled the sheet over his face.

Wearing his goalie mask, Jamie giggled. ''Knock, knock.''

''Who's there?'' Logan said, smiling widely. His eyes twinkled with joy. She'd been right, the man was gorgeous when he smiled. No photograph could hold a candle to the real thing.

''Amory.''

''Amory who?''

''Amory Christmas and a happy new year!''

''Hear, hear!'' someone piped in.

Between the laughter and the tears, the crowd spontaneously broke out into song. Hand in hand, Logan and Beth joined in.

# Epilogue

*Thanksgiving a Year Later.*

Jamie and Logan walked into the garden-like kitchen, shaking snow from their boots. The scent of roasting turkey filled the room and enticed growls of hunger from Logan's stomach. Sniffing madly, Max trotted straight to the oven and slanted Beth a pleading look.

"We found one, Mom." Jamie's coat fell to the floor, his hat and gloves followed in quick succession, marking his path. "We found the perfect Christmas tree."

Logan smiled at Beth. "A six-footer with the perfect conical shape."

"You don't say." Beth set two mugs of hot chocolate on the table along with a plate of gingerbread men.

She squealed as Logan grabbed her by the waist and waltzed her around the kitchen.

"Oh, no. You guys aren't gonna get mushy again, are you?" Jamie asked, stuffing a cookie in his mouth.

"Yeah, we are. Very mushy." Logan dipped Beth and planted a loud kiss on her lips.

"Ew, gross."

Beth laughed. "We don't have time for this. The guests will be here any minute."

Logan chuckled. "They won't mind."

"Have I told you how much I like to hear you laugh?"

"Tell me again."

"I love you, Logan."

"I love you, too." He waltzed her into the hall. "More and more every day."

He stopped at the living room doorway, holding his wife tightly in his arms. They'd furnished the room with an eclectic collection of treasures found at garage sales and lovingly refinished. The walls were cream, the wallpaper a subtle print, the floor a cordial polished honey. A fire glowed in the hearth, throwing warmth and welcome.

Here in this house, the dream he'd thought forever lost had finally come true. He placed a hand gently over Beth's stomach, over the child growing in her womb. This baby would be an Easter present to celebrate the rebirth of their hearts.

A family. His family.

Never had he imagined he could be so happy, so content. "Where do you think we should put the tree?"

"By the table."

From frames on the small occasional table by the window, Sam and Jim smiled their approval.

\* \* \* \* \*

## AVAILABLE FROM 20TH DECEMBER 2002

### SINGLE WITH TWINS Joan Elliott Pickart

His brother had broken Heather's heart and left her pregnant with twins—but she was irresistibly drawn to world-famous photojournalist Mack Marshall. Was he certain heartbreak...or the husband of her dreams?

### THE GROOM'S STAND-IN Gina Wilkins

Rugged Donovan Chance had agreed to watch over romantic Chloe Pennington, his best friend's prospective fiancée. Forced together by a kidnapping, could his loyal resolve restrain his unexpected desire?

### IN LOVE WITH HER BOSS Christie Ridgway

*Montana*

Lori Hanson wanted to make a fresh start—not fall in love with Josh Anderson, her dangerously attractive boss! So how would he ever capture the heart she was so determined to protect?

### ANOTHER MAN'S CHILDREN Christine Flynn

Lauren Edwards found looking after her brother's children much easier with the help of rugged bush pilot Zach McKendrick! But the tenderness of the mesmerising male made her long for a family of her own...

### THE CHILD SHE ALWAYS WANTED
### Jennifer Mikels

*Family Revelations*

Soft-hearted Rachel Quinn had hoped for a life with rugged Kane Riley years ago. Now watching his orphaned niece warm his hardened heart revived her lost dreams—but could she finally make him hers?

### ON PINS AND NEEDLES Victoria Pade

*A Ranching Family*

Sceptical Sheriff Josh Brimley found it hard enough to seek treatment from beautiful Megan Bailey *before* he knew her parents were murder suspects. But she was a very hands-on practitioner...